Previous Books in the Waterspell Series

The Karenina Chronicles:
A Waterspell Novel

I0670628

"Superb. Engaging from page one. I found myself engrossed."

"Exceptionally vividly realized. Wonderful characters, each with their complexities of make-up and backstory."

"Excellently written and enjoyable."

"What a journey! Nina is such a strong character."

Waterspell Books 1–4
Warlock, Wysard, Wisewoman, Witch

"A must-read for fantasy enthusiasts who enjoy immersive world-building, well-developed characters, and a storyline that seamlessly blends magic and human emotion."

"Addictive epic fantasy with drama and adventure. I binged through the books, eager to see how the story unfolds."

"The last fantasy I read that was memorable was by Tolkien. That was until I found the first Waterspell book in my large 'to be read' pile. I was entranced from the beginning. The world-building was amazing but the characters pulled me in."

"An impressively immersive quality in Deborah J. Lightfoot's writing draws you in and keeps you there as the pages turn. The quality of her writing is excellent and she has the knack of engaging the enduring interest and sympathy of the reader as they follow the twists and turns of the plot."

"I stayed up late many nights to read what happened next in this series. It's definitely a page turner and keeps you guessing."

"Imaginative, entertaining, and much more than just a delightful read. The characters came alive on the pages."

"Grabbed my attention and kept it. This is a series not to miss."

"An extremely well written fantasy story. Flows well with a very readable style that holds your interest throughout. The world building is solid and intriguing, the magical aspects well drawn and versatile and characterisation is energetic."

"It's no wispy piece of fluff fiction! Plenty of mystery and twists and turns."

"Wonderfully written. I was hooked right away and loved that I couldn't predict what was to come next."

"A riveting series. Well written, excellent world-building with an engaging plot in each book and well-developed characters. I was gripped right from the start with twists and unpredictability."

"If you like epic fantasy that sweeps you to amazing, immersive worlds and while following intriguing characters, be sure to add this series to your to-read list."

More reviews & review attributions @ waterspell.net

The Fires of
Farsinchia

A Waterspell Novel

BOOKS of WATERSPELL

Original Quartet
Book 1: The Warlock
Book 2: The Wysard
Book 3: The Wisewoman
Book 4: The Witch

Nina Sequels
The Karenina Chronicles
The Fires of Farsinchia

The Fires of Farsinchia

A Waterspell Novel

Deborah J. Lightfoot

Seven Rivers
Publishing

Seven Rivers Publishing
P.O. Box 682
Crowley, Texas 76036
waterspell.net

Cover design by Tatiana Vila, Vila Design
viladesign.net

Ore Hills detail map by Tiffany Munro, cartographer
feedthemultiverse.com

The Fires of Farsinchia: A Waterspell Novel (Book 6) / Deborah J. Lightfoot
First paperback edition: November 2024
First electronic edition: November 2024

Summary: With the revival of magic in the world of Ladrehdin, an ancient foe reawakens. Lady Karenina is called home to wield her wizardry against a power far older and deadlier. Will she survive? Who will hear her call for help?

ISBN 978-1-7377173-6-2 (Paperback)
ISBN 978-1-7377173-7-9 (Ebook)
ISBN 978-1-7377173-8-6 (Audiobook)

This book was written by a human, not AI.

For L.H. Blocker (1934–2023), my high school English teacher who set a high standard and challenged me to meet it.

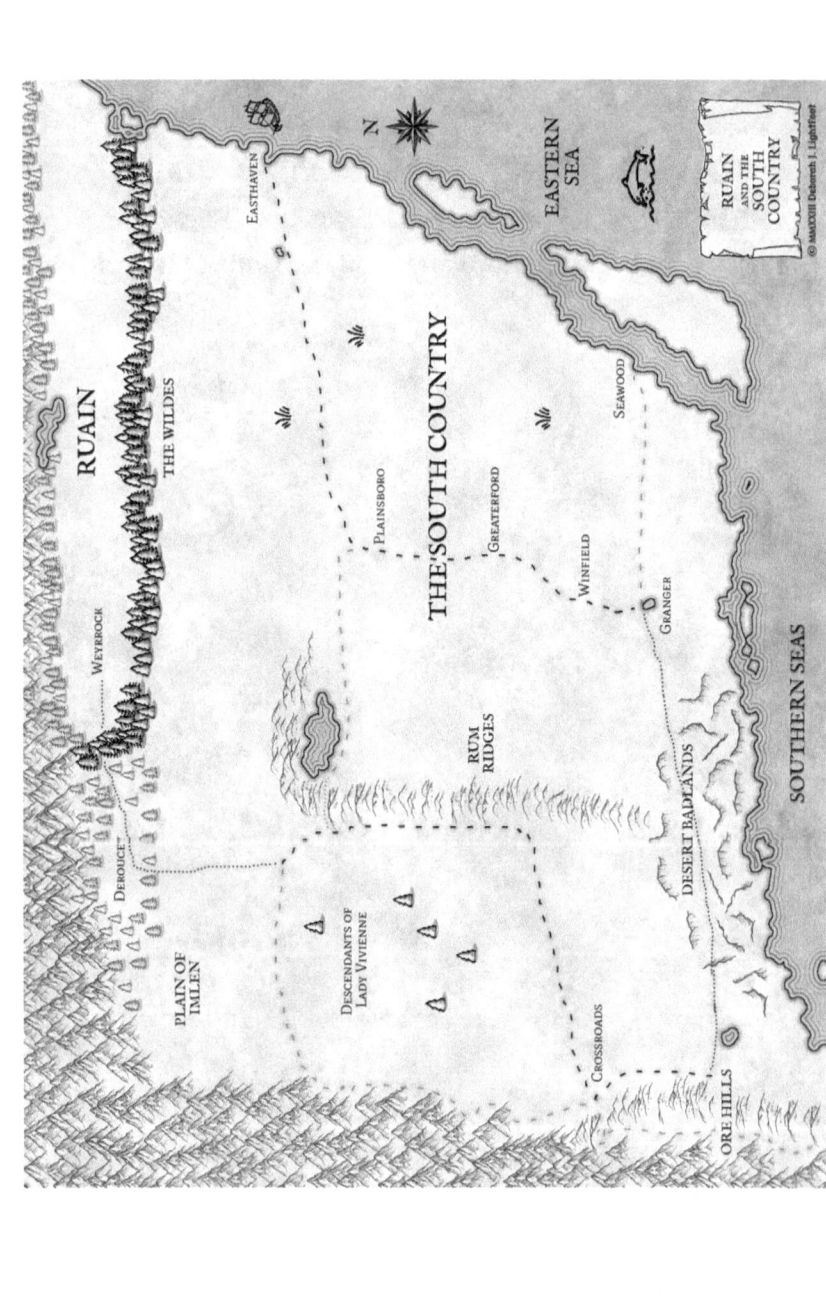

Contents

"Do a good deed and throw it in the river.
One day it will come back to you in the desert."

Jalāl al-Dīn Muhammad Rūmī
13th-century Persian poet and Sufi mystic

Chapter One

"What the—? Ow!"

Heat flashed in Karenina's hand as she snatched the heavy pendant from under the neckline of her sleeveless blouse. The solid chunk of metal was threatening to burn her. As she held the pendant away from her skin, fire gleamed in the depths of the blue steel and flickered in the nuggets of pure gold with which her brother Galen had fashioned the jewelry. In that instant, Nina saw the flaming forge of the metalsmith, though Galen's magical workshop lay at a great distance beyond the void that separated her adopted home from the faraway world to which she and her brother were native.

Nina not only saw—and felt—the fire of her brother's spellcraft, she heard his voice within the flames.

"Come quickly!" Galen cried, his words echoing across the formless oblivion. "Jacca needs you."

"What's happened?"

Nina yelled into the pendant as though shouting through cupped hands. But the flames had died and the metal had already cooled. The brief link between the worlds was broken, leaving Nina staring at the exquisite piece of jewelry she'd always known was enchanted. When Galen pressed it into her hands at the hour of their last good-bye, she had felt the magic within the metal: magic from the hands of its maker. Until this moment, however, she had not guessed the pendant held the power to breach the void.

Such power had been wielded by only three *wysards* of Ladrehdin, all of them female. Nina herself had been a little girl, not quite six years old when she first crossed the void on magic of her own making. Going back a generation, Nina's legendary mother—Lady Carin of Ruain—had also made the crossing at a young age, although her passage had not been by choice. Carin's first journey through the nothingness had been forced upon her by dark magic. She'd been abducted from her childhood home by a blood sorceress whose name would never again find utterance among the true *wysards* of Ladrehdin. Though now condemned and forgotten, that ancient sorceress had been the only other adept of Ladrehdin who'd had the power to create otherworldly bridges.

Which made Nina stare all the harder at the pendant crafted by Galen of the Ore Hills, the metalsmith *wysard* who had worked void-breaching potency into his parting gift for his sister. Nina tried squeezing the chunk of metal between her hands, attempting to re-invoke its power. When she got no response, she dropped the pendant under the neckline of her shirt and pressed the now-cool steel to her naked flesh. Behind closed lids, she pictured her brother at his smithy, and called to mind Galen's daughter, the green-eyed girl named Jacca—the magian child who had the gift of fire at her fingertips, a fire even hotter than Galen's ore-smelting furnaces.

"I'm coming," Nina whispered into the silence that followed Galen's brief, magical entreaty. She was only distantly aware of ocean breezes sighing through the palm trees of her island home on this alien world where she had lived since the age of thirteen. Carried upon the breezes, tropical birdsong came faintly to her ears. Nina noted the far-off booming of surf upon the shore, and heard a ship sound its horn as it approached the distant harbor. Her thoughts, however, remained riveted upon the world to which she had been summoned.

Nina recalled her first glimpse of the foothills where Galen made his home and practiced his art. Up from the desert canyonlands, she had ridden to the hills hot and sweaty, reining her horse beside the gritty nomad who had been her guide to that remote corner of Ladrehdin. Nina had drunk in the sight and scent of the pine trees that climbed those hills and lightly greened the mountain slopes rising beyond them. After weeks in a barren desert, she had needed the moist coolness under those trees like a fish needed the sea. Southern Ladrehdin's sunbaked deserts were no place for a water-sylph who carried the ocean in her veins.

And yet, Nina had sorrowed to reach the Ore Hills and bid farewell to the nomad named Corlis. During their time together, struggling to survive in a nearly waterless desert, the man had become more to her than a guide.

The nomad's lean, sun-bronzed face swam before her mind's eye as Nina tucked away her necklace and leapt down the slope to her cottage in the papaya orchard. This latest abode of hers was tiny, but the two-room hut was all she'd had since returning to her island world. She'd come back to find her descendants comfortably lodged in the larger house below the towering wall of rock, the house on the beach of the sheltered bay.

She'd once shared that home with a mortal man, a non-magian native of these islands. But Makani was dead now, victim of his mortal years, leaving Nina widowed and restless. Seeking the solace of family, she had jumped the void to visit not only her brother Galen, but every wizardly relative she could locate in the world of her birth. She might have stayed in that world, might have remained at home in Ladrehdin amongst her magical kinfolk, if her sense of duty to her own descendants had not drawn her back to these islands.

Once here, however, Nina had discovered that her progeny no longer required her maternal, guiding hand. Her children's children had spread throughout the archipelago, devoting their talents to rebuilding a world previously devastated by an otherworldly plague.

There had been only one thing she could do for them now. Upon her return to this revitalized world, Nina had acted swiftly to close off a potential source of new peril to the ocean planet called Earth. From the garden shed behind the house on the bay, she'd grabbed an axe and a shovel and climbed to a lonely spot inland from the beachfront property. In that place, high up the forested slope behind the house and un-seeable from any window, a misshapen tree had grown—a strange and twisted thing that did not belong in this world. Nina had proceeded to chop it down. Then she'd dug up its roots and tossed every shred of the tree onto a bonfire. For good measure, Nina had salted the burned ground and come back weekly thereafter, to watch and be certain nothing pernicious regrew in that hidden place.

She'd been up there making her regular inspection when Galen's message came through. Now she was back in her tiny hut, the two rooms her descendants called a "granny flat."

Nina snorted. She did not look or feel like a granny, or care to live like one. But here in this world she was a grandmother and a great-grandmother, many times over. Truth was, she'd lost track of how many "greats" now attached to her matriarchal status. She and Makani had known five generations of the family they made together. Of the descendants continuing on from there, however, Nina now had only a vague notion. More than a century had passed, after all, as reckoned by the passage of time in this world.

These days, islanders whose names she did not know would address her as "Noni Nina" and approach to offer tentative hugs. She found these encounters increasingly awkward, not least because the longevity granted a *wysard* of the true Power made Nina seem like a woman of twenty-five: a strong, healthy woman whose athleticism contrasted painfully with the decrepitude of her oldest living offspring.

"You're doing it again," Nina muttered to herself as she busied around her small rooms. Into a satchel of soft cloth, she threw spare clothes, then shouldered her bow and quiver of arrows as she headed for the hut's narrow door. "You are running from the brevity of mortal life. You're fleeing the pain of deathbed vigils."

This time, however, Nina had an irreproachable reason for running. Her niece Jacca needed her.

Unlike the people of these islands—people whose years were measured by the limited timescales of their mortal world—Jacca was imbued with magic. From her wizardly ancestors, and by the favor of the Elemental Ones to whom the Power ultimately belonged, the girl had inherited a great gift of fire-magic. When first it manifested, Jacca's gift had overwhelmed the child. Nina had been forced to conjure waves of water to quench the inferno that threatened to burn the girl alive.

So great was Nina's concern for the child, she had made herself her niece's guardian. But then Jacca had been properly apprenticed to a master *wysard*, a fire-mage like the girl herself, a mage who could teach the girl to harness her gift. That master was none other than Galen the goldsmith, he who had fathered the child out of wedlock and for a time had refused to acknowledge her, or to admit the affair that had produced her. It had taken Nina's cajoling—and the display of Jacca's extraordinary powers—to convince Galen to accept his responsibilities, both as the child's father and as her wizardly tutor.

But now something was amiss. *"Jacca needs you,"* Galen had said. Although distorted by its passage through the magical pendant, his message had carried notes of urgency. Had Jacca's gift overwhelmed even the master fire-mage who had been conjuring and controlling infernos since his babyhood? Was Galen desperate once again for the quenching power of Nina's water magic?

As she hurried past the main house, toward the coral-sand beach of the secluded bay, Nina paused to speak to one of the urchins who played in the shallows, splashing like a porpoise and laughing. The boy was her direct descendant, but by how many generations she couldn't be bothered to calculate. She certainly did not remember the child's name. Her Earthly progeny were uncountable by now. Her offshoots had spread through the islands, many of them sailing away year by year to populate distant shores. Nina did not ask the boy's name as she beckoned him over. He clearly knew who *she* was, and that was all that mattered.

"Child," she said, crouching to address him at eye-level, "there's somewhere I need to be. Tell your folks that 'Noni Nina' has gone traveling." As the boy reached with pudgy fingers to trace the curve of the bow in Nina's hand, she crooked a smile and added, "Tell them I won't be needing the granny flat."

Chapter Two

Nina's leap across the void ended with her splashing into waters even warmer than the tropical seas she'd left. A strong sidestroke brought her to a familiar ledge of rock at the edge of the hot-spring pool. She and Jacca had sat together on this very ledge, back when the girl first showed Nina the spring that bubbled in secluded secrecy in the Ore Hills, up behind Galen's lodge. The warm waters had been their place of bathing and swimming during the days when Nina and Jacca had shared a tent in a hillside pinewood, while Galen had tried—and failed—to figure a way out of his parental responsibilities.

The hot spring was exactly where Nina had wanted to land. She'd crossed the void with perfect precision—a feat not assured, given that all of her previous transits between the worlds had been to and from the wizardly stronghold of Ruain. In that hidden province, the realm of her birth, Nina had called upon Ruain's vast magical potencies to carry her through the nothingness. She had not been certain that her own powers of water magic would be sufficient to bridge the gulf between Earth's Pacific Ocean and Galen's Ladrehdinian spring.

As she climbed from the water, Nina whispered her thanks to the unseen but always felt Source of her wizardly gifts. Hard experience had taught her: magical power belonged to the Elementals and must never be taken for granted. Never a day passed, now, when Nina did not express her gratitude for what she had been given.

Crouched on the ledge near the pool's upper rim, Nina caught her long braid of raven hair and swung it like a sodden rope over her shoulder. Tied to the end of the braid, as always, was a strip of satin-shiny, iridescent fabric, its colors shimmering through every shade of purple, violet, blue, and woodland green.

"Grog, my old friend," Nina called down into the pool, directing her voice through its depths, downward to the fractured rock where heated water welled up from the sunless, stony roots of these hills. "I have returned." She swished the end of her braid in the water, the fabric floating and twisting, making a tiny disturbance that was unlikely to catch the attention of the King of the Underworld. But she must try. "I'm in the hills west of that desert lake where last we met. I would love to see you. I've missed you."

Not awaiting an answer—Grog could be thousands of miles from here, and a hundred miles deep—Nina scrambled up off the ledge. From the rim of the pool, she made straight for the trail through the pine trees. Her clothes and hair dripping as she walked, she followed the trail down to the frigid cave that had once been Jacca's refuge from the child's blistering fire-magic. Nina stuck her head in, but saw by the conjured light of an Ercil's orb that the child's former "bedchamber" was empty. Nothing now remained of the water cask, the candle stubs, or the heaped blankets with which the cave had once been furnished.

Farther downhill, Nina left the trees and approached the back gate of Galen's lodge. She did not tarry there, or call out to whoever might now dwell in that house. The last time Nina had seen the place, Galen's mortal wife had been resident within, the woman seething with fury over the revelation of her husband's affair and the by-blow the affair had produced. Nina saw no reason to seek Galen within the walls of that house. More than likely, his wife had thrown him out.

A surer place to find Galen, always and ever, would be the metalsmith's forge. Nina continued on down the lane and around the corner, out into the sun that baked these hillsides only a little less ferociously than it scorched the desert that stretched eastward from their feet. She followed the street she had climbed on the day she'd first reached the Ore Hills, and retraced her steps down near the stables where she had left her horse on that initial visit.

As she neared the shadowy alleyway in which she had taken her leave of Corlis—bidding the nomad farewell with a last, passionate kiss—Nina faltered. With an impatient shake of her head, she pushed the memory aside. She could not, however, stop her sidelong glance down the length of the alley as she stepped past to pull open the door of Galen's workshop.

The smithy was surprisingly cool inside. A back door stood open, and through it Nina glimpsed the blue-white glow of a roaring fire in the adjacent courtyard: Galen's forge in operation. But whether by clever placement of the furnace or magical restriction of the heat that it threw off, the front of Galen's shop offered customers a cool and sparklingly illuminated room in which to admire the metalsmith's craftsmanship.

Displayed were tiers of fine jewelry in gold and silver, steel and copper, many embellished with precious gemstones that glittered against the polished metals. Alongside the jewelry, Galen's sought-after blades filled a glass-fronted case. On offer were daggers, stilettos, short swords, cleavers, boning knives, and even scythes. Occupying two walls were examples of Galen's larger smithcrafts: gates made from iron bars that he'd twisted into the fantastical shapes of wild animals and mythical beasts: hooded snakes, fringed lizards, fire-breathing dragons.

Nina took it all in with a glance that encompassed an apprentice who sat at work in a far corner, the boy so focused on the gold wire he was braiding that he hadn't looked up when the jingle of the bell over the shop door announced her arrival. The clerk behind the counter, however, took immediate note of Nina's presence.

"May I help you, madam?" the gray-haired beldame asked in the crisp voice of a practiced saleswoman. "A beauty like yours needs draping in gold." The woman gestured at the heaviest, most ostentatious collars and necklaces on display—the priciest items in the shop, Nina felt certain. Though why the woman would think Nina could afford such treasures was beyond her. She'd arrived in Galen's showroom penniless, and decidedly bedraggled from her submersion in the hot spring, her dusty walk down the chalk-layered hillside, and her sweaty traverse of shadeless streets. Though now, out of the sun and standing in the chill interior of the shop, Nina felt goosebumps rise on her bare arms. Her knee-length trousers and thin, summer blouse stuck to her with clammy dampness where they had not yet dried.

"Is Galen out back?" she asked with the casual confidence of someone who felt entitled to deal with the owner directly, bypassing the hired help at the front counter. "He's expecting me."

The saleswoman lifted her chin and eyed Nina narrowly. But then she gave a brief nod and stepped to the doorway where the sound of forging drifted into the shop, a muted roar from the furnace yard beyond.

"Sir!" the woman yelled into the middle distance. "A lady here to see you."

No change ensued in the hiss of flames or the rhythmic clanking and hammering that filled the space beyond the open door. But presently Galen stood framed in that doorway. The sun and the white fire from the open yard behind him conspired with the glitter of gold and jewels in his showroom to strike sparks from his tousled copper hair. His green eyes flashed with the clarity of emeralds as his gaze swept the room and lit upon Nina.

"Sister!" he cried, and lunged from the doorway to fling open a hinged slab in the display counter so she could join him in the back. "I wasn't sure you'd received my message." His voice sounded muffled as he embraced her and pressed his cheek against hers. "I thought you had, but that was many days ago. I was afraid you would not come."

"Days?"

Nina extricated herself from Galen's enveloping arms, arms that bulged with a blacksmith's musculature. She frowned up at her brother. "I was on my way here within an *hour* of scorching my hand on this magical messenger of yours." From under the neckline of her blouse, Nina pulled out the beautiful pendant with its ocean waves crafted of blue steel, the symbol of her element gleaming under the brilliant whitecaps that Galen had worked in polished silver. "I barely took time to grab my bow and a few spare clothes." Nina dropped her squishy satchel on a bench in the sunlit furnace yard and rested her bow beside it, then unshouldered her quiver and belatedly checked that she hadn't lost her arrows in the hot spring. "What can you mean, that you called me days ago?"

Galen lifted his hands, his sooty palms up and fingers spread, signaling his uncertainty. "It's been days for *me*," he said, gazing at her. "I guess there's no knowing, though, what time does or how fast it passes for you ... out there in the great beyond."

"Of course!" Nina smacked her forehead in sudden comprehension. "Island time."

The conventional meaning of that phrase, as Nina had learned it during her sojourn on the ocean world, referred to the easygoing, live-in-the-moment attitude that many islanders could embrace when their day-to-day survival was no longer their chief concern. Conditions in the archipelago had improved dramatically since Nina's earliest introduction to those islands. Back in the last century, by the count of Earthly years, staying alive was all anyone could do or think about. Nowadays, however, the people had leisure for playing games, making art, chasing butterflies and generally "goofing off," as they put it.

But for Nina, "island time" had quite a different meaning. That's what she called the mind-bending disparity between the elapse of years on Earth and the way moments were reckoned on Ladrehdin. She'd been barely six years old the first time she set foot on the ocean world. Her mother, anxious for Nina's safety in a place torn apart by pestilence and bloody violence, had forbidden any return journeys until Nina's wizardly tutor released her from apprenticeship. It wasn't until Nina was nearly thirteen that her parents accepted her tutor's assessment, and the young *wysard*'s own, that she was ready to make the leap. Nina, however, had arrived in the islands a second time to find that a scant twenty-four months had passed in that reality while she'd been home in Ruain for a full seven years.

Much more recently, the pattern had repeated when she'd toured the south country of her homeworld for nearly a year, and then returned to the islands to ensure the continued security of her adopted realm. No one in the archipelago had even noticed she'd been gone. A year in Ladrehdin had translated to a few days on Earth.

And so it was again. Here in the Ore Hills, Galen had been watching sunrises come and go, despairing of Nina's return although she had sprung back immediately, from her perspective, upon hearing Galen's call.

"Island time," Nina repeated, and squeezed Galen's grubby hand. "It plays tricks. But I'm here now." She looked around the furnace yard, seeking her niece amid the noise and smoke of smelting and forging. "Where's Jacca? Is the girl all right?"

"She's traveling," Galen muttered. "Safely away from here. I had to get her out of the hills and let folks simmer down."

"Simmer down?" Nina echoed. "What happened? What has she done?"

"Nothing," Galen almost snapped, his emerald eyes glittering. "My daughter has done nothing wrong. She's harmed no one. But things have been happening here that people can't explain. They've decided to blame Jacca, since they cannot find anyone else to blame for their troubles."

"What troubles?" Nina started to ask, but held her tongue as the words continued to flow from Galen. Her brother had begun life as a happily mischievous but untalkative child. Over the years, however, Galen had grown fluent in his speech, an alteration that still tended to startle Nina, it seemed so different from the nearly wordless boy she'd grown up with.

"Maynor started the slander," Galen said, fuming. "Mostly to get back at me." He snorted. "The man will not challenge me to a duel that he knows he'll lose. So he's spreading rumors and lies to hurt me and defame Jacca." Galen frowned as he rubbed the back of his neck. "I need you to help me keep a level head, Nina." He shot her an earnest look. "I need you to quench some fires—my own maybe, to stop me burning Maynor alive. He has tried my patience until I'm about ready to fry him."

With a sharp snap of his fingers, Galen evoked a long tongue of white-hot fire from the mouth of the nearby forge.

"But mostly, Nina," he added as he dropped his hand and turned back to her, "the people of these hills need you to quench whatever those fires are, the sparks that come in the night and set haystacks alight, and barns, and now a couple of houses. People are scared, with good reason. But they've got no reason to think Jacca is setting the fires. She is innocent. While she's gone from here, we'll prove it. You and me, we'll find out what's going on. We'll prove the girl is blameless."

Nina studied her brother, absentmindedly fingering the now-dry strip of fabric at the end of her braid. Then she stooped to pick up her bow and quiver. The damp satchel of clothes, she thrust at Galen, not remembering the dark soot on his hands until he'd caught the soggy sack. Nina winced at the smudges he left on the pastel tropical weave.

"The last time I came here," she said, turning toward the door to the shop's interior, "you stuck me in a tent and never invited me into your home. That's not happening this time. I want a proper bed and a tub with hot water, and somewhere to cook that's not a campfire. A table with chairs would be nice, too. You got any of those?"

A grin creased Galen's face. For a moment he looked like the impish little boy who had summoned fires while Nina conjured floods, back in their half-wild childhoods. "At your service, my lady," he said with a bow half mocking, half sincere. "You shall have all that I possess, as an honored guest in my humble home. Just let me bank these fires before we head out."

He shouldered Nina's satchel, freeing both his hands to work his magic. With quick snaps of his fingers, Galen reduced the inferno within the forge to a redly glowing bed of coals. Across the way, molten metal splashed into a smooth iron mold and grew still when the firemaster flicked a settling spell at it. The yard fell silent around them as Galen stood in the doorway magically suspending every operation of smelting, casting, forging, and hammering.

"If that's how you do it," Nina said, grinning back at him, "then I wonder you can get so dirty." She looked askance at his sooty hands. "Why touch anything if all you have to do is cock an eyebrow at it?"

Galen snorted. "Be content if you will, sister, to summon your own magic with an aloof wave of your hand. I, however, must *touch* my element. My soul craves the feeling of fire at my fingertips, and the weight of solid metal in my grasp. I practice my art as close to it as I can get without it burning me to a crisp."

Nina considered him, then nodded understanding. "Thus it has always been. Even when we were babies together, you risked burning yourself with your conjured fires—and later with your melted metals. But as your more sensible big sister, I knew how to make waves without drowning in them."

"That's a talent which may prove invaluable, in the present instance," Galen muttered, a thoughtful frown replacing his smile as he ushered Nina through the shop door and out into the sun-washed street. "Come up to the house—the abode I now call home—and let me explain the problem. If I *can* explain it, that is," he added cryptically.

Chapter Three

I t's simple," Nina said, far too glibly, when Galen had concluded his account of recent events in the Ore Hills. "You've got an arsonist running around. Are you sure it isn't Maynor setting the fires? He seems the type. Bitter and resentful."

Galen shook his head. "That's what I thought, at first. But I've had him watched. My men tell me Maynor is sleeping on his front porch, weapons ready to kill anybody who comes near. He hasn't stirred on any night when there has been a fire. It can't be him."

"And you're sure it's not Jacca."

Nina meant to declare the girl's undoubted innocence. But Galen frowned as though he'd heard a question in her statement.

"I'm *certain* it's not Jacca," he growled. "By her own insistence—to rule out the possibility that she's been sleepwalking, or entranced, or anything of the sort—I've locked her in her room at night." Galen gestured up the stairs of the cozy stone cottage that he now called home. He had shared the simple abode with his daughter since returning to the Ore Hills and finding his wife unwilling to cohabit with either himself or the child of his illicit affair. "You're welcome to examine the door bolts and the window shutters. Jacca could not have got out—unless she's able to dissolve into smoke and drift through the cracks."

Nina laughed. "I believe that you yourself were once accused of possessing such powers. Didn't our honored mother suspect that you evaded her vigilance in exactly that manner?"

Galen's frown dissolved into a chuckle. "She leveled the charge at me while hauling me back to bed by my ear one night. I denied it then, and I'll deny it now on behalf of my daughter. I am not a shapeshifter, and neither is Jacca." Galen's grin turned pensive, then fled altogether. "The girl has, however, taken a shine to a certain shapeshifting youth who is known to you."

"Wolfram?" Nina exclaimed, naming the only possible candidate. "My wolf cub? How in the world does Jacca even *know* Wolfram? I left that young man a long way from here. The last I saw of him, he was leaping through the Rum Ridges, chasing outlaws and ready to tear them apart with his fangs."

"Wolfram's been here to the hills several times since you parted from him," Galen replied. "He makes himself available as a messenger, a go-between to Vivienne's clan up near Imlen." Galen rubbed the back of his neck. "It never entered my thick skull that I might be playing matchmaker when I sent Jacca to Lady Marsial for the summer. At the time, it seemed a good idea to let Wolfram escort the girl on a visit to her cousins. Marsial and the rest of those *wysards* up yonder can teach Jacca all manner of skills that are beyond me. Not just magic, you know, but ... woman stuff." Galen averted his gaze and heaved a forlorn-sounding, slightly embarrassed sigh.

"Raising a girl by yourself must be hard," Nina murmured, sympathy rising in her. Galen had once hoped for a reconciliation with Jacca's mother, the hillwoman named Taji, his former mistress. Evidently, he had not gotten his wish.

Galen shrugged, a self-conscious twitch. "A girl growing toward womanhood needs other females to show her the ropes. Jacca is always keen to go up to her cousins. Every time she comes home, she's full of all the new spellcraft she has learned, the new skills she's mastered—everything from weaving chainmail and wielding a sword, to conjuring roses and summoning rain. I hardly know the girl, it seems now, she's grown up so much these past years."

"I wonder if I'll even recognize her," Nina muttered, beginning to realize that Jacca was no longer the little girl who had once been under her guardianship. Time had passed, and passed swiftly here in the world of Ladrehdin. "How old is Jacca now?"

Nina shot the question to Galen across the dining table where they sat nursing cups of tea. Upon arriving at her brother's cottage, Nina had barely taken time to unpack her satchel and hang her damp clothes to dry in the kitchen doorway where it opened upon a small, enclosed garden. Galen had scrubbed the soot from his hands, made a pot of tea, and settled himself and Nina at the table for their long exchange of news. Nina had little to impart, given that she'd hardly set foot on the islands of her adopted world before answering Galen's summons and making the leap back to his desert hills.

Her brother, however, brimmed with new developments. The more Galen talked, the greater the impetus on Nina to recalibrate her internal clockworks away from "island time" and accept that years had passed in the lives of her loved ones here.

"Jacca is fifteen," Galen said, looking across at her with furrowed brow. "Plenty old enough, I'm belatedly realizing, to notice boys. She's definitely noticed Wolfram. You'll think me a fool, and such I am, to have allowed that fellow to escort the girl—unchaperoned—all the way to Vivienne's clan and then back to the Hills. If I was thinking at all, I suppose I thought of Wolfram like he was just another cousin of hers." Galen rubbed the back of his neck again, as if to ease a sprain. "That was before I saw the way Jacca looked at him."

Nina laid her hand on Galen's where it rested on the tabletop. "May I remind you, dear brother," she said, smiling gently, "that I, too, have traveled with Wolfe 'unchaperoned.' The boy behaved toward me as a perfect gentleman."

"What else could he do?" Galen demanded, his gaze narrowing. "Wolfram knows as well as I do what you would have done to him, had he insulted or offended you."

"He also knows what *Jacca* will do to him." Nina squeezed Galen's hand. "Maybe you did not hear the advice that I gave the girl, that afternoon when the hunting party surprised us on the trail through the foothills. Harmless though they were, those men gave Jacca a terrible fright. She tore her skin to ribbons, hiding from them in the briars." Nina clucked her tongue, remembering. "When I finally got her out of those brambles, I impressed upon her what my mother had told me and Vivienne, both of us long ago in our girlhoods: The daughters—and granddaughters—of House Verek have the power to slay any man who threatens our lives or our bodies. I told Jacca to never withhold her magic, should any man menace her, or offer her an insult. I told her she must do to her attacker what she'd done to that timber snake."

Nina chuckled at the expression that befell Galen's countenance, a look both heartened and alarmed.

"You remember that snake, don't you, Galen?" she asked. "To protect you, Jacca burned that viper to ash. Do you really think Wolfram would risk the same fate? I believe you can rest easy, brother. Wolfe is not only a gentleman, he's surely *wysard* enough to know that he's no match for Jacca. Not when it comes to slinging deadly spells, I mean," Nina hastened to add. "As a suitor, however, and eventually a husband to her, I would consider the young man to be an exceptionally eligible match. I came to esteem Wolfram highly during our travels together."

Galen answered with a short shake of his head. Though he said nothing to contradict her, he gave Nina the impression that he was not sold on the idea of a shapeshifter as a son-in-law.

"I'm not sure I ever told you," he muttered after a brief pause, "how grateful I am for the guidance you offered the girl, in the short time she was with you—how you helped Jacca overcome her fears and embrace her gifts." Galen patted Nina's hand, then reached for the teapot to refill his cup and hers. "I have often wondered if the girl wouldn't have been better off, if I'd kept to my original intention to hand her over to you, then bid the pair of you a fond farewell and slink home to my very angry wife."

"But think what you would have missed!" Nina countered, raising her teacup to him in a mock toast. "You wouldn't have had the excitement of training the most extraordinary fire-mage to come along in this present age. And you wouldn't be the anxious father losing sleep over his daughter being out with a boy." Nina saw in Galen's grimace the confirmation of her assumptions. "That's where Jacca is at this moment, right? You sent her off with Wolfe again, to get her out of the public eye while you figure out what's happening with these fires."

Galen put down his tea and leaned back in his chair. He ran the fingers of both hands through his uncombed hair. "The fellow is taking her back to her cousins," he said with a vexed sigh. "They haven't been gone long enough to have reached even the crossroads by now. But that's enough distance, I believe, to keep Jacca safe from the wild rumors and angry accusations that are flying around these hills."

He rocked forward again, and twisted to stare out through the cottage's open front door. "Another reason I can't pin the fires on Maynor, besides him never leaving his porch at night, is that his place is up in the hills a little north and east of that cave where you camped with Jacca. But all of the fires have been down in the river valley that runs west of here, a goodly way from Maynor's house. That's where we need to start looking for answers, as soon as you're ready, sister."

"What do you propose?" Nina looked at him, her head atilt. "Shall we camp in the valley and catch the culprit in the act?"

Galen nodded. "Let's ride there first thing in the morning. There's someone living at the edge of that valley who has wanted to meet you for years. She still has questions about the sandfly maggots that you dug out of Corlis."

"Your ancient herbalist?" Nina exclaimed. "She of the cucumber lotion that I slathered on Jacca's burns? I'm a little surprised the woman is still alive."

"She seems not to have aged a bit, these past seven years." Galen gave a shrug. "I'm beginning to think the old lady is immortal."

Chapter Four

They rode out at dawn, Galen mounted on the same horse that had carried him up the foothills trail when he'd served as "escort" to Nina and Jacca, during his failed attempt to solve his problems with women. Nina, however, was now bereft of her big-hearted roan, the gelding named Traveller who had once carried her from one end of the south country to the other. Trav belonged to Wolfram now, and the news of Jacca's interest in the shapeshifting youth brought Nina hope that she might see the horse again, as well as the young man. She had said good-bye to them both with scant expectation of ever meeting them again, and certainly with no thought of their reuniting this soon.

Making up for Trav's absence was the lithe, compact mare that Galen brought from the stables for Nina to ride.

"That looks like the breed Corlis favors," Nina exclaimed upon being introduced to the animal. "Small and white like those desert horses that thrive on sun and sand."

"It is one of his," Galen confirmed. "A spare from his herd. He brought it back from way down south, the last time he surfaced from his trading jaunts there among the warlords." Galen shook his head. "It's a mystery how the man can wander through that country and not get himself killed. Why don't those chieftains just slit his throat and rob his corpse? Instead, they pay him handsomely in raw gold, precious gems, and sometimes horses. Well-trained horses, at that."

Galen clicked his tongue, and the "spare" came to attention as if awaiting instructions. "I believe you will find this beast a pleasure to ride. She's smart and fast."

"What's her name?" Nina asked. "And why do you have her if she belongs to Corlis?"

"He called her Thorn," Galen replied. "But you can name her anything you want. Corlis said he didn't need her. He had a good packstring, and he wasn't ready to replace any of them or change his riding horse. He didn't want to pay to stable the mare indefinitely, so he traded her to me for a bag of my best knives." Galen ran a hand down his cheek and over his chin. "I haven't yet decided which of us rooked the other. It pains me to think he might be one up on me. Put this mare through her paces, if you please, and tell me whether I got a good deal."

Nina already knew the mare was worth the price. She'd bonded with the creature before she swung into the saddle. Looking into the mare's large, dark eyes, she glimpsed something more than animal intelligence. There was intellect in that equine brain.

"Thorn," Nina whispered into the mare's close-set, curved ears, "talk to me when you're ready. I know you can. I almost hear you now." Nina had learned the language of the dolphins that swam in the waters of her island home. Now she rode away from Galen's cottage convinced that this mare could communicate with her in its own way, not with a dolphin's clicks and whistles, and not even the recognizable moods conveyed by a horse's ear-flicking and head-bobbing. Nina wondered if Corlis had sensed something uncanny in the animal, and that was why he'd left Thorn behind.

His loss, came the unspoken thought into her mind.

She followed Galen along a side street that ran southward from his cottage. They passed a smattering of similarly modest abodes, many of them wattle and daub, a few built of stacked stone. Galen's new neighborhood was less elegant than the lodge with the fountain-filled grounds that he'd once shared with his wife Sheyla. Never having been invited inside that house, Nina had no idea of its interior aspects, whether it felt like a home or a museum. His current residence, however, the two-story cottage with its solid walls of native rock and enclosed private garden, had a warm and happy feeling within, as though imbued with the contentment of those who inhabited it.

The street climbed to the shoulder of the hill that overlooked Galen's cottage and his immediate neighbors. There, the lane ended at a well-marked trailhead. Galen reined his horse onto the trail. Nina followed, glad for the shade of the pine trees that thickened as they ascended the hill. The trees thinned again, however, as they topped the crest and dropped down into the wide valley that lay directly west of the Ore Hills. Ahead, mountains rose to dizzying heights, snow visible on their highest peaks in defiance of the blazing sun that parched the desert east of the Hills. The sun held less sway over this low strip of fertile land between the foothills and the mountains. But still its power had Nina sweating by the time Galen brought her to a pocket canyon that was tucked into one side of the valley, below a stony ridge.

Within the small, sheltered space, a miniature forest of pines and hardwoods shaded a ramshackle cottage. Chickens scratched busily in the grassy yard, and a herd of goats clambered up the slope behind the house. In a sunny garden alongside, vegetables ripened in colorful rows: red peppers, purple cabbages, yellow squash. Herbs abounded too, most of them instantly recognizable to a trained healer like Nina. She saw and smelled lavender and sage, peppermint and lemon balm, feverfew, chamomile, and countless others.

Sitting shaded on the cottage's front porch was a lean, whipcord figure who wore her long white hair pulled up into a topknot. Wisps of hair escaped the knot and floated around the woman's face like cobwebs. Her face was deeply lined, and yet retained a vestige of beauty: the woman had been lovely in her youth. Even now, she radiated magnificence, and an aura of power.

Of the true Power, Nina realized as the woman's gray eyes caught her gaze and locked on.

Nina was off her horse in an instant, breaking eye contact as she dropped a deep curtsy. Her sideways glance found Galen still in his saddle and looking confused.

Urgently she motioned him to dismount, speaking from the side of her mouth. "Show respect!" she hissed. "Can you not recognize an Old One who is right in front of you?"

"Wh-what?" Galen stammered as he obeyed Nina's gesture, but once afoot only stood staring at her stupidly. "Who? Where?"

From the direction of the porch came a throaty laugh.

"You are more perceptive, my lady, than your thickheaded brother." The Elder smiled benignly. "The fumes that Master Galen breathes in his forge have done his wits no good, I fear." The woman turned to Galen, who continued to stare idiotically, now with his mouth hanging open. "How many years, sir, have you been coming here to consult me, with never a thought that I was anything more than a hill-country herbalist?" She chuckled again. "Stop catching flies on your tongue, Galen, and introduce your companion."

Galen's teeth clicked together audibly as he snapped his jaws shut. He recovered enough of his composure to give the Elder a stiff, formal bow. As he straightened, he reached for Nina's hand and drew her forward.

"Lady Karenina of Ruain," he intoned with the gravity of a court herald, "eldest daughter of House Verek, firstborn amongst the children of Lady Carin, the blessed reviver of magic in this world, and first daughter of Lord Theil Verek, head of that honored House and sovereign of its lands and realms. May I have the privilege of presenting you to ..."

Here Galen faltered, his confusion returning as he groped for the honorifics appropriate to an Elder of wizardry who outranked him to such a degree, he now found himself tongue-tied in the presence of the Old One.

The whipcord figure rose from her seat on the porch. Age had not bent the woman's back. In the shade under the eaves, she stood straight and majestic as she beckoned her visitors to join her.

"Call me Mother Labéht," the woman said, stressing the *bet*. "It's how I've been known in these parts since I came down from the mountains. That was so long ago, I hardly remember any name to the contrary." As Nina stepped up on the porch, Labéht gave her a congenial nod and gestured to a rustic chair of wickerwork. The women took their seats in the cool shade, leaving Galen to settle on the top step, half in the sun and an object of curiosity to the chickens that came clucking up to him, pecking at his pockets as if expecting treats. Galen's efforts to shoo them away were restrained and cautious, as if he feared to ruffle a feather of any bird belonging to an Elder.

"Now that you know where to find me," Labéht said, fixing upon Nina a piercingly direct gaze, "I'll expect you for a long visit. I wish to know, in precise detail, how you dealt with the sandflies when you were in the desert with that vagabond Corlis. I have received two accounts of those events: your written description of purging the maggots, and the version Corlis spread around about ridding himself of the worms amidst veritable swarms of sandflies—a story I cannot credit. When you've the time, I'll desire the pleasure of your company for a leisurely talk about your experiences in the Badlands."

As Nina nodded, still too awestruck to say much in the presence of this living embodiment of Ladrehdin's wizardly antiquity, Labéht turned to the equally silent Galen.

"I thank you, Master Goldsmith, for showing your honored sister the way to my door," she said, settling back in her chair. "I will not detain either of you this morning, however, for you must be about the business of catching the latest plague of flies to afflict this land. I speak, of course, of 'fire-flies'—the drifting things that have set thatches and haystacks alight."

"Flies!" Galen and Nina exclaimed together, but not in the same voice. He reacted with incredulity; she, astonishment.

Labéht inclined her head. "Not the kind you're thinking of, I'll wager. They are not insects. I'm not certain they can properly be regarded as having 'life' in the way that life is commonly understood to exist. If I were pressed to describe the few that have drifted clearly into my view, I might call them cinders. Except," the Elder added, rubbing her thumb on her chin, "cinders may kindle whatever they touch. If the 'flying fires' that are wafting into this valley were so indiscriminate, every farmhouse, field, and barn would have gone up in flames by now."

"Wafting," Nina repeated, attentive to the woman's eyewitness account. "Like they're floating in on the breeze? From where?"

"From up there." Labéht twisted in her chair to indicate the mountains that rose steeply on the valley's far side, opposite her small, private canyon. "At night, I fancy I glimpse a dim glow in those heights. But I cannot be sure of what I see, nor can I tell you where to seek its origins. It seems to emanate from no fixed spot." Labéht twisted the other way, to reach behind her chair and drag out a burlap bundle. She used her foot—clad in a no-nonsense ankle boot with a flat heel—to push the bundle toward Nina.

"I have sacked up burn remedies for you." She nudged the burlap with her toe. "You may need them. In the bag, you will also find empty jars for collecting specimens. I suggest you show the dunderheads of these hills incontrovertible evidence, if you wish to disprove the accusations against young Jacca. Further, I recommend you take a witness with you, someone who is not the girl's blood relative, and whose word is beyond reproach. Take Warthog."

Labéht stood, signaling an end to this brief visit and the instructions she had issued. Although neither Galen nor Nina had broached the subject of mysterious fires in the valley, nor spoken of the slanders that had been drummed up against Jacca, the Old One seemed to know every reason that brother and sister had for riding into the valley this morning.

As Labéht rose, Nina shot to her feet and bowed her head respectfully. Her eye caught Galen's where he still sat on the steps trying with exaggerated gentleness to dislodge the chicken that had settled in his lap like a broody hen on a nest. With a sigh of exasperation, Nina scooped up the hen and carried it down the steps, reuniting it with the flock in the yard as Galen scrambled up and awkwardly made his obeisance.

"Be easy, goldsmith," Labéht said, chuckling. "If I've not yet turned you into a toad for your insolence, in all these years, I'm unlikely to begin now." She waved her hand dismissively. "Be about your business. Come back when you can tell me, with certainty, what makes those 'flying fires' and whence they arise."

Galen's response was an inarticulate mumble. He stumbled down the steps and all but vaulted into his saddle, taking his horse to a canter as he fled the Old One's presence. On her nimble desert mare, Nina followed at the same pace, and caught Galen at the mouth of the narrow canyon where he had slowed to a walk.

"How is it *possible*, brother," Nina demanded when she reined alongside him, "that you never recognized your 'ancient herbalist' for who and what she is? That woman's power took my breath away the instant I drew near."

Galen hung his head. "I cannot explain it. It's as though my eyes were covered with scales, and only when I saw her through your eyes did those scales fall away."

Nina adjusted the burlap bag that she had slung across the saddle in front of her. "I suppose it's in the nature of an Elder," she said, thoughtful, "to value privacy above almost any other consideration. Perhaps 'Mother Labéht' deliberately concealed her identity from you. In any case, you don't seem to have earned the woman's enmity. More than anything, she seemed amused by the impertinence you have shown her through the years." Nina frowned. "Even if she'd been only a village herbalist, however, her age alone should have commanded your respect, Galen. I hate to think you've been rude to her."

He flung up his hand in denial. "Never that. I've always esteemed her. We have been on civil terms for longer than I can remember." He tilted his head back and gazed with narrowed eyes at the hazy blue sky above the valley that they were now crossing widthwise. "Truth be told, I cannot say how long I have known the woman. Was she here generations ago, when first I came to the Ore Hills as apprentice to a master metalsmith?" Galen dropped his chin and gave a shrug. "My mind retains no memory of a first meeting with Mother Labéht. When I plumb my recollections for a moment of introduction, nothing surfaces except thoughts of her chickens."

"Chickens!" Nina exclaimed. "You've had an Old One within hollering distance all this time, and you're oblivious to all except her hens?"

Galen shrugged the other shoulder. "Those pesky birds fly at me every time I get near. They seem to expect treats, disregarding the fact that I have never once fed them." He rubbed his neck and gave a groan. "They try my patience beyond endurance. I fling them off, not hard enough to hurt them ... but with considerably more vigor than you saw from me this morning." He laughed, grimly. "Now I suppose I must suffer the creatures to roost upon my head and peck my ears. For I will never again dare to shoo them away."

Nina rolled her eyes, wondering if Labéht was correct about the diminished state of Galen's wits. "The solution couldn't be simpler, brother. Always bring pumpkin seeds—in a sack, not your pockets—to tempt them aside and out of your hair."

Galen grimaced, as if picturing himself scattering chicken feed like a flower girl with rose petals at a wedding. "Drisha's fist!" he swore. "Gives new meaning to the phrase, 'hen-pecked.' But I'll feed the damned chickens if it keeps their mistress from turning me into a mealworm or something."

"A wise decision. Now, if you're done smoothing feathers," Nina said, moving things along, "will you tell me, please, where we are to search for 'fire-flies'? And why we need a warthog with us?"

"A hog wallow could prove beneficial, if we're caught in a swarm of burning cinders," Galen muttered. "Warthog is not an animal, however, but a resident of this valley. He goes by that name because he spends his days in mud, making bricks from muck and clay. His handiwork is in every bread oven and pottery kiln in the Hills. I use his fire bricks in my forge. As Labéht said, Warthog is a man with an honest tongue—a sharp tongue, some would argue." Galen chuckled. "Let's just say that he is blunt in his speech. He tells the truth as he sees it."

"An impeccable witness, then," Nina said approvingly. From her absent niece's wardrobe that morning, she had borrowed a straw hat. Now she settled the hat more firmly on her brow, squinting at the intense sunlight that shimmered through the valley. "How long before we reach his wallow? In this heat, a splash of mud sounds enticing."

Chapter Five

Of mud, Nina got more than a splash.

The man called Warthog did not pause in his mucky work, but he nodded brusque agreement when Galen explained the purpose of their visit. The fellow affirmed that he, like Labéht, had seen embers drift into the valley from the high mountains to the west.

"I'll hunt 'em with ye," Warthog said in answer to Galen's request. "I see 'em most every night. Never thought to catch one." He motioned for Galen and Nina to dismount. "Get your boots off and give this mud a stomping. I ain't out to go nowhere 'til these bricks are made and dryin'."

Thus, Nina found herself up to her calves in a pit of wet clay and sand, tromping straw into the mixture with her bare feet and working up a sweat despite the coolness of the mud that oozed between her toes. Warthog kept them at it all afternoon, with only a brief pause for a lunch of bread and cheese. The brickmaker's "wallow" had a roof of sorts, a thatch of twigs and reeds supported on poles. The thatch provided enough shade from the sun to make the work bearable, but Nina's leg muscles were cramping and her feet stumbling long before Warthog called a halt.

In his build, the man was stocky like his namesake, with a crest of brown hair on his head and bristly tufts on his cheeks. Also like the animal, he was tough. Warthog labored without pause out in the open sun. Methodically the man cast mudbricks in fixed molds, forming smooth-sided blocks that he slapped onto a patch of bare ground to bake dry. The afternoon heat had Nina drinking perpetually from the waterskin that hung shaded under the thatch. The brickmaker, however, never paused for a sip until he had scooped the last of the mud from the pit, molded and trimmed it, and set it in the sun.

"That'll do," he grunted as he washed his hands in a water trough beside a brick-enclosed well in the yard of his brick-built house. "Clean yourselves up."

Galen was obliged to let down a bucket into the well and draw up fresh water, several bucketsful before he and Nina had sufficient for ridding themselves of their coatings of mud and muck. Though both had rolled up their trousers legs before wading into the pit, they'd ended their labors spattered from knee to neck.

That man better do a bang-up job of clearing Jacca's name, Nina thought. She scowled at the narrow front doorway through which Warthog had disappeared into the shadowy depths of his home, leaving his visitors sitting on the well-curb as they dried their feet and pulled on their boots.

Nina was about to grumble to Galen, that she had not expected to work so hard for the man's testimony, when Warthog reemerged into the fading light of the day. He held in his hands a two-handled clay jug.

"Come around back and get supper," he growled. "I ain't out to singe my whiskers on an empty stomach."

Nina's quick glance caught Galen arching a quizzical eyebrow at their taskmaster turned host. He said nothing, however, only gestured for Nina to proceed him past the coppice of hazel where their horses had spent the afternoon grazing, loafing out of the sun. Along one edge of the grove, behind Warthog's single-story home of stacked mud bricks, she found the man sloshing wine into clay cups beside trenchers of glazed terracotta. Arrayed on a sideboard under the eaves, across from a weather-beaten table of rough wood, were platters of cold meats, crisp vegetables, and crusty bread.

"Eat," Warthog grunted. "I ain't out to pack it all away myself." He ran a hand over his crest of stiff hair.

The man poured wine for himself and stood back to drink it as his visitors filled their plates with the unexpected bounty. When they sat down at the table, Warthog joined them but made no attempt at conversation. He only grunted wordlessly—a sound very like that of a hog—when Nina expressed appreciation for the food and ventured to compliment the straight, evenly spaced rows of bricks that formed the square walls of the man's squat home.

With Galen equally indisposed to talk—too fixed on his plate to bother with dinner-table civilities—Nina fell silent. She ate buttered bread and gazed out over the valley that sliced between the mountains and the Ore Hills. Warthog's property sat about midway across, his home and brickyard occupying a low bluff with a good view of the river that flowed through the valley. Below the bluff, the river moved lazily, murky with sediment. Away to the north, however, a clear stream rushing down out of the mountains fed a stretch of turbulent, foamy whitewater.

From Warthog's backyard, a meadow of surprisingly green grass sloped down to the river. The meadow angled off the shoulder of the bluff and descended through scattered willows, oaks, and a dark stand of stonebark trees. Neat walls, running the length of the greenway from yard to river, bordered the pasture. The walls were of brick— many rows of mudbrick stacked tall—but they would prove no obstacle to the dozen or so goats that cavorted down near the river. Those animals could come and go at will, easily leaping the walls.

Nina marveled at the work that had gone into enclosing the pasture. Those walls must have taken Warthog years to build, brick by mortared brick. She wondered why he had bothered, but she got her answer when the man pushed his plate aside. He swiveled around, put his fingers in his mouth, and send a piercing whistle down the backyard slope. Instantly, two mules came trotting out from the dense cover of the stonebarks, shadowed by the nearest wall as they scampered toward their master, their long ears pricked with interest.

"Be dark soon," Warthog grunted as he rose from the table. "I ain't out to cross the river in the black of night. Get your horses."

Nina and Galen scrambled to their feet and made for the hazel grove toward the front of the house. By the time they'd collected their horses and led the animals through a gate into the back pasture, Warthog had one of his mules saddled and the other loaded with tarpaulins. Nina contrived to brush up against the pack mule, unobtrusively examining the load, concerned lest Warthog was hauling combustible materials on a hunt for flaming embers. The man had anticipated the danger, however. The tarps were not oilcloth, but wool tightly felted, the fabric's hard surface impervious to virtually everything, including fire.

With a faint twitch of uneasiness—unacknowledged until now— she mounted, and followed as Warthog led the way down the sloping meadow to the river's pebbled bank. For a short distance, he reined his mule back along the bank, riding toward the foot of the bluff and to the slow-moving section of river directly below his homestead. There, Warthog splashed across to the river's far side, his mules crossing with surefooted confidence.

Galen's mount and Nina's new horse showed no hesitation to wade in, but both riders crossed warily, unable to see the riverbed in the murky water. The lack of clarity did not deter the horses from quenching their thirst as they stood knee-deep in the current. The coppice of hazel had offered shade and browsing, but no water through the afternoon.

Their slow crossing put them well behind Warthog, who had ridden onward without a backward glance. The man headed northwest, toward no discernible landmark in the mountains, but presumably toward a place from which he had seen glowing embers drift into the valley on errant night breezes.

The dusk was deepening to full dark by the time Nina and Galen caught up with their guide. Warthog had reined to a halt, and he sat astride his mule surveying the mountainside and the ridges, cliffs, and terraces that loomed, barely visible, upon the slopes.

"Up there, last I saw," he muttered, and pointed as his followers joined him. "Now we wait."

They dismounted, and made themselves as comfortable as possible in the rocky scree at the foot of the mountains. There would be no camp here tonight—no campfire to impede night vision, and no un-saddling of horses. They must be ready to move, and move quickly, should "flying fires" arise in the dark. Nina had no idea how difficult it would be, or how dangerous, to "bottle" a satisfactory sample of drift-ing embers. But she took note of the only item that Warthog unloaded from his pack mule. The man shook out a thick blanket of wool felt, not to cushion his seat on the ground, but to create a shelter. Draped over a tumble of larger rocks, the covering protected a crawl-space down amongst the boulders—a space big enough to shield a man of Wart-hog's stocky build, should fire gust down from the cliffs tonight.

Nina considered pulling the remaining wool blankets off of Wart-hog's pack animal, to ready them for herself and Galen. *But Master Warthog doesn't know,* she realized, *that I have the power of water at my command.*

Could she protect them all? She had once argued with Galen when he'd claimed that his element—fire—was of lesser potency than hers. Nina had contradicted him, maintaining that fire and water, although opposite, were equal.

Perhaps we will settle the argument tonight, or in nights to come, Nina mused, preparing herself for a vigil of weeks if that's what it took to prove that Jacca was not setting fire to her neighbors' roofs and hay-stacks. She sighed, feeling disgust mixed with anger at the girl's former stepfather, Maynor.

Maynor had emotionally abused the girl when she'd lived under his roof. Now it seemed that he'd been nursing his spite for the past seven years. The unexplained fires in the river valley had presented a perfect opportunity for Maynor to cast the girl as a malevolent witch. From what Galen had said of the matter, Nina surmised that most of the local population believed Jacca had been sneaking around in the dark of night, using her magian powers to burn barns and houses. How easy it would be to whip the people into a vengeful mob—ready to burn Jacca at the stake, should any individual die in one of those mysterious blazes.

Nina gazed up at the mountains, their bulk looming against the starry night sky as the last trace of twilight faded behind them. Ceaselessly she scanned the slopes, watching for any flicker. This was the closest she had ever been to the mountains that dominated the west of Ladrehdin—mountains that had sheltered the Old Ones when the Wizards Wars drove them out of the south, long ago. Most Elders of the craft had made their way to the far northwest, to high peaks thickly forested and capped with snow year-round. Some, however, had taken refuge along this southern spine of the mountains, where winters were milder but water less abundant due to the often scanty snowpack. Nina heard the river burble down the valley, and fancied she even heard the slender mountain stream as it rushed to join the river, creating the whitewater she had glimpsed from Warthog's bluff.

Otherwise, the night was silent. Nina's two companions said nothing, both of them as watchful as she. Occasionally one of the men would shift his position among the rocks, seeking comfort for his backside or relieving the strain on his neck from gazing too fixedly upward. Once, all three of them rattled the small pebbles at their feet, their muscles jerking reflexively as a wolf cut loose with a howl far up the slopes. The animal's cry was answered by another, farther away.

As silence again enveloped them, Nina turned her head to check on the horses. Both stood with Warthog's mules, none of the animals drowsing on their feet now, but roused to alertness by the wolves' cries. In the starlight, Nina saw Galen's mount and the two mules eyeing the same mountain slope that she had been studying into what felt like the wee hours of the night. Her own horse, however, was gazing farther north. Thorn's white coat stood out from the other animals, and revealed the mare standing with her attention fixed upvalley, her ears flicking with interest.

Nina followed the mare's gaze, and shot to her feet with a suddenness that startled her companions. Both men jerked upright. Galen had his hand stretched out, his fingers spread, ready with magian fire to scorch any potential attacker.

"Look there!" Nina exclaimed. She grabbed her brother's hand and used it like a pointer, pulling him around to see what she was seeing. "There's a swarm up there ... like fireflies. Fluttering along that spur yonder. See them?"

Before Galen could reply, Warthog was out of his crawl space and trundling past, his woolen blanket gathered in his arms in untidy folds. "That's them," he grunted as he flung the blanket onto his pack mule. "Ride."

In moments they were mounted and hastening toward the specks of light that had looked, from a distance, like a swirl of glowing insects. As they neared their quarry, however, Nina saw nothing living, only sparks like those that shot up the chimney when logs exploded in a fireplace. The sparks threw off heat as well as light, warming the chill night air that had settled in the valley like a cold shroud.

Nina reined up and dropped from her saddle. She fished in the bag of burn remedies and other supplies that Mother Labéht had given her, and pulled out the empty jars for collecting specimens.

"Don't risk your animals," Nina warned as she handed the glass containers to Galen and Warthog. "I'm going in on foot. Wet yourselves down. Just because these sparks are not setting the grass ablaze is no sign they won't burn skin."

Nina upended her canteen and soaked the straw hat she'd almost forgotten she wore. The borrowed hat hadn't left her head since she'd doffed it to Labéht, and then replaced it upon leaving the Old One's porch.

With water trickling through the loosely woven straw, dampening her hair and wetting her shoulders, Nina plowed into the sparking swarm. She swept the wide mouth of her uncorked jar through a particularly dense cloud of glowing particles, aiming to scoop up all she needed in one pass.

She caught nothing. The sparks swirled away, evading capture.

Time and again Nina tried, noting from the corner of her eye that Galen and Warthog were having similar difficulties. Warthog kept mostly clear of the swarm, sticking only his arm in amongst the sparks, jabbing his open jar one way and then another, haphazard in his efforts. But Galen was in the thick of it with Nina. As hot sparks landed on the backs of his hands, he emitted yelps of pain but only plunged in deeper, batting at the sparks and attempting to herd them into his jar.

Nina kept ducking to keep the sparks out of her eyes. The dripping brim of her hat mostly protected her face, but her bare arms were blistering under the onslaught of tiny glowing embers. As she bent to sweep her jar past her knees, aiming for the knot of sparks that hovered there momentarily in a sizzling cluster, she realized her trousers were smoldering. Her nostrils filled with the smell of burning linen.

"Give up, Galen!" she shouted as she lunged out of the swarm. Nina dropped her jar's cork stopper, leaving her with one hand free to snatch off her hat and beat her clothes with the damp straw. She snuffed hotspots down her legs and across her lower back. "Get out of there!" Nina yelled again when she looked up and saw Galen still in the midst of swirling flecks of fire. His clothes smoked, the shoulders of his shirt charred through as he struggled to secure the evidence that would lift the cloud of suspicion from Jacca.

Nina crammed her hat back on her head and darted again into the swarm. She sprinted toward Galen, her empty left hand reaching for him while she continued to hold the open jar ready in her right. As she rushed through the burning swirl, Nina found she was pushing sparks ahead of her, concentrating them in the constricted space formed by her two outstretched arms. Sparks packed tightly in the air between her torso and Galen's back, in the moment that she reached him.

Nina did not squander her chance. She plunged the jar into the mass, filling the container with blazing flecks as, lefthanded, she tore the shirt from Galen's shoulders. Wadded into the mouth of the jar, the fabric prevented the sparks from escaping.

"I have them!" Nina shouted into Galen's face. He had whirled at her touch, startled to feel his garment leave his back. Now as he stared at the glowing jar which she held before his eyes, he broke into a grin, seemingly oblivious to his blistered skin and smoldering trousers.

But Nina's numerous burns throbbed, radiating pain down her arms and legs. She turned to backtrack through the swarm, with a jerk of her head bidding Galen follow. He hurried after her, batting sparks away from both of them as best he could, but still letting many through to sear Nina's arms anew.

Warthog had backed off by this time. He waited with his mules beyond the swarm's edge. As Nina reached him, the man offered her the cork stopper he had retrieved from the ground where she'd dropped it. Swiftly, to give the sparks no chance to escape around the edges of the makeshift fabric plug, Nina corked the jar with the fabric still in place, like a thick liner under the stopper. The sparks were consuming the linen of Galen's shirt, eating their way through the material like predators gorging on a carcass.

Watching them, Nina shivered under her thin, damp, summer blouse. Judging by the lacework of pin-holed scorch marks that marred the garment wherever it had not received a protective wetting, she'd now be nearly shirtless in the chilly night if not for her soaking. Nina winced as goosebumps rose on her blistered arms, arousing fresh prickles of pain from every burn.

She was turning to the white mare, wanting the burn remedies from the bag tied to Thorn's saddle, when a shout from Galen brought her spinning back around.

"Firestorm!" he yelled. "Coming fast."

Nina squinted at the harsh brightness that assaulted her vision. Rolling toward them down a spur of rock was a low wall of fire. Within the glare, individual sparks danced, but they packed together so tightly, they presented a solid front.

Galen flung out his hand, sending the power of his element against the face of the wall, fighting fire with fire. The bolt that shot from his fingertips struck with the force of lightning and with a deafening crack of thunder. Shock waves reverberated across the valley. Warthog tumbled into the rocks, knocked off his feet. The brickmaker's mules brayed in terror and ran. Galen's mount reared, screaming with panic, and joined the mules in a headlong retreat.

The power of Galen's thunderbolt sheared away one side of the oncoming wall of fire and extinguished that side like a booted giant grinding sparks underfoot. Half of the wall remained intact, however, the speed of its advance undiminished by Galen's spellwork.

Nina pressed the jar of captured sparks to her chest, instinctively protecting the hard-won evidence as she flung up her free hand in the beckoning motion that she'd used all her life to summon the might of her own magic. The wizardry answered her: water surged against the rocky spur, as loud as storm surf against sea cliffs. A great wave hung suspended for a heartbeat, high above the rock, reflecting the glare of the firestorm. Then the wave broke upon the advancing wall of sparks.

Steam exploded upward and out, a tremendous cloud of vapor that roiled along the mountain spur and billowed downslope. Galen let out a whoop, a gleeful sound of approval as he hastily backed away to get clear of the blistering steam cloud.

Nina strained to see through the vapor, searching for surviving sparks. So intense was her focus, she did not notice Warthog scramble to his feet and leave the scree of rocks at the foot of the spur. She jumped when the man's piercing whistle split the darkness that had again enveloped the night.

Hoofbeats sounded behind her. Nina turned to discover Warthog's two mules returning, obedient to the man's summons. Thorn was there too, standing alert but seemingly unperturbed by the night's commotions. Galen's horse, however, had fled the vicinity and was nowhere to be seen.

"Sir," Nina said sharply as she intercepted the brickmaker before he could mount his mule and also quit this place, as was clearly the man's intent. "Take this."

She pressed the specimen jar into Warthog's hands. Sparks still glowed within it, but in diminished numbers now. Either they were exhausting their fuel, having consumed the linen that lined the cork stopper, or they were running out of air. Time was short for presenting this evidence to the court of public opinion.

"I beg you will ride into the hills tonight, without delay, and tell the people what you have witnessed here." Nina locked gazes with the man. She stood eye level with him: Warthog was about her own height. Enough light gleamed from the jar, and from the stars above, to reveal both wonder and alarm in the man's face. Whatever Warthog might know or think about the magian fires that Master Galen commanded in the furnaces of the smith's forge, the magic on display in this valley tonight must surpass any wizardry the brickmaker had ever experienced.

For generations, the people of the Ore Hills had lived as next-door neighbors to mountain-dwelling magian hermits. For the most part, the hillfolk were comfortably familiar with magic. Many family lines in the foothills carried traces of the Gift, inheritors of magian talents that ranged from slight to substantial. Jacca's maternal line was one such family. The girl had a grandmother in the northern end of this valley where it sliced between foothills and mountain peaks. That beldame was a renowned dowser with a gift for finding veins of ore and precious gemstones.

Familiar with magic though Warthog might be, however, as one who resided cheek-by-jowl with it, the man was shaken by what he had seen tonight of Galen's powers, and Nina's. Sympathetic though she was, Nina would not release Warthog from his duties as witness.

"Go," she bade him, her tone as commanding as her gaze—the darkly brilliant, imperious gaze Nina had inherited as a daughter of House Verek, child of a "warlock" whose glance could strike terror. "Tell everyone what you have seen. Show them these sparks"—Nina indicated the jar now gripped tightly in Warthog's hands—"and give your testimony. Inexplicable though these events seem, with the source of the sparks yet a mystery to us all, everyone in these hills must now concede that Galen's daughter is wrongly accused."

Warthog gave a short nod. "I'll speak for the girl," he grunted. The bristly tufts on the man's cheeks nearly brushed Nina's face as he spun away, his hurry to be gone written in every motion as he caught the lead rope of his pack animal and swung into the saddle of the mule that he rode. Nina watched the man stuff the glowing jar down inside his shirt, its light vanishing as he reined toward the river and his destination beyond: the hills at the valley's eastern edge.

"I would wish to go with him," came Galen's voice at Nina's elbow. The fire-mage had approached her so unobtrusively, Nina had not noticed him standing with her until he spoke. "I would like to judge the effect of his words on those who hear him tonight."

"Do you trust him to faithfully discharge his errand?"

"Of a certainty. Warthog is perhaps the only witness in the whole of the southwest whose word is incontestable. His reputation for honesty is unrivaled."

"Then it's best that he goes alone," Nina reasoned as she stepped to her horse to fetch the bag of burn medicine. "Your presence could not lend weight to his testimony, it could only detract. Take this," she added as she turned her hand palm up and conjured witchlight, letting the orb float above her fingers. "Hold it where I can see your burns. Those sparks roasted you."

Nina slathered ointment on her brother's arms, his shoulders, his back and chest. Then she treated her own injuries, which were fewer than Galen's but throbbing nonetheless. By the magical witchlight, Nina examined her blisters, all of them small, hardly larger than pinheads, but hurting like the stings of fire ants.

"How could those sparks burn skin and not set grass afire?" she marveled as she stoppered the ointment. Nina turned with Galen to survey the ground where they had battled the hot particles. The base of the mountain spur was muddy where Nina's conjured wave had soaked it. But beyond the rocky scree, the valley floor was covered in grass, rank with dry, feathery seedheads that would go up like torches if exposed to ordinary flame. No spark had caught in that grass, however, and Mother Labéht had mentioned the "discriminating" nature of the cinders—that they did not burn every flammable thing they touched.

"If I understand what you told me earlier," Nina continued when Galen offered no immediate reply, only a thoughtful frown, "people around here had ruled out wildfires—natural fires—because no grassland had burned. Only haystacks and barns ... structures that people had built. Folks assumed that some person must be setting the fires, deliberately and maliciously destroying the work of their neighbors' hands."

"Some person?" Galen repeated. "The arsonist you proposed to catch in the act tonight?" With a sweeping gesture of his arm, he indicated the mountain slopes that loomed above them. "Anyone could hide up there, easy enough. But not just 'anyone' would have the power to tell the sparks what to burn, and what to leave alone."

Nina rubbed her lower lip. "What are you willing to bet that we've spooked our mysterious quarry? Whoever's behind these fires, they've now seen the might of your thunderbolts and my water magic. If they've gone to ground, hiding up there, we can nose them out." She jerked her chin at the rocky spur down which the sparks had swirled, their patterns loose at first like fireflies swarming, but then coalescing into a solid wall of fire. "Let's climb. In the dark, we may see the glow of the firebug's lair and put an end to this maliciousness, tonight."

"Lair?" Galen muttered, casting a sidelong glance at her. "I wish you hadn't put it like that. You've got me remembering those tales of ogres and dragons and mountain trolls that our tutor used to read us for bedtime stories."

Nina inclined her head. She wouldn't want to admit it, but those same old stories had risen, unbidden, to her own thoughts. Just what kind of "arsonist" were they dealing with?

Chapter Six

Only a short climb up the mountain spur, they came upon embers trapped amongst rocks. The scattered fire "flies" appeared to have lost the power of flight. A faint breeze arose with the first hint of false dawn, but it failed to lift the embers into the air. Where they lay on the bare ground, a few stray sparks took new life from an errant puff of wind, but their renewed brightness did not last. The sparks faded, dying to ash ... but not before they had outlined a trail of sorts, leading upward through the dark rocks.

The fast-dimming glow on the ground guided Nina and Galen up to a crack that opened below the ridgeline of the spur. The crack was narrow and of no great length, but fire seethed deep in its belly. Alerted by yellow-white light seeping from the fissure, they approached warily, watching for a sign of the quarry they pursued.

But when they had climbed high enough to peer down into the crack and feel its heat on their faces, they saw no one and nothing crouched there—only fresh swarms of sparks. These were dense and bright, not fading like the stray particles that languished outside the protection of the fissure. Nina, mesmerized, watched the sparks dance in their subterranean vestibule. As they roiled and tumbled, the sparks resembled water in a boiling pot.

"Boiling," she muttered, mostly to herself.

Then she looked at Galen, who stood near, also observing. "Brother, I'm going to pour water into that pot of fire. Lots of water that will make lots of steam. If you don't want the two of us parboiled where we stand, then I suggest you be ready to seal the crack. Throw the power of your element upon its rim and melt the edges together. Fuse the rocks solid so that neither spark nor steam may escape."

"Tricky magic!" Galen exclaimed, staring at Nina in the combined glow from the fissure and the thin predawn light. "You suppose I can seal the crack fast enough to stop a burst of steam from blasting us off this slope? Even if I succeed, the explosion will shake this mountain. You would risk such perils, to douse a cloud of sparks that seem safely contained for the present?"

"I want the explosion," Nina insisted. "I want the combined power of our wizardry to send a spasm through this mountain. Recall what Mother Labéht said about the 'flying fires' that drift in the night, how they seem to emanate from no fixed spot on this side of the valley." Nina pointed at the ground under her feet. "Remember, too, that Warthog guided us to a slope south of the ridge upon which we now stand. He led us to where he had seen sparks arise in the night. But we soon found out that they may erupt from a different place altogether."

Galen frowned, but slowly nodded. "You think this crack in the rock is connected to others. You seek to make an explosion so powerful that steam will boil through the branching passageways and snuff every spark that burns in the bowels of these mountains."

"I do. With a single stroke, we may end this demoncraft."

Galen's rust-colored eyebrows shot up, nearly to the waves of hair that fell over his forehead. "That's an odd choice of words. From whence comes your talk of 'demons'?"

Nina took a moment before replying. In memory, she replayed her last visit to the south country, when she'd glimpsed an underworld she never would have guessed existed. She'd met a magical being who came from that place and called it his home.

In her mind's eye, Nina pictured her friend Grog, the shapeshifting man of rock who had wandered up from the depths to dwell for a melancholy time in the surface world of sun and sky. Grog's joy had been palpable when he'd found his way back to the netherworld. He'd disappeared through a smoldering rift in the bedrock—a crack not so very different from the fissure that housed the dancing sparks at Nina's feet.

She could not explain to herself, much less to Galen, how different this crack felt from the steaming rift that had opened in the grasslands to give Grog his safe passage home. The longer Nina lingered above the fire-filled vent in this mountain spur, the stronger the impression of malice that rose from it—an impression at odds with Grog's aura of immense but gentle strength. Something spiteful was stirring at the mountain's roots. It wished harm to the farmers of the valley and to the artisans in the neighboring foothills. Nina had never supposed that Grog lived entirely alone in the vast, unknowable reaches of the underworld. Nor had she forgotten the stories that she and Galen had learned in their childhoods—the ancient tales of demons, dragons, wyverns and wyrms that were said to live in the fiery depths.

"Let's just call it a feeling," she finally said in answer to Galen's questioning look. "I want to do this, and I need your help." Nina raised her hand, prepared to hurl a river of water down into the depths. "Are you ready? I'll flood the crack in one stroke, fast as I can. You cap the fissure and seal the steam inside. Don't try to be neat," Nina added, mindful of her brother's exacting standards when he smelted ores in his forge. "Speed and strength are all that will count."

Galen looked apprehensive, but he'd never been able to say no to his big sister. He shifted toward her and squared his stance, ready to summon magian fire so hot, it could melt mountains.

"On three," he said with a quick glance at Nina. "Count us down."

She nodded. "One ... two ... *three!*"

No mortal eye could have followed the speed of the siblings' spellwork. The downward sweep of Nina's arm blurred to invisibility. Steam hissed as her conjured flood engulfed the densely packed sparks. In an instant that could not be measured in time, but existed in the indefinable spaces between moments, Galen's thunderbolts struck the fissure's edge. His incandescent fires melted the rock, fusing the edges together and trapping the steam within.

Under their feet, the mountain bucked. Nina and Galen hit the ground, digging in with fingers, elbows, and the toes of their boots, fighting the ridge's efforts to shake them off. With her face in the dirt and her ears filling with grit, Nina heard steam rip through the granite under her. It exploded through stony fractures and cleaved new channels in the rock.

For what seemed minutes but might have been only seconds, the mountain quaked. Boulders tore loose and tumbled down the slopes, treeless slabs of rock crumbled and fell, and under Nina the bedrock groaned. As the shaking began to subside, the groaning continued. Nina remained flat on the ground, absorbing the shudders of the rock and listening as stone creaked like the walls of a timber-framed house in a gale-force wind.

The creaking gave way to grinding, stone against stone. The sound put Nina in mind of massive teeth grinding together in a gigantic, clenched jaw. She heard rumbling too, like the gut-rumbling of something huge and hungry.

Not until the sounds had faded below the threshold of hearing did she lift her head from the ground and raise up. She found Galen half sitting, staring past her as he absently brushed stone dust and dead pine needles from his shirtless chest and arms. His garment was nothing now except shreds of scorched linen. Nina had yanked the entire back out of it to use for a plug when she'd captured her jar of flying fires.

Galen seemed oblivious, however, to the tattered state of his attire. Something farther up the ridge held his attention. Nina turned her head to look, and glimpsed leftover steam drifting from a vent in the middle distance. Through the thinning cloud of vapor, lights became visible, gleaming yellow-white from at least a dozen stony cracks.

"Beggar it!" She swore vehemently at the evident failure of her plan to extinguish the source of the fiends'-fire in one great, magical, underground flood. Nina leapt to her feet, lunging upward to continue the battle. She would drown the surviving sparks one by one, if that's what it took.

"Whoa!" Galen called, halting Nina before she'd taken four steps. "The sun will soon rise, and it will bake these slopes like it scorched the badlands when you crossed the desert, sister. At least in those canyons in that time of your foolishness, you found a little shade. But there is none to be had on this exposed rock." Galen shook his head and motioned for Nina to backtrack. "We must go down and get supplies. We need food and hiking gear, if it is your intention to push higher into these mountains."

"On that question, we have no choice," Nina snapped, knowing Galen was right to force this delay upon her, but chafing at the necessity of it. She jerked her arm to indicate the glowing cracks in the rocks above and beyond the ridge. "Look what has sprung from my brilliant plan to quench the fires and rout the arsonist! I've made things a hundred times worse. Instead of extinguishing the sparks deep underground, I've driven them nearer the surface, to a dozen battlements from which they may launch attacks upon this valley and your hills."

Galen rose to his feet to stand facing her. "Having the sparks at the surface might work to our advantage," he argued, calmly knocking dirt out of his hair. "They might be easier to reach and eradicate. In any case," he added as he began searching out a downward path through the slope's rubble, "the 'flying fires' appear to dislike sunlight. No one has reported seeing sparks by day, and every burning of house-thatch, haystack, or barn has occurred in the dark of night." Galen reached for Nina's hand to help her past a boulder that partly blocked their descent. "Perhaps your plan did not succeed as you envisioned, to douse the fires at one stroke. But I fancy the sparks that you have forced to the surface will wilt today under our southern sun. Most things do." He grunted tiredly as they regained the valley floor at the foot of the ridge.

"I certainly have wilted," Nina muttered. Weariness leadened her steps as she plodded to the mare that had patiently awaited her all this time. Thorn had found a patch of grazing in summer-shriveled grasses near the foot of the mountain spur. The mare looked up languidly as her rider trudged toward her, seeming not to resent a full day spent under saddle. At cockcrow yesterday morning, Nina had been riding with Galen to confer with Labéht and seek the help of Warthog. Now a new dawn had come, without the mare seeing the inside of a stable, or Nina catching a wink of sleep.

"It's good that Thorn has taken a shine to you and stayed near," Galen remarked as he caught the mare's trailing reins. "She will have to carry us both home. My useless horse is nowhere to be seen."

"But take me only as far as the river," Nina directed when Galen had mounted and pulled her up behind him. "I want to soak my blisters ... and remain here in the valley where I can watch for outbreaks from those new nests of fire-flies."

"I believe there's no need." Galen spoke over his shoulder. "The sparks have never been seen on the wing during sunlit hours."

"Nevertheless, I wish to wait for you at the river. Go get whatever we will need for climbing these slopes. While you're at your house," Nina added, "grab my clothes. Stop at the apothecary, too, and get all of the calamine powder he has. I can make a paste with it to protect our skin from burns."

Galen grunted acknowledgment, and said nothing more during the brief ride to the river that wended its way southward along the valley floor. He dropped Nina on the willow-shaded bank at the water's edge. The trees promised cool refuge from the morning sun that had risen above the Ore Hills and now glared down into the valley, its rays hot despite the relatively early hour. Galen did not dismount but sat quietly while Thorn slaked her thirst and Nina forced her sleep-deprived brain to think ahead, to consider what they had and what they might yet need.

"Don't rush back on my account," Nina said, looking up at her brother. "You must rest, too." She paused before adding, "But I'd like you to arrange for Jacca's immediate return, if you believe it's now safe for her to be here—if you find that Warthog's testimony has convinced people she's had nothing to do with the fires."

"Why bring her back so soon?" Galen asked, scowling. "If it's just that you want to see your niece, I'd prefer to wait until you and I have ... secured the battlements."

"Of course I want to see her," Nina exclaimed. "She was a child of eight when I left her with you, and now you tell me she's fifteen." Nina shook her head in wonder. "Doesn't seem possible, but I've learned not to argue with time. What I've really got in mind, though, is Jacca's new ability to summon rain. Didn't you tell me she'd learned weather-working from her cousins?"

A smile replaced Galen's scowl. "Indeed, she has." He nodded under-standing. "You want her to park rainclouds over this valley, to stop barns from burning."

More than that, Nina thought. *I want her in the mountains with us, wet-ting us down so we don't burn.*

But Galen would fiercely oppose any such suggestion, Nina was cer-tain. He would want his daughter safely tucked away—a sensible atti-tude, but one that Nina could not share. Jacca's skills might tip the balance in whatever battle lay ahead. Nina glanced at the mountain slopes that already shimmered in a haze of heat. Lost in the morning sun were the faint glows from the spark-filled crevices. Yet Nina could feel their seething menace almost as sharply as she'd felt their hot stings on her skin.

"This river is calling me—I want a swim." Nina returned her atten-tion to Galen as, with a nod, she accepted the spare jar of burn oint-ment that he handed down from the supplies Labéht had packed for them. Nina's arms cried out for a fresh application of the soothing ointment, but her pain must be negligible compared to Galen's. He had blisters on his arms, his bare torso, and even his throat and one cheek. "Let me put more of this on you before you go," Nina said, eyeing him critically. "You walked through fire last night."

Galen shook his head. "It's time I got home and heard the word on the street. I suspect the news has gone 'round, of what Warthog saw and reported. It's sure to be on everyone's lips." He shaded his eyes against the sun reflecting off the water. "If I find no cloud of suspicion still hanging over Jacca's head, then I will send a rider to fetch her back, as you wish ... and Wolfram with her, as needs must. Both of them will be glad to see you again, sister."

Maybe not when they learn what I have in mind for them, Nina thought as she waved Galen on his way. She sat on a streamside boulder to remove her boots and stockings and slip off the belt that secured her throwing knife in its leather sheath. Fully dressed otherwise, she waded into the river under the shade of gracefully arching willow branches. The water stung her blistered skin but then felt cool and comforting as it washed away the dust and grit she had picked up on the mountain spur. Nina lay back in a shallow eddy, only her face above water as the gentle current swept over her.

She was nearly asleep when voices roused her. They came from some distance upstream, along with a muffled thumping and thudding of purposeful activity. Nina sat up, seeking a glimpse of what sounded like a good-sized crowd. But through the drooping branches of the willows, she saw no one. With a tired sigh, she stood and sloshed up the riverbank. Moving to investigate, her knife in her hand and silent on bare feet, Nina kept to the narrow strip of grass that greened the bank in a lush ribbon, its presence testifying to the vital role this river played in the life of the valley.

Where the stand of willows thinned and opened the riverbank to a wider view, Nina paused, her attention on the crowd that had assembled upstream, still some distance from her. With a fair amount of shouting and jostling that diminished as she watched, the people organized themselves into a bucket brigade. Straw-hatted farmers and smallholders lined up, making a chain that snaked away from the river, its endpoint reaching past a hedgerow in the valley up beyond Nina's line of sight. Along that chain, buckets of water passed from hand to hand.

Fire! was Nina's first thought upon witnessing this scene. The people had come together to fight a fire.

She glimpsed no smoke, however. And as she studied the bucket brigade, Nina detected no great urgency in the people's movements. They worked steadily, intent on their task but unpanicked. Several of those in the human chain cast frequent glances, though, over toward the mountain spur where a firestorm had dashed itself to pieces last night, against the combined magian powers of Nina and Galen.

Aha, she thought as realization dawned. *They're not fighting a fire now. They're trying to prevent one.*

At the end of the chain, beyond the hedgerow that obstructed Nina's view, there must be a structure: a house or a barn that the neighbors were wetting down. She could only surmise that Warthog's eyewitness testimony had prompted this flurry of activity. People had hastened along the valley and down from the neighboring hills to protect one another, the populace coming together in a time of trouble.

I wonder why they didn't do it before? Nina mused as she backtracked to where she'd left her boots. *Too busy pointing the finger of blame, I suppose, to consider what they might do for themselves. Too easily divided by malicious rumors, when they should have been standing shoulder-to-shoulder as they are now.*

Satisfied that the spark-infested slopes were under close observation this morning by eyes other than her own, Nina relinquished the watch. She dabbed ointment on her many blisters, then stretched out in the shade of the willows and fell into the soft arms of sleep.

Chapter Seven

Nina awoke in late afternoon to the sound of horses splashing through the river below her sun-dappled willow grove. Galen rode the animal that had bolted in fear last night. Evidently the creature had made its way back to the safety of its stable in the hills. Nina's steadfast Thorn followed behind, the mare loaded with bulging knapsacks. At the sight, Nina glanced over her shoulder to check the sun's position. Before night fell, she'd be strapping one of those bags on her back and climbing into the mountains, to search out nests of fiends'-fire.

But first, something to eat.

"You better have brought food," Nina grumbled at her approaching brother. She rubbed sleep from her eyes. "I'm starving."

"You told me not to rush back." Galen handed her a wax-coated bundle. "I need a meal, too, and I haven't slept. Been busy all day."

The bundle, unwrapped, revealed a feast. In the shade of the willows, Nina and Galen tore into succulent roast chicken, herbed cheese, and crusty loaves of brown bread.

Between mouthfuls, Galen recounted his day's efforts. It hadn't taken him long to learn that Warthog's testimony had convincingly persuaded the locals that Jacca was innocent of the valley fires. The brickmaker had attracted a crowd when he stood in the middle of the high street and told of sparks swirling down from the mountains. Some of the sparks Nina had captured were still glowing in the jar she'd entrusted to him. Warthog had kept the jar tightly stoppered until Maynor pushed his way to the front of the crowd, the man's face dark with anger at the words which contradicted his accusations against his former stepdaughter. When Maynor drew near, seeming to think he could intimidate the brickmaker into silence, Warthog uncorked the jar and flung sparks into Maynor's face.

"I'm told the fellow bawled like a baby." Galen spoke around a bite of bread. He washed it down with a swallow of tea, then continued. "Maynor collapsed in the dust of the road, wailing and crying, laid low by the pain of those burns. People crowded around, no one trying to help him, but everyone wanting a look at his blistered face." Galen's grin expressed wicked satisfaction, for which Nina could not blame him. "Confinement seems to have stoked the heat of those fire-flies," he added. "They lit into Maynor so hard, one or two burned clear through his cheek and singed his tongue. It's what he deserves for slandering Jacca." With his knife, Galen gave the cheese a savage cut, as though slicing the tongue from Maynor's mouth. "I'm not the only one to say it, either. All day today while I was in town, people sought me out, shamefaced and full of apology for listening to Maynor's lies."

"Then it's safe for Jacca to come home." Nina leaned to catch Galen's gaze. "Have you sent for her?"

He nodded. "A messenger on a fast horse left before noon, down the foothills trail. I expect him to overtake Jacca and Wolfram before they've reached the crossroads."

Nina leaned back, and sighed. As much as she wanted to see the girl again, their reunion would necessarily be delayed. By sundown tonight, she and Galen needed to be up in the mountains, searching for sparks and doing their magian best to snuff every nest.

At least they had a backstop now, a secondary line of defense against any sparks that might get past them and drift into the valley. While Galen bagged what was left from their supper—cheese and bread to take with them up the mountain spur—Nina told him about the bucket brigade she had seen at the river. Warthog's demonstration with the captured "fire-flies" had not only silenced Maynor, the brickmaker had roused the people to act in their own defense. Hot sparks would have a harder time catching fire in newly dampened thatch.

As she talked, Nina made a paste with the calamine powder Galen had brought from the apothecary. She dabbed the pink goop on his arms and face, noting with relief that Galen's skin was less blistered now. His burns had responded well to the single application she'd given him, last night, of Mother Labéht's ointment.

Nina's own injuries had also healed with remarkable speed. Finished with Galen, she daubed calamine on herself and found no lingering tenderness on the soft skin of her arms. Nina slipped into the heart of the willow thicket, toting the sack of her spare clothes that Galen had collected when he'd stopped by his house. In deep shade curtained by drooping branches, she disrobed and checked her body for blisters. A few persisted on her legs, but with the fluid already drained and healthy new skin forming under painlessly dead surface layers.

Nina donned fresh clothes to replace those nearly burned off her last night. *I believe,* she mused as she dressed, *the Old One mixes magic into her remedies.* The thought held comfort. Going into battle against fiends'-fire, she would welcome all forms of benevolent magic, from any source that offered.

* * *

Warthog was waiting to take their horses when Galen and Nina reached the foot of the ridge where sparks had swarmed down upon them last night. In the fading afternoon light, the brickmaker appeared keen to be away. As soon as the two *wysards* had dropped from their saddles and shouldered their overstuffed knapsacks, Warthog gathered their horses' reins and mounted his mule.

"I ain't out to burn in a devil's bonfire," the man said as he stroked the tufts of hair on his cheeks. "If you make it to the high pass, be *certain* the South Trail is clear before you give me the signal. Dead certain, you understand?"

With that, Warthog rode away, tugging the horses after him. Both animals snorted as though surprised by the speed that Warthog coaxed from his mule as he headed for the river crossing nearest his mudbrick home.

"Signal?" Nina shot her brother a quizzical look. "What's he talking about?"

"I've made a plan with him," Galen replied. "Somewhat against the man's wishes. But once Warthog gives his word, he keeps it. I'll tell you when we get up there." Galen jerked his head at the long, undulating ridge that rose to form a steep-sided spur thrown out from the main body of the mountains to the west. He settled his pack on his shoulders. "Let's climb before it gets dark."

They scrambled up the ridge to the point they had reached last night, above the narrow crack from which the firestorm had emanated. Galen's molten seal held firm. The rock had cooled smooth and glassy, its surface unbroken but coated with the dust and pebbles that the violence of the underground steam blast had shaken loose from higher up.

"We won't do that again," Galen muttered, echoing Nina's unspoken thought as he eyed the sealed crevice. Not only had their combined efforts failed to suffocate the fires that smoldered within these mountains, their magian assault had quaked the ground out from under them. They could not risk a repetition. If they lost their footing, the drop would be long indeed. Nina ran her gaze high up the ridge they were following, then swallowed in a dry throat as she surveyed the valley below. A fall from any height above this point would be fatal.

They climbed onward, picking their way up the stony hogback, up and over boulders and the occasional downed tree. Pines struggled to grow on the dry, rocky ridgeline. Every tree had a distressed look, with wind-twisted branches and lightning-scarred trunks. Rain must be rare in these desert mountains. But when storms broke upon these slopes, they would bring deadly flash floods and stone-shattering thunderbolts.

Dusk had closed in by the time Galen and Nina reached a small plateau, a narrow bench of relatively level terrain that jutted out from the mountain spur. There, they ceased their climb for the present. The plateau afforded a good view of the fractured crags from which fiends'-fire had glowed last night, dimly betraying new nests of uncanny sparks.

"Can we reach them from here, if they show up again?" Nina panted, her breath coming short from carrying a heavy pack up a steepish incline. "I believe I can conjure waves at this distance. But I'm unfamiliar, brother, with the uttermost range of *your* spellcraft. Do I not remember that, in your boyhood, you liked to work magic up close? Close enough to singe your hair, as I recall."

Galen shrugged out of his pack's shoulder straps and grunted as he dropped his knapsack on the ground. "That was long ago, and I was young. I'm a mite more practiced in the art nowadays." He unslung his water bottle and took a long drink. "Dig out that leftover cheese and bread, will you? If fire-flies swarm us like they did last night, we might not get a chance to eat or drink again until dawn."

They made no proper camp that evening. After consuming a light, second supper, they stowed their supplies, reserving only water bottles and the fireproof tarpaulins that Warthog had left with them. For safety against drifting sparks, they stuffed their canvas knapsacks into a gap in the rocks behind them. Nina covered the gap with a tarp weighted down by stones.

Another of the felted woolens pillowed Galen's head. He stretched out under conjured witchlight and fell soundly asleep, for his day had been busier than his sister's sunlit hours. While Nina lay napping in the shade of leafy willows at the river, Galen had chased around the Ore Hills gathering news, securing supplies, dispatching messengers, and making secret plans. The fire-mage had yet to tell his water-sylph sibling what signal Warthog would not wish to see until the coast was clear.

Nina did not learn the answer that night. She extinguished the witchlight and sat in the dark, listening to Galen snore while she watched for sparks. Toward midnight, the breeze picked up. It sighed through the scattered pines like a melancholy wraith. Goosebumps rose on Nina's calamine-coated arms. After sundown, these mountains seemed to hold heat longer than the desert sands did, down past the foothills. Back when she had traveled those empty badlands in

company with Corlis, nighttime had brought plummeting tempera-
tures the moment the stars came out. Up on this mountain ridge, however, she hadn't noticed a chill in the air until the wind began to moan
in the trees.

Nina huddled under the last wool blanket and thought of Corlis. By
her reckoning, she had parted from the nomad only months ago. She'd
left him in the heat of the southern summer, and subsequently she'd
quit her homeworld while the northern snows flew during that following winter. Now she was back in the south—back in the nomad's territory, or close to it. Nina had not expected to see the man ever again.
But could she now look forward, perhaps, to a reunion with him?

"Will he *want* to see you?" Nina muttered under her breath, careful
not to wake Galen. "Months for you have been years for Corlis." Seven
years had passed in that man's world, same as they'd passed for Galen
and Jacca. By now, Corlis might have forgotten his temporary lover,
his water-witch of the desert. In seven years, he could have bedded any
number of women ... a succession of temporary lovers held close in his
sinewy arms, and then forgotten.

"Let him go," Nina counseled her heart as she had in her final days
with the nomad. "He is mortal, you are magian. You can have no future
together."

Her heart did not listen. It never had.

Deep into memory it took her, into the desert when Corlis had
nearly died and Nina had struggled to save him. She'd struggled, as
well, to view the nomad as merely her guide and then her patient, a
wounded man who required the ministrations of a skilled healer. From
her first glimpse, however, of his wiry frame and sun-weathered face,
Nina had been intrigued, her interest aroused. At a lake of conjured
magic, surrounded on all sides by barren desert, she had opened herself to Corlis. Their lovemaking had been beyond passionate, rising to
transcendent, nearly mystical.

He has not forgotten, Nina's heart insisted. *He could never forget. Just as
you cannot forget.*

So lost was she in thoughts of Corlis, in dreams of his embrace and
the intimacy they had shared, Nina nearly missed the sparks that

arrowed in on the breeze. For an instant, her distracted imagination mistook them for the harmless lightning bugs they resembled—except no insect ever shot through the air with the speed of those approaching particles.

"Galen!" Nina shouted as she sprang to her feet. "They're back."

With a sideways kick of one booted foot, she bestirred him to consciousness. Galen came up cursing, but Nina had no time for a gentler wakeup. She was fully engaged in dousing sparks. Her two-handed conjuring raised sheets of water that reduced the flecks of fire to puffs of steam—so many puffs, she could not see through the curtain of vapor that stretched past the plateau and up the opposite slopes.

"My turn!" Galen yelled as he elbowed alongside her. The fire-mage sent a scorching blast through the curtain. The heat of his magic obliterated the vapor and opened a clear view of the battlefield—for such it had become. Sparks flew at them from at least a dozen crevices in the crags across from their position.

They fought until dawn. Nina dashed endless waves against the rocks, the noise of her wizardry echoing from the mountains like the pounding of high surf on a stormy coast. At her side, Galen pummeled the crags with magian lightning. The thunderbolts that flew from his fingers snuffed every spark in their path and blasted deep into the fractured rock, annihilating nests of blazing particles before they could take wing. The air grew thick with the acrid stink of sulfur and smoke. By the time the sky brightened in the east, Nina was gasping for breath.

All that remained was to put out hotspots. Most of the nests had been destroyed overnight, and the few which endured were greatly diminished. In the glare of the rising sun, their weakened glow disappeared. Even after he could no longer see the sparks, however, Galen continued his magical assault upon the infested crags. His thunderbolts fragmented the slopes and sent rubble tumbling to the valley below.

"Enough!" Nina cried, her hands clapped over her ears. "Save your strength for tonight when we can *see* the enemy. I've no doubt, there're more of those things waiting to strike at us." She grabbed Galen's outstretched hand. "Time for breakfast, brother. Then I must sleep. I'm exhausted."

They dragged their knapsacks from under the protective tarp and made a meal on hard bread, crumbly cheese, and brittle strips of dried meat. Galen claimed to have packed a bag of figs, but neither of them had the energy to dig through their supplies in search of the fruits. Once they'd breakfasted, they collapsed where they were, on flat ground thinly shaded by sparse pines.

They awoke toward noon, sweating in the sun. Bleary-eyed, Nina squinted against the orb's glare and shouldered her knapsack, determined to find some place cooler than the exposed plateau. Farther up, higher on the mountain spur they were following, a spot of blackness promised shade. She gestured to Galen, and began climbing.

As they neared it, the black spot became recognizably the mouth of a cave, low to the ground. A shallow furrow led out from it. Though now dry, the furrow was lined with pebbles that, over time, had been shaped and smoothed by running water.

"I'll bet it's damp in that cave," Nina said as Galen came alongside her. "We'll find fresh water in there—I'll stake my water-working reputation on it."

"But what else will we find?" Galen countered. "As Warthog might say, I'm not 'out' to come face-to-face with a mountain cat ... or whatever else lives in there." He pointed at the cave's low mouth. "Getting in will be a belly crawl."

Nina shrugged out of her knapsack. "Let me try evicting the current tenants. They can have the cave back when we're done with it, but right now I need that cool, damp shade."

With her eyes clenched shut against the dazzling sun, Nina sent her magian senses to probe the cave's interior. She detected a pool of standing water, a faint current stirring in its dark depths. Nina bent her will upon that current, and it obeyed. Up from the depths, water rushed to overtop the pool's rim and spread through the cave.

The flood was gentle but persuasive. It flushed out two skunks. Swept into the furrow, the disturbed animals scrambled into the sunlight and waddled away. On their heels, a rat-tailed snake floated from hiding and rode the current out through the cave's mouth. Finding itself beached at the edge of a rapidly flowing streamlet, the creature wriggled its way to nearby rocks and slithered out of sight.

Nothing else of any size emerged, only crickets, long-legged spiders, and a few luckless blind fish that flopped helplessly in the bottom of the furrow as Nina's conjured flood drained away and stranded the fish on sun-drenched pebbles. Nina scooped them up and flung them in the direction the skunks had gone, offering a free meal as compensation for driving the animals from their snug shelter.

Nearly too snug, as she and Galen discovered when they had squirmed through the low opening. They pushed their knapsacks ahead of them to fend off anything that might yet lurk in the dripping interior. As soon as she had a hand inside, Nina flung witchlight into every corner, bringing sunlike brightness to a space that had never seen the sun since time began.

The orbs revealed glistening walls and reflected from the surface of the small pool, its waters ebbing to their usual level with the cessation of Nina's conjured flood. Fish darted in the pool, colorless creatures that lacked eyes and thus could not see the magical lights. Nina watched them for a moment, then dipped her head and drank deeply of the cool water.

"Careful!" Galen exclaimed. He put his hand on her shoulder as if to yank her back. "It might make you sick."

Nina came up wiping her hand across her mouth. She smiled. "It's perfectly fresh, and some of the best water I've ever tasted. You can rely on my judgment, brother. I'm a recognized authority on the subject, after all."

Galen laughed. "No arguing with that." He looked around their refuge, which was so small it barely held the two of them with their knapsacks. But it was cool and refreshing, smelling of moss and soothingly dim once they extinguished most of the witchlights. Nina brought out the bread and cheese again, and Galen found the figs crammed stickily in the bottom of one pack.

Both curled up then, needing hours more sleep before nightfall brought another threat of demon fire. As a precaution, Galen blocked the cave mouth with a low curtain of cool blue flame, his benign spell-work proof against any intruder.

Too comfortable in their bolt-hole, they overslept. Darkness had come by the time they crawled from the cave. Beneath a canopy of stars they scrambled back down to the plateau, anxiously scanning upslope and down for escaping sparks. A thin stream of fiends'-fire drifted from the crags opposite, the sparks reminding Nina of tiny soldiers limping down a steep battlefield. Few of those "soldiers" had avoided annihilation last night. Now, none of the embers survived a renewed attack by the magian siblings.

Higher in the mountains, however, pockets of fresh fire glowed. The new sites had sprung up like luminescent mushrooms after a rain.

"Do you get the feeling," Nina said as she stood with Galen, both of them hands-on-hips as they studied their new targets, "that we are being lured up these slopes? That something is tempting us to climb ever higher?"

"Or *taunting* us," Galen muttered. "Let's go back to the cave. If the skunks haven't reclaimed it, we can stay there until sunrise. Then I want you to return to the valley. Get your horse from Warthog and ride to my house. You should be there when Jacca gets home. She'll want to see you."

"As I want to see her!" Nina exclaimed. "But first things first, brother." She pointed at the seething glow high up the slopes. "We've got fires to douse."

Galen shook his head. "This isn't your fight, Nina. I asked you here for Jacca's sake. Deep down, I was worried that the girl might be doing exactly what she was accused of doing." He waved aside Nina's attempted protest. "Not on purpose, of course. I knew she wasn't roaming at night. I kept watch to be sure. But I wondered if she might be starting fires in her dreams ... somehow projecting her bottled-up anger out into the waking world."

"Her anger at what?" Nina asked, frowning.

Galen massaged the back of his neck, tension showing in his starlit profile. "Not everyone around here was happy when I brought Jacca home," he muttered. "Maynor's friends and allies have scorned the girl, calling her a bastard child. Never to my face, of course. But I hear things." He paused, his shoulders drooping as if weighted by disappointment. "Those friendly to my ex-wife have also been vile toward Jacca. They hold her responsible for the breakup of my marriage."

Nina kicked at a mound of pebbles underfoot, letting out a little of her own abruptly risen anger. How small-minded people could be! And how cruel toward a girl who was innocent of any sin that might be laid to the account of her parents. It was not Jacca's fault that Galen and the hillwoman Taji had been unfaithful to their respective spouses. Galen's wife Sheyla, a haughty and imperious woman, had rejected Jacca out of hand when she learned who the child's father really was. And Taji's cuckolded husband Maynor had evidently spent much of the last seven years engaged in whisper campaigns and rumormongering as he sought revenge on the *wysard* who had impregnated his wife, and on the magically Gifted child of that liaison.

"I'm sorry," Nina muttered, looking up at Galen. "You warned me that trouble would come if you openly acknowledged Jacca as your daughter. It was the right thing to do—I still believe that." She sighed. "But I'm sorry it's been hard for you and for my niece. I can see why Jacca might be angry enough to lash out. You're satisfied now, though—aren't you?—that she has nothing to do with the fires spawning in these mountains."

Galen nodded. "At least she'll not be having *those* accusations flung in her face when she gets home. But I want you there to greet her. I don't like the thought of Jacca being home alone, especially with Maynor slinking around, nursing a new grudge because he's been proved a liar." Galen clicked his tongue. "Warthog's testimony dealt a serious blow to Maynor's credibility. He'll be looking for a way to hit back."

Nina conjured witchlight, brightening the night with two orbs. She flung the lights ahead on their path as they began ambling upward, retracing their steps toward the cave but with no intention, on Nina's part, of crawling back into it.

"I won't leave you up here to battle fiends'-fire by yourself," she said, her tone firm and brooking no argument. "From what you've told me,"

Nina added when Galen attempted, nonetheless, to object, "Jacca is not alone. She's riding with Wolfram, and I hardly think that young man will abandon her when they reach the Ore Hills and find you gone." She raised a hand to stave off Galen's next attempted interruption. "But surely there must be some older woman—besides myself—who can look after the girl in your absence. How about that clerk who works the counter at your shop?" Nina gave an exaggerated shudder. "That woman could cow any man."

Galen laughed. "She is a steely-eyed, hard bargainer, for whom I am grateful daily. No one gets the better of her when they cross my threshold determined to haggle." He fell silent for a moment, then clicked his tongue again. "I believe Jacca would do better, however, with Mother Labéht."

"Of course!" Nina struck her forehead with the flat of her hand. "Exactly right. Jacca and Wolfram must go to the Old One. With her, they'll be safe, and Jacca will be well positioned, tucked there at the edge of the valley, to summon rain for quenching any flying fires that get past you and me."

"But how to arrange it?" Galen's grin yielded to a slight frown. "Unless you go down to meet the girl and tell her the plan, how is Jacca to know what she must do?"

They had reached the mouth of the cave. Standing in the dry wash below it, they took a moment to adjust their knapsacks to ride more easily upon their backs. A long climb awaited them. They'd need to trudge into the wee hours and beyond, to approach within striking distance of the simmering sparks that were luring them onward. Nina felt the near presence of the pool inside the cave, her magian senses drawn to those cool, gently stirring waters. She had bent them to her will before, and now the waters invited her to work further magic upon them: to send a message through them.

At this hour, however, deep in the night under starry skies, Jacca and Wolfram must be sleeping, somewhere along their return route through the foothills. Better to wait for dawn, when travelers would be washing their faces, making morning cups of tea, or otherwise lingering near water.

"Leave it to me," Nina said as she stepped out to resume the night's climb. "Women have our ways."

Galen cocked his head, studying her through narrowed eyes. But he made no reply, only summoned one more witchlight and set the orb with the others to light their way upward.

The climb became a hard slog, the slope growing steeper as they hiked the ever-narrowing crest of the boulder-strewn ridge. Night was nearly spent by the time they reached a point below the next pocket of glowing sparks. Warily they edged along a rock shelf, Nina taking care not to look down as they positioned themselves to avoid possible burial under falling stones. If Galen unleashed the full might of his thunderbolts against the flickering nest, a big chunk of mountainside could go crashing down to the valley below.

"The sparks appear to be waiting for us to make the first move," Nina muttered as she and her brother stood together on the ledge, out of the way of any impending rockfall. "Before you blast them, let me attempt a gentler dousing."

She raised both hands, ready to summon a double flood, but she called up only a stream at first. The stream flowed down from the nearly vertical headwall above the sparks. Water trickled into the nest, hissing as it met the fiery flecks. It extinguished all that it touched. Emboldened, Nina increased the flow. The hissing grew louder, and steam boiled from the side of the stony crack that held the nest.

The steam partially hid the sparks' counterattack, but a rumbling within the mountain gave warning a split second before a firestorm blazed out. The incandescent brilliance of the inferno nearly blinded Nina, but she threw her magic upon it so quickly that no degree of its blistering heat reached her skin. Her double waves of water hit the firestorm with hurricane force. Every spark died in a ground-shaking explosion of steam.

Steam rolled like a tidal wave downslope, swooping toward the valley below with power enough to flatten buildings. An even more enormous cloud of vapor billowed into the sky, ballooning past the high peaks of the mountains above.

Nina was barely on her feet now, staggered by tremors in the rock under her, but more so by the potency of her own spellwork. *Drisha's teeth!* What damage had been done down below when that tremendous steam-blast hit the valley? Could it have reached the river, and even as far as Warthog's brickyard?

"By the Powers, sister!" Galen swore. His hand on her arm steadied her. "Did I not once tell you that water is mightier than fire? I recall that you wished to argue the point. After what you just did, however, you must concede that I am correct."

Any reply that Nina might have offered was washed away in a sudden downpour. The steam shooting up into the predawn sky had cooled, condensed, and returned to liquid form. Fat drops rained down upon them. Nina had inadvertently brought a summer cloudburst to these arid mountains.

The deluge continued for some minutes, then ended as abruptly as it had begun. Galen and Nina took care with every step on the rain-slick shelf of rock as they levered themselves back onto the ridgetop. Even with half a dozen witchlight orbs brightening the night, they dared not attempt any higher ascent before sunrise.

In any case, they now had no clear destination. When they had settled as securely as possible on the wet, narrow ridge, to wait out what little was left of the night, they extinguished the witchlights and sat in the fading dark. Both strained to catch any remaining glimmers of fiends'-fire. If sparks still cowered, however, in rocky clefts or crevices, no glow rose on the mountainside to betray the embers' location.

But this isn't over. Nina kept the thought to herself, unwilling to break the profound silence that wrapped the slopes in a kind of shocked stillness. It seemed the mountains themselves needed time to recover their composure after experiencing the might of Nina's water magic.

Deep within the silence, down at the roots of these mountains, she sensed a vast malevolence—withdrawn and quiet for the moment, but still steaming and stewing. Nina glanced at Galen and saw him scowl at the rocks upon which they sat.

He feels it, too, she thought. *Maybe he doesn't believe in demons and netherworld fiends, but he knows we're contending with a dark intelligence.* Whatever the form or nature of the "arsonist" they were chasing, it had a mind that could think and plan and pick its moments.

It's smart enough to set traps, Nina warned herself. *Take care you don't blunder into one.*

Chapter Eight

Dawn purpled the eastern sky, but the sun had not yet risen above the Ore Hills. Nina crouched over a shallow puddle on the ridgetop where a depression in the rocks held water from last night's cloudburst. She sent her thoughts questing toward Jacca, seeking the child she had known while trying to imagine her niece as Jacca was now: a fifteen-year-old novice *wysard* who hadn't many years left in her apprenticeship.

As the world slowly turned and the sun peeked over the low hills across the valley, Nina's pool caught a faint, soft ray of its light. "Now," she muttered to the water, invoking her power over its elemental nature. "Show me Jacca."

The pool clouded. When it cleared, the girl stared out from the puddle, Jacca's face framed by her copper-streaked hair, every strand agleam in the strengthening daylight.

"Water lady!" Jacca exclaimed, her green eyes wide with surprise, and her lashes like delicate, silken fans against her skin. "I've missed you. Where are you?"

"In the mountains with your father." Nina's reply was rushed, for time was short. This magical link would not survive the glare of a fully risen sun. "When you get home, go directly to Mother Labéht. Stay with her until your father comes for you. We're up here fighting fires. You can help us by bringing rain to the river valley. Understand?"

"Yes!" Jacca cried. Alive with excitement, the girl clearly relished having a part to play.

And maybe she's happy to retain her escort for a few extra miles, came Nina's shrewd thought, for undoubtedly Wolfram would accompany the girl down the backslope of the Ore Hills and into the valley beyond. This supposition found confirmation when Jacca started to say more but did not get past "Wolfe and I—" before brilliant morning sunlight slanted into the pool and severed the connection.

"Wolfe, again," muttered Galen. "Always Wolfe."

He had hovered close at Nina's shoulder during this exchange but made no attempt to speak directly to his daughter. As every man of House Verek knew, this was women's magic. Nina had learned it long ago from her great-aunt Megella. Meg had not only given Nina her earliest training in herb-lore, the northern wisewoman had shared the secret of "tea-dreg tidings"—a delicately tenuous method of magical communication. Whether in a teacup, water bucket, wishing well, or roadside puddle, a successful connection depended entirely on the angle and quality of the light that suffused the water. By night under the moon, or very rarely in a slanting ray of sun, the relentless spin of the world meant the link could not endure more than a few seconds.

"Jacca could do much worse," Nina said in response to Galen's unspoken but clear disapproval. "If you've trusted Wolfram with your daughter to this point, surely you can go on trusting him until she's safely in the care of Mother Labéht."

Galen only grunted as they rose from their crouch over the pool and slung on their knapsacks. He proceeded up the mountain spur, leading the way with purposeful steps even though they had spotted no new flareup of sparks after Nina's spectacular dousing of the previous nest.

But these were Galen's mountains, in the sense that they rose directly across the valley from his home in the hills. Undoubtedly he had been up these slopes before—had even prospected for valuable ores in these peaks, the silver, gold, iron, and copper that he used in his smithery. He must have a destination in mind, and Nina hoped to reach it before the sun grew much hotter. By midmorning it blazed down upon the exposed ridgetop, the strength of its rays pressing upon her back as though the orb was close enough to squash her.

The heat had, in fact, nearly flattened Nina by the time they crested the ridge and dropped down into a sheltered hollow on its back side. She collapsed in the shade of pine trees that grew thick in the bowl-shaped depression, and took a long pull from her water bottle. Galen flopped down beside her, slumped against a tree trunk as he also quenched his thirst.

For half an hour, neither spoke, both needing time to slow their breathing and cool their sweat. When finally she could shape words, Nina posed what might be an indelicate question, but it had been on her mind since Galen confirmed that Mistress Sheyla was now his *ex* wife.

"I don't mean to pry, brother"—a lie, for obviously she *did* mean to—"but what became of Taji? Did she leave her husband?"

Nina was glad to see no grimace cross Galen's face, no outward sign of discomfort. He only nodded. "She and Maynor got divorced. She packed up and left the Ore Hills ... went far up the valley to live with her mother." Galen jerked a thumb over his shoulder in a vaguely northward direction.

"Does she ..." Nina paused, hesitant but pressing onward nonetheless. "Does Taji take an interest in Jacca? Has she kept in touch?"

Galen tilted his head in a noncommittal half nod. "More so, recently. The first three years that Jacca was with me, we saw nothing of her. Taji's neglect of the child angered me. Jacca missed her mother terribly and cried tears of longing—tears that broke my heart." Galen's sigh was tinged with sorrow. "I sent word to Taji more than once, telling her how her daughter pined for her. I offered Taji a house of her own, in the hills above my current abode." He shook his head. "But I heard nothing from her—only stony silence."

"Does she see her other children?" Nina asked, frowning. "As I recall, she had four with Maynor—two girls and two boys."

"Maynor has forbidden his offspring to speak to their mother ever again." Galen's voice sharpened, anger displacing sadness. "The wretch poisoned them with his own bitterness." Galen picked up a stone and threw it hard at a nearby tree, as if glimpsing Maynor's face in the bark. The stone hit with bruising force. It knocked reddish-brown flakes from the trunk and made such a noise that mountain birds rose squawking in all directions. Heretofore unseen flocks abandoned their shady perches in the pines and darkened half the sky as they winged away into the noontime heat. Their cries of protest shattered the sleepy silence that had blanketed the slopes.

"Drisha's fist," Galen muttered. "I shouldn't have done that." He shot Nina a rueful glance. "But Maynor disgusts me ... although no more than I disgust myself. Taji lost everything because of me. She lost her husband, her family, and her home." Galen rubbed his chin. "I should have kept my distance. I knew it was wrong to be with her. She was married, and so was I. But Nina," he added with a look of pleading in his green eyes, as if seeking forgiveness or understanding, "Taji and I had something real together—something genuine and deep, and precious to me. I loved her. And I love the daughter she gave me."

Nina laid her hand on Galen's arm. "Without Taji, you wouldn't have your daughter," she murmured, locking gazes with him. "None of us would have Jacca. House Verek would be poorer for never having given rise to such an adept as she—a fire-mage of the first rank." Nina patted Galen's arm, then gave her head a little shake. "Taji has not lost everything. She still has Jacca. And I think perhaps she could still have you, brother, if only the two of you could find your way back to each other. Taji told me she had loved you as you'd loved her."

"She said that?" Galen's eyes widened. He sat up from his slouch against the tree. "She really said that to you?"

"She did," Nina affirmed with a nod. "I spoke with Taji at some length when I stayed with Jacca at the cave where she'd hidden the girl away. Taji professed her love for you, and declared that she would love her daughter always." Nina frowned. "I confess it surprises me to hear that the woman has shunned Jacca and ignored your overtures."

"Not lately!" Galen exclaimed, new resolve showing in his glistening eyes. "Not nearly so much, lately. I'd almost given up hearing from her ever again, but then Jacca and I received an invitation from Taji's mother."

"The old lady with the dowsing rod who finds sapphires and garnets?" Nina leaned forward to study her brother's face. "You had hoped the beldame would support your decision to publicly acknowledge Jacca. Did she?"

"With alacrity." Galen grinned. "I might even say, with relief. She made it clear that she'd known Jacca was mine, not Maynor's. She'd known it all along, perhaps from the hour of the child's birth. I got the impression that she had argued with Taji many times, had told her the girl was gifted and must be apprenticed to a *wysard* to be properly trained." Galen settled back against the tree, still smiling. "Since I was the only qualified *wysard* personally known to the old lady—and father of the child, to boot—she willingly signed the apprenticeship contract. Jacca was bound to me before Taji knew what was happening."

"No wonder Taji did not speak to you for three years!" Nina burst out. "You ganged up with the old lady and ran roughshod over her. Tah!" Nina shook her head at her brother's clumsiness. "After such treatment as that, I can't imagine it was easy for Taji to go live with her mother. The tension under that roof must have been thick enough to cut with a knife." Nina arched her eyebrow. "But did you accept the old lady's new invitation? Pray tell: what kind of welcome awaited you?"

Galen sobered under Nina's withering gaze, but the grin did not entirely leave his face. "I am happy to say that Jacca made a joyous reunion with both her grandmother and her mother. We stayed for a week. I mostly kept out of the women's way—"

"Wise decision," Nina interjected.

"—but I was always close enough," Galen continued, ignoring the interruption, "to watch for signs of distress from Jacca. Had the girl looked uncomfortable for even a moment, I would have bundled her out of there and back to the hills. But Jacca was happy—deliriously so—to be welcomed back into her maternal family."

"What of you, brother?" Nina asked softly, no thought now of chastising him. "Were *you* welcomed? Did Taji speak with you?"

"Briefly," Galen replied, stroking his cheek. "But cordially. She asked how Jacca was faring with her change of circumstances, and how her studies were coming. I told her of the girl's summertime visits with her cousins, up in the city of Vivienne's clan. But I mostly kept magic out of it. You know Taji has always been uneasy with *wysards* and our doings."

Nina snorted. "If Taji were all that 'uneasy' with *wysards*, brother, I don't believe she would have had 'doings' with you: you, the resident mage of the hills, as everyone here knows. It is my opinion that she suffers more from feelings of inadequacy than from fear of magic. Taji thinks she has nothing to offer Jacca because her child is Gifted—powerfully so—and she is merely mundane, an ordinary hillwoman."

Galen stared. "Did she tell you that?"

"Not in so many words." Nina shrugged. "But I read it in the woman's plea that I take the child away and give her to a master *wysard* who could teach her well and wisely. That was before you decided to claim the girl yourself."

Galen looked up at the treetops. For a time, he seemed far away. Then he refocused on the present.

"We need to be moving," he muttered as he got to his feet. "Come nightfall, we should be where we can see fire from a long way off."

* * *

They had to go down to go up. Nina followed her brother along a steepish descent through the pines. At the bottom of the tree-lined hollow they found water. A streamlet trickled in a bed of gravel barely deep enough for refilling their water bottles. Goat tracks and game trails crisscrossed the area: mountain wildlife made regular visits to this place. From the streambank, Galen picked out a well-trodden track leading upward. Soon they were out of the wooded dell and back in the rocks where trees grew thinly if at all.

The track climbed to a ledge that hugged the shoulder of the mountain. The ledge was a smooth shelf of rock that appeared to have no end, zigzagging southward as far as Nina could see, following the profile of the mountainside. In places the ledge clung to the slopes, too narrow for comfort, but most of the way it widened out reassuringly.

"Welcome to the Sky Trail," Galen said, gesturing at the path ahead. "People have been climbing up here for … well, for millennia, I suppose, ever since the first folks settled in the valley, back in the night of time. It's a religious pilgrimage. Not popular this time of year, though, when there's no shade from the sun all morning long. People mostly come up here in the early spring to pray for rain, and then in autumn to give thanks for the harvests and pray for snow." Galen craned his neck, peering upward as if hoping to glimpse Drisha, deity of the mundane, non-magian world. "In wintertime, this way is usually impassable. Too much wind up here. If it snows, the blizzards are deadly."

"I can imagine!" Nina exclaimed. She shot a glance at the peaks that towered over them. Mostly, however, her attention was on the valley that stretched below her. In the relatively green ribbon that separated these tall mountains from the shorter, gentler slopes of the foothills beyond, she could make out Warthog's brickyard. His property appeared as no more than a red blotch standing proud above the river in the distance. But from any point within his mudbrick walls and fences, he would have a clear view of this "sky path."

"I see now how you can signal Warthog," Nina said, turning to her brother. "Do you mean to wave a torch some night, and send him a message in your own secret code? He must see it down there." She gestured toward the brickmaker's premises. "But how is he supposed to bring our horses up here? Goats could climb the ridge that we took to get this high, but no horse will manage it."

Galen shook his head. "We're not ready for horses yet, and Warthog won't be looking for a signal from here. The Sky Trail takes days to walk, end to end." He settled his knapsack and strode forth, leading the way toward the first visible narrowing of the ledge. "We'll have to make our way in the afternoons," he added, speaking over his shoulder, "when the mountains block the sun and throw this ledge into shade. Mornings, it's too exposed—we'd cook in the heat. At sunrise, we'll have to hunker down and sleep."

"And every night, we'll watch for sparks, I suppose," Nina put in, scanning the vista that opened out before her as they proceeded along the ledge. From this high shelf, they had a panoramic view of the slopes ahead, behind, above, and below them. "If any fire flickers up here in the dark, we'll see it."

"Let's just hope," Galen said as he reached the narrow place in the trail, "that we aren't forced into battle while hanging on by our finger-nails." He said it with a grin. But butterflies fluttered in Nina's stom-ach as she watched him inch his way along a rapidly tapering sill of crumbling rock. Galen turned his face to the mountainside and pressed his chest against its solid bulk, balanced on one leg at a time while he stretched with his boot-toes for secure footholds, and jammed his fingers into any available crannies.

Nina held her breath until Galen was safely past the constricted place. Then it was her turn.

"It's not as hard as it looks," he said in a voice so calm, one would not have thought he'd just defied death. "I went slow so you could see where I was putting my hands and feet. Just face the mountain and lean into it, giving it your weight. Slide along little by little, and *don't* look down."

Nina fought a rush of panic. She'd never been afraid of heights, but neither had she been expected to cling to a sheer slope like a wood-pecker on a vertical tree trunk.

Water, came her sudden recollection, and with it a calming of her nerves. *If I fall, water will catch me*—just as it had in her childhood when Nina the impetuous nymph had summoned a magical wave and plopped her small body down upon it, cushioned by billowing swells that supported her as softly as feather pillows.

"All right then." Nina flashed her brother a smile. "Anything you can do, I can do better."

She was past the narrow spot in seconds, leaving Galen gaping at the speed of her movements.

"Lead on," she ordered, and gave him a little push to get him re-started down the trail. "I trust you will find us a less precarious perch for the night watch. If we're dousing sparks after darkfall, I'd prefer solid rock under my boots, not thin air for three thousand feet."

Chapter Nine

Two nights passed before a twinkling glow on a lower slope revealed the presence of a fresh nest of sparks. Nina and Galen dealt with it speedily and with frugal use of their powers. The fire-master needed only a flicker of lightning to blast the nest apart. Most of the sparks succumbed to that single stroke. The handful which escaped met their end in Nina's shimmering, precisely controlled wave. A sheet of water, scarcely thicker than Warthog's felted tarpaulins, extinguished the remnant embers and disappeared in a gentle splash down the mountain slope. Nina strove to avoid an explosion of hot steam such as that which had earlier billowed into the sky and tumbled down to the valley, withering everything in its path. Her purpose here, she reminded herself, was to protect the valley's farmers and smallholders against uncanny fire. They'd be no better off if their crops wilted and livestock died in clouds of scalding steam.

With Galen continuing in the lead along the Sky Trail, day after day they worked their way across the eastern face of the mountains, heading generally southward. Nests of sparks appeared, on average, every other night, and few lasted more than an hour under a salvo of magian thunderbolts and conjured waves.

"Just enough to keep us up here," Galen remarked at the end of a night's work, when they were spreading and staking Warthog's tarps to make an awning, for shade from the rising sun. "Just enough to keep luring us along." He clicked his tongue. "I might have been a little doubtful, sister, when you spoke of an ill-intentioned awareness behind the sparks, an entity with a mind capable of cunning and craft. Be assured: I harbor no doubts now. These 'fire-flies' arise from no natural phenomena. There's thought behind them, and malice."

"It is the inescapable conclusion," Nina agreed, her head atilt. "The sparks tried at least twice to overwhelm us in a firestorm—to sweep us away, so they could get back to burning homes and barns unopposed. Failing in that effort, they have ceased to seriously challenge us. Now it's just breadcrumbs. Our 'arsonist' is dropping little morsels in front of us, enough crumbs to tease us into continuing our onward march."

"To what destination?" Galen grimaced as he rubbed his shoulders. Their knapsacks were lighter now, half empty of the provisions they had packed along. Even with the diminished weight, however, their muscles felt the strain of backpacking for miles every day along a narrow and often boulder-clogged ledge. "This pilgrimage path ends at the South Trail," he said with a tired gesture at a rock pile that partly blocked their forward progress. "We're halfway there. I'd give much to know what awaits us at that juncture." Galen stretched out in the shade of the makeshift awning and closed his eyes, ready for sleep. "That's assuming, of course, that our adversary does not strike while we are still plodding along this ledge."

"The South Trail?" Nina was half asleep already, her wits dulled by the tedium of watching most of last night for sparks that chose not to appear. Sunrise had brought a wash of heat to the east-facing slopes, blanketing her in warmth that felt good, at first, after another chilly night on the exposed mountainside. Nina tried to stay awake long enough to remember what had been said about the South Trail, when Warthog spoke to Galen of "signaling." But sleep took her, forcing the question from her mind.

* * *

The next days blurred together with little to break the monotony, until the delicious scent of rain filled Nina's nostrils and stopped her in her tracks.

"Look there!" She grabbed Galen by the arm, yanked him around, and pointed at the valley below. "See the clouds? Spreading back toward the north. I think the farmers along the river are getting an unaccustomed summer shower."

"It's Jacca!" Galen shouted, and broke into a grin. "She's home. Well, she better not be 'home,' exactly. The girl had best be staying with Labéht like you told her. But those are Jacca's rainclouds, I'll warrant." He puffed up with fatherly pride. "That's a fine display of the weather-working she's learned from Vivienne's bunch."

"Very fine indeed."

Nina stood breathing the delightful scent of rain-washed air and rich, damp soil. Her magian "nose for water" was as keen as any horse's, and regularly drew her to any nearby source, as it had alerted her to the pool hidden in the skunks' cave. Several times on the dry, stony ledge they were following along the mountainside, Nina's water-sense had detected hidden rivulets that trickled down from the peaks above, remnants of snowmelt from last winter. The clear-running rivulets served to refill their water bottles, and allowed for washing the dust from their faces and soaking tired feet. None of those trickles had the power to fill the air with the sweetness of Jacca's magical rain-clouds, however. As Nina gazed down upon the tops of the clouds, visible below as fluffy puffs of white, she longed to turn around and race back the way she had come, back past the skunks' now-distant den and down the long ridge to the valley, to go dance in the rain of her niece's conjuration.

"They're all safe now," Galen said. He laid his hand on Nina's as if to recall her to her present location and her purpose for being here. "Nobody and nothing in the valley can burn now," he declared in a tone of satisfied certainty. "Jacca's spellwork will keep off any sparks that may get past you and me." Galen snorted. "Ironic, isn't it, that the same folks who accused Jacca of torching their property are now indebted to her for preserving it."

Nina smiled. "In the faraway islands where I lived for so long, I think people might say it's 'kismet'—their word for an outcome that is written in the stars. The girl who is presumed to be the destroyer is in fact the protector. Now that we've got Jacca backing us," she added, "how about we go on offense, brother?" She tore her gaze from the alluring rainclouds and looked ahead along the ledge that was leading them she-knew-not-where. "Instead of following breadcrumbs, let's look for the whole loaf, if you get my drift."

Galen nodded. "A loaf that I mean to blacken to a crisp, when we find it." He resettled his knapsack on his shoulders and set out once more along the skyway, his steps brisker than before. "You may have a nose for water, honored sister of mine, but I can smell what's burning. I've known for days that we're getting closer to whatever witch's cauldron has cooked up all this trouble."

Chapter Ten

They barely avoided getting the entire cauldron dumped on their heads.

The first hint of impending peril appeared as a glow high in the mountaintops, upslope from the ledge but farther south, and visible morning, noon, and night. Nina and Galen watched the radiance strengthen with every passing day as they kept to their established routine. In the heat of each morning they slept, their unfurled tarpaulins keeping off the sun that baked the slopes. After midday, when the towering mountains blocked the direct rays of the westering orb, they walked the ledge, quickening their pace in anticipation of meeting their adversary face-to-face. The Sky Trail being too treacherous to hike by night, they devoted the dark hours to trouncing the occasional nests of sparks that glimmered on the slopes down below the ledge. The nests had a perfunctory feel now, and posed no threat. Nina and Galen kept wary watch, however, on the gleam high in the peaks. Up ahead of them it waited, and from time to time tendrils of its heat seemed to brush their arms.

What betrayed the ambush, seconds before the trap was sprung, was no drifting tendril of warmth, but a veritable furnace-blast in their faces. With Galen leading as usual, they rounded a bend where the ledge curved past a stony outcrop. Hidden behind that crag, a narrow crevice sliced up the mountainside. The long, steep crack was hemmed in by sheer walls all the way to the top, forming a rock chimney. Racing straight down that open-faced chimney was a river of lava: liquid rock glowing brilliant orange and fiery red.

"Look out!" Nina shouted as she flung up both hands and summoned water, a great white-capped wall of water that she raised directly in the flow's path. The speeding lava struck her conjured wave with a quaking shock that nearly knocked her off her feet. The mountain shook, boulders tumbled, and the ledge heaved under her. Nina glimpsed the lava turning black where the forefront of the flow had hit her immovable wall, the molten rock hardening instantly upon contact with cold water.

All was immediately obscured, however, in billows of steam. Through the dense white vapors, Nina could no longer observe the battle between fire and water. But she felt the lava press heavily against her conjured wall, the thick flow piling up high and higher, attempting to overtop her defenses.

"No!" she screamed, and reached for the fullest measure of her Gift.

Deep within, Power answered. Above the mountaintop a tempest rose, wilder than any storm at sea. Waves surged, their roar deafening as they thundered down into the rock chimney and crashed upon the massed lava.

Steam exploded with the force of a bomb. The shock front slammed Nina to the ground. She landed on her back with the breath knocked out of her. As she lay sprawled on the ledge, perilously close to going over, she still had both of her hands raised—sustaining the magic that flowed into her from the Elementals and out through her stiffly spread fingers.

From this position, she watched gobbets of molten lava fly skyward, their color ruddy amidst boiling clouds of steam. Flung up at the moment of impact when surging waves struck liquid rock, the hot blobs cooled as they rose. From the top of their lazy arc through the sky, the blobs fell back as lumps of iron-hard stone—several on a line to hit Nina and take her on over the edge.

She started to shout for Galen. The fire-mage, however, had spotted the danger, for he had been looking up all this time.

Galen stood aside from the mouth of the crevice, away from where the steep chimney sliced downward to meet the ledge. Past the outcrop of stone at that juncture, he had taken a position out of the way of Nina's wizardry, where he had a clear view of the boulders that continued to bounce and lurch down the mountainside. Shaken loose in the ground-rumbling collision of uncanny forces, the boulders clattered down on either side of the crevice. Those that fell at some distance, Galen spared. Any that threatened to fall upon his head or Nina's, however, he blasted to dust with well-aimed thunderbolts.

Now as the lava-lumps streaked the sky and plummeted toward them, Galen countered the onslaught with his head back, his feet planted, and his arms raised high. He clapped his hands together and then flung them apart, his palms turned skyward. From his palms, fire spread upward in a dazzling canopy, unfolding like an umbrella of pure white flame. Midair over the ledge, the umbrella hovered, a blazing barrier between themselves and the chunks of falling lava. Red-hot lumps hit the white flames and disappeared in puffs of gray smoke.

"Well done!" Nina exclaimed, or started to. But she hadn't the strength to speak. Every particle of her power remained focused on her conjured waves, the magic she could feel but not see through all-enveloping clouds of steam. The rock chimney was wreathed in roiling, tumbling vapors.

Galen's canopy of white fire, in contrast to Nina's water summoning, seemed not to require his undivided, two-handed attention. His barrier remained in place even when he swept one arm downward and flung a gesture at the crevice, his motion like scooping air. A blast of dry heat grazed Nina's face as a withering wind screamed off the canopy and into the crevice. The scorching wind dissipated the steam, giving Nina her first clear view of the magic she had wrought.

Up and down the crack in the mountainside, the river of lava lay black and dead like a monstrous, shriveled snake. Nina's conjured waves had prevailed, water again emerging victorious in its elemental struggle against fire.

Though that struggle had produced vast quantities of steam, a huge volume of liquid water yet remained. The sheer walls of the rock chimney now held what was essentially a vertical lake. Clear blue water filled the chimney from the distant top of the crevice all the way down to the hardened plug of lava where molten rock had piled up against her wall of wizardry.

But now that wave-formed wall was beginning to slump. Nina could not sustain the magic much longer: the wall must break. When it did, the entire lake would surge down the length of the crevice, a thundering torrent of water as through a burst dam. The torrent would cascade over the ledge and roar down to the valley below—its splendid, frothing power taking Nina's crushed body with it.

Now I know how Jacca felt when the girl got scorched by her own magic, Nina thought. Fire-mages like Jacca and Galen could burn if their spellwork went awry. A weather-worker like Nina's brother Dalton—captain of the Eastern Seas—could drown in a violent storm of his own conjuring. Even a stonecrafter like Nina's youngest brother, Legary the mason of Granger, must take care with his wizardry if he did not wish to die beneath a toppling slab of granite. Never before, however, had Nina placed herself in danger through the working of her own special power, her mastery of water.

"Move me!" Nina shrieked at Galen, finding her voice as her arms began to quiver and the first crack opened in her spellcraft. Water came running down the steep, rocky crevice. A trickle reached the ledge and flowed toward Nina. Dampness spread far enough past the protruding crag to become visible to Galen, where he stood watching for threats that might yet fall from the sky, though by now every high-flung splatter of lava had expired in his flaming canopy.

"Drisha's bollocks!" he swore. His eyes widened as he spotted the trickle and instantly comprehended what it meant. Abandoning his canopy, Galen sprinted to where Nina lay sprawled. He grabbed her ankles and yanked her toward him along the ledge, away from the mouth of the crevice.

Her head had barely cleared the danger zone when water came roaring down, a flood of such power that it cut straight through the ledge. Rock split, cleaved asunder as the flood smashed its way to the valley below. Taking boulders and trees with it, the torrent raced downslope through the jagged gap it had made in the skyway.

Nina scrambled to her feet, pushing Galen behind her as both of them backed away from the collapsing edge. A rockfall stopped them before they got far: their way was partly blocked by debris that had been shaken loose from higher up the mountain. Secure for the moment, however, they huddled together, breathing heavily, and watched as the flood slowed to a dribble. When it ceased altogether, Nina ventured to the broken edge and looked over, marveling at the mighty force of Nature she had unleashed ... recoiling, too, in the face of it, to know that her conjured flood would have killed her, if not for Galen's swift action.

She turned back to him, minded to thank him for the rescue. But Galen broke out swearing before she could speak.

"Guts and gall, sister!" he exclaimed. "Make do with a little less water next time, would you? These parched mountainsides buckle under such quantities." With a somber look clouding his face, he added, "I fear our local pilgrims will be dismayed, when next they walk this path." Galen gestured at the void that yawned in what had previously been a solid shelf of rock. Nina's flood had sliced crosswise through the Sky Trail like a hot knife through a slab of butter. They were now effectively cut off from the many miles of mountain-hugging ledge that stretched back away to the north, the way they had come. Their only course, going forward, was to clamber over and past the rockfall and continue southward.

Unless we climb to the top of the chimney, Nina thought, *and gain the heights from which that attack was launched.*

Galen dismissed her suggestion out of hand, however, same as he dismissed her apology when Nina expressed regret for sundering the ledge, and then proposed that they should ascend straight up the lava-filled crevice.

"That break in the path can be bridged, in time," he said. "A determined pilgrim could do it with planks and ropes. But we have no ropes with us, sister. Even if we did, that crack is too steep to climb—and the lava which fills it is still too hot. Do you not smell it, the odor of burning rock? That smell of sulfur tells me there's red heat trapped under the black crust." Galen shook his head, decisively. "Even if we could get up there—which we cannot, given the steepness—the soles of our boots would melt and our feet would burn off to the ankles before we made it to the top."

"Not if I kept us soaked and the lava wet," Nina argued, stubborn. "Up the chimney must be the quickest way to the demon's lair. The attack we just repelled *must* have emanated from the heart of our adversary's stronghold, do you not think, brother?"

"Perhaps." Galen had shrugged out of his knapsack. He settled atop the rockfall to search his supplies for the makings of the midday meal they had not yet found time to eat. "Be that as may," he said, not looking up, "you are too exhausted at present to summon the protection of water, even were we foolish enough to attempt such an impossible climb—which we are not."

"I'm too exhausted?" Nina echoed, frowning. "What makes you think it?"

Galen shot her an answering scowl. "I am not blind. I saw your arms quiver. And when your spellwork caved in and released the water, I saw the shock of realization on your face, when you comprehended that not even you—Karenina of House Verek, this world's greatest worker of water magic in a thousand years—not even *you* could constrain a force of Nature indefinitely."

Nina started to protest, but subsided as intense weariness engulfed her, and with it the recognition that Galen was correct. She had expended prodigious effort to summon all that water and then hold it in check. At present, she had nothing in reserve. Hotfooting it up a broiling spillway of lava would be impossible without the cooling armor of water, and in her current condition she could not summon a drop.

With a sigh of resignation, Nina slipped out of her knapsack and tried to knock off some of the ground-in dirt. Her pack and her backside had suffered from the unceremonious way Galen had seized her ankles and dragged her to safety. The canvas of her knapsack was ripped, as was the seat of her summer-weight trousers. Nina fished out her spare clothes and changed the ruined garment for sturdier attire.

What little food her pack still held, she gave to Galen for safekeeping, since his knapsack had no hole in it.

"We're running out of anything to eat," Nina commented as she parceled out hard crusts of dry bread. "Perhaps our adversary need only wait for us to starve to death on this ledge."

Galen passed her a mug of tea, brewed in water he had heated with a snap of his fingers.

"We're nearly to the South Trail," he said around a bite of dried fig. "Though I don't suppose Warthog will meet us there now, or willingly haul the mule-load of supplies I had hoped he would bring up. Like everyone else in the valley and the hills, the man must see that ominous glow in the peaks." Galen gestured overhead where the threatening radiance bathed the summits, visible even under the glaring desert sun. Though Nina had blocked the river of lava, the hot brilliance of that mysterious high glow implied the source of the lava remained intact. "I doubt there's any signal I could send," Galen added with a woeful shake of his head, "that would entice Warthog up the trail with his mules and our supplies."

"You've lost me," Nina said as she settled beside Galen on the rockpile and reached for a fig. "Are you saying it's possible to ride into these mountains on horseback—or muleback?"

"Possible, but rarely attempted."

Galen proceeded to sketch the lay of the land and the plan he had made with Warthog. Down the valley a fair distance from the brickmaker's property, a bridlepath cut through the scree at the base of the mountains and climbed the slopes. The trail was steep, narrow, and rocky, but shaded by pines clear to the top. In all the many years Galen had lived in the Ore Hills, he had ridden up that South Trail only a handful of times—chasing rumors of rich new ore deposits out that way, rumors that seldom panned out.

But it was lovely country up high, Galen said. Greener by far than the exposed stone ledge where he and Nina now sat. Galen had planned their route as a loop: up the mountain spur where they'd first met the blistering attack of uncanny sparks, then along the skyway ledge until it converged with the South Trail at a spot which now lay no very great distance from them. Galen had hoped to signal Warthog while they yet walked the ledge. The brickmaker was to watch for a sign, a blaze of symbols the fire-mage would trace in the air to say that all was well and Warthog could safely ascend. The man had been charged with bringing not only food up the trail, but also horses, so that Nina and Galen could continue their "mountain tour" astride. Galen had thought to ride to the summit, to show Nina a grand vista of pine-covered peaks and surprisingly green mountain valleys.

"But that was assuming we would snuff every spark and arrive triumphant at the trail," he added ruefully as he peeled a shriveled fig from its sticky wrapper. "Had we succeeded as I had hoped, I would not scruple to summon Warthog. But alas, he will not come, and I cannot blame him for being a sensible man." Galen put away their meager leftovers and got to his feet, swinging his pack onto his shoulders in smooth, well-practiced movements. "Let's push on, sister. We can decide our further course when we reach the trail: either down it to the valley ... or on up higher, in search of whatever is making that ill-omened glow in the peaks."

Nina frowned but said nothing in reply. She had all she could do to scramble up and over the rockfall that impeded their progress on the skyway. Future pilgrims would need ropes, planks, and shovels to restore this path of religious devotion. Boulders clogged it, mounds of loose stone piled high in the path, both ways. Back behind, however, gaped the most severe damage that walkers-to-come would have to negotiate. Below the mouth of the lava-plugged crevice, the old ledge was gone altogether, swept from existence by the force of her magical flood.

The missing section slipped from view—and from Nina's thoughts—when she had cleared the rubble and she walked once more on solid bare ledge. For a time she followed Galen without speaking, weighing the choices they must soon make. Without bread and sustenance, carrying the fight to the enemy might prove suicidal. If they pushed on toward their adversary's perceived stronghold—that glow in the heights—they could find themselves called upon to summon vast powers of magic from bodies too starved and weak to endure the strain.

But if they retreated, if they took the trail down to the valley to get the horses and food they needed, would that not allow the malevolence in the mountains to grow and strengthen unopposed? Without two *wysards* of the true Power standing in its way and keeping it occupied, what devastation might that unknown evil wreak upon the people of the valley and the hills?

Nina could little doubt that their adversary *was* evil, and she felt equally certain that the intervention of herself and Galen had saved the local farmers from far worse than burned haystacks. She and Galen had drawn to themselves the malice of the unknown entity, distracting it from its attacks on non-magian folk. Could they now walk out of the mountains and leave those high passes unguarded, knowing what their adversary was capable of: rivers of lava coursing down mountain slopes, molten rock entombing everything in its path?

"Tell me," Nina said, breaking her silence and moving up closer to Galen, to make herself heard over his rapid, crunching footsteps. "Do deer live in these mountains? Or goats?"

"Plenty of goats," Galen answered without breaking stride. "But deer mostly stay north where summers are cooler."

"Goat meat is fine," Nina said, nodding satisfaction. "We won't starve."

Chapter Eleven

Nina's hunting prowess would not be put to the test. Not in pursuit of goats, at any rate. Awaiting them at the junction of skyway and South Trail were their two horses and a great quantity of food and supplies, but no Warthog. Instead, it was Jacca who greeted them.

The girl threw her arms around her father and gave Galen a great hug. The two held each other tightly, although Galen protested against Jacca's presence, softly demanding to know why she wasn't safely ensconced with Mother Labéht as he had instructed.

"I have permission," the girl replied, her green eyes flashing defiance as she gently broke her father's embrace and stood facing him. "Mother Labéht gave me leave to come up here with your horses and things. When I showed her what I could do with rain, she said I'd be safe enough." Jacca shrugged. "She told me to stay hidden in the trees, and of course Wolfe is here with me."

"Of course he is," Galen muttered, looking both relieved and perturbed as Jacca's devoted escort emerged from the late-afternoon shadows under the pines.

Wolfram the shapeshifter—human-formed at present—made obeisance to the fire-master with a formal, respectful bow. Then the young man turned to Nina, greeting her in like fashion, silent, but with a sparkle of pleasure in his hazel eyes. Clearly he wished to speak, perhaps to exclaim aloud his excitement at this reunion. Wolfe hung back, however, as if conscious of the blood-ties which bound all others in the little group, but excluded him.

Nina gave him a reassuring smile, and proclaimed her pleasure at seeing him again. Speech between them would have to wait, however, for Jacca had now flung herself into Nina's arms.

"How I've missed you, water-lady," the girl declared in a voice Nina hardly recognized, a voice older and more confident than the bashful child she had left behind—a child from whom she had parted only months ago by Nina's reckoning, but with a full seven years gone by in Jacca's world. "I've got much to show you," the girl said, her eyes shining with eager anticipation. "My fires go where I want them to now. And I've even learned a little water magic. I always wanted to, after I saw what you could do with water. I wasn't sure, though, that I would ever master a drop without it turning to steam."

"That's wonderful news, Jacca," Nina murmured. She felt absurdly pleased to know the young adept had taken such inspiration from her, that Jacca had been moved to learn wizardry diametrically opposed to the girl's natural Gift. The thought returned unspoken to Nina's mind that Jacca's twin talents—firebolts and cloudbursts—might prove invaluable in battling the enemy that lurked in these peaks.

Galen will never allow it, Nina cautioned herself silently. *He'll have the girl down the mountain and back to Mother Labéht before you can say diddly.*

"We saw your beautiful rainclouds," Nina said, smiling at the girl as they walked together to join Wolfram. "Back along the pilgrimage path, we could look down on the fluffy cloud-tops where you'd brought rain to the river valley." Nina tilted her head to shoot the girl a questioning look. "As delighted as I am to see you—and to find you grown capable and strong—I worry that you have abandoned your post to bring aid to your father and myself." She laid a hand on the girl's arm. "The food is much appreciated. We were running out. But uncanny fires still threaten the farmers in the valley. Oughtn't you to be down there, sustaining your magic to protect them?"

"I can do it from here!" Jacca exclaimed. She pointed at a ridge, barely visible through the screen of pines, that bordered the South Trail and overlooked the valley. "I walk up there every evening and look for a signal along the river. If nobody waves a torch, I know they are still plenty wet from the last rain and not worried about catching fire. But if I see torchlight, I summon new clouds and give the valley another good soak." Jacca shrugged. "I worked it all out with the brickmaker and his neighbors before Mother Labéht let me come up here. They all know it's me with the rain now—and it was never me with the fires," the girl added, her fleeting frown expressing a twinge of resentment at having been falsely accused.

"What a turnaround," muttered Galen, who had joined his daughter in the conversational knot, where everyone was talking except for Wolfram. "Did the brickmaker tell you, girl, what he'd done for you? How he risked singeing his whiskers to capture sparks in a jar and show everyone what was really starting the fires?"

Jacca nodded. "He told me a little. I heard more from Mother Labéht—enough to know that I am in debt to all of you for proving my innocence." The girl stretched to give Galen a kiss on the cheek, and accorded Nina the same. "Now let me fix your supper." Jacca grinned as she added, "I hardly ever burn the bread anymore."

The girl and her father moved off to where bags and bundles of supplies waited on the ground on carpets of pine needles. As the pair launched into preparations for the best meal to come Nina's way since her rearrival in the Ore Hills, she stood on tiptoe and passed along to Wolfram's cheek the kiss that Jacca had given to hers.

"My lady," the young man mumbled. Wolfram blushed but looked pleased.

"How have you been keeping, wolf cub?" Nina used her old term of fondness for the youthful shapeshifter, but immediately she recognized its impropriety if Wolfram was now a fully qualified *wysard*, no longer answerable to any master, as appeared likely from his demeanor. Wolfe had bowed to both Galen and Nina in the stiff, ceremonious way of proud young *wysards* showing respect to their seniors in the craft, just as Nina had made obeisance to Mother Labéht upon recognizing that woman's status as an Old One.

"I see you're parted from Master Gelgeis," Nina said, seeking to confirm her supposition. "Was the old fellow well, when last you saw him?"

Wolfram relaxed a little, but he still held himself ramrod straight and decorous. "I thank you for asking, my lady," he said in a voice deeper and more mature than that of the seventeen-year-old novice with whom Nina had once traveled. "My old master has returned to his hermitage in the high north. Before he released me from apprenticeship, he bade me use my gifts in service to others. So now I patrol the roads, and I escort any traveler who needs my protection along the byways from the Ore Hills to the forests of Ruain."

"Ruain!" Nina exclaimed. "You have been to my ancestral home?"

Wolfe nodded. "To the doors of Weyrrock itself. Last summer, Master Galen bade me escort his daughter to the city of her cousins— a place that I know well." At this, Wolfe allowed himself a small, wistful smile. "From the *wysards* who rule those lands, I then carried a message on north to Ruain, to tell your honored parents of Mistress Jacca's progress with her studies."

"Had you any difficulties at the border?" Nina asked, acutely interested to learn of this new channel for communication among her westward-living relatives. "Ruain does not readily admit those who are not native to that province."

"Your brother anticipated my need for safe passage. He gave me this." Wolfram fished under his shirt collar and pulled up a pendant on a double chain of fine steel links. "This piece is the work of the master's own hands, vouchsafed with magic to allow me across that border."

"It's beautiful." Leaning close to study the pendant, Nina saw a stylized wolf head that was crafted in gold to suggest a wolf's tawny coat, with silver for the lighter fur around the animal's muzzle. Two gleaming beads of amber mimicked the color of Wolfram's eyes. "My brother is indeed a master of his craft," Nina murmured. She pulled out her own pendant, the silver-crested waves of blue steel in which Galen had seemed to capture the power of Nina's water magic. "I have been honored in like manner. Though the goldsmith of the Hills may offer many fine works for sale, his true masterpieces he gives as gifts to those he esteems."

Wolfram stood even straighter at this, his pride evident, and also his gratitude for Nina's recognition of his status. Although Galen might harbor fatherly reservations about leaving his daughter alone with the young man for weeks on end, as the pair journeyed together, the smith clearly thought well of the shapeshifter. Safe passage into Ruain, to the very gates of the ancient manor house called Weyrrock, was a privilege granted to only a few select individuals who were not of the bloodline of House Verek.

"What are you riding these days?" Nina asked as she slipped her pendant back under the neckline of her blouse. "Still have the roan gelding?"

"Certainly!" Wolfram exclaimed, looking shocked by the question. "I would never forsake Traveller, nor he me." The young man turned toward a particularly dense patch of shade under close-growing pines. "Come say hello. I believe we've two horses here who will be glad to see you."

There were, in fact, three animals eager to greet her. Nina was practically mobbed when Wolfram led her into the shade, then past it into an open, grassy glade. She stepped out from under the trees to discover the party's horses grazing alongside a fast-flowing mountain stream.

Nina's new white mare, the desert-bred Thorn, was the first to notice her. The mare threw up her head, nickering with excitement, and trotted straight to her. The warmth of the animal's welcome was a surprise, given how little time Nina had spent with the mare to this point. But they had forged a bond at their first meeting, a wordless understanding between them like a meeting of minds.

That understanding was immediately tested as another horse left the streamside and loped toward Nina. Thorn bared her teeth at the approaching animal, and in her head Nina clearly heard the warning: *"Stay back or I'll bite."*

"It's all right, girl!" she exclaimed, and laid a reassuring hand on the mare's neck. "I know that gelding. Traveller's his name, and he is my friend. But he's no longer my horse. Trav belongs with Wolfram now."

In response, Thorn offered a soft whicker and stood aside, allowing the roan to come close. Nina smiled at the mare's protectiveness, and then at the eagerness of the gelding who crowded up, gently nudging her and nuzzling her cheek.

"No apples today, Trav," she murmured into the roan's ear. "But I'll see if I can find you a sticky fig."

The equine reunion was not yet ended. Next, a big, bobtailed horse came plodding up, more from curiosity than affection, Nina thought, for on her previous visit to the hill country she'd had little to do with Jacca's oversized mount. Both the mare and the gelding moved aside, however, to let the big horse enter the circle that was centered on Nina. She chuckled at the way both younger animals showed respect toward their lumbering elder, much as fledgling adepts made obeisance to master *wysards*.

"Bobby, old fellow," she murmured as the animal stood looking down at her, its withers higher than her head. "No offense, big guy, but I would have thought you'd be out to pasture by now."

She looked to Wolfram for an explanation. "Jacca's still riding this beast?" Nina asked, one eyebrow raised. "A wind-broke nag would be swifter. From time to time you must want a little speed along the chancy roads that you ride with the young lady."

Wolfram's face lifted into a grin, allowing Nina a glimpse of the wide-eyed youth she had known.

"Jacca loves that horse." He rubbed the bobtail's broad nose. "I don't mind traveling at the pace Bobby sets. The old fellow is not fast, but he can outwalk any horse that ever lived, mile after steady mile." Wolfe's smile took on the wistfulness Nina had earlier detected. "Moving slowly on the trail gives time for conversation. Mistress Jacca has spoken to me at length about her early childhood and her unhappiness in her first home, and she's told me of the journey that she and her father made in your company, from the hills to the crossroads."

Wolfe ducked his head for a moment, then looked at Nina with an expression of pure gratitude. "I am in your debt, my lady, for so many things—for befriending me when I was trapped in the shape of a savage animal, for conducting me to the only *wysard* of Ladrehdin who could free me from that form ... and for persuading Master Galen to keep his daughter at home. Jacca told me the question hung in the balance: Would she travel onward with you, as your apprentice, and perhaps leave this land forever? Or would she remain in the country of her birth?" Wolfram flexed his fingers as if to grasp a thing that had nearly eluded his reach. "Without your wise counsel to Master Galen that Jacca should stay with him, he might have given her up. Had she left the Ore Hills, I would not now have the privilege ... or more, the pleasure," he added in a lowered voice, "of escorting that fine young woman."

In Wolfe's every mention of Jacca, Nina heard the notes of yearning. They chimed through his words like soft, clear bells. She eyed the young *wysard*, unable to suppress a chuckle.

"'*Escorting*' her?" Nina repeated, noting the way Wolfe had said it. "The word you are wanting, I believe sir, is *courting*. You do wish to marry the girl, do you not?"

Wolfram looked alarmed. "Are my intentions obvious?" he gasped. "If Master Galen believes that I have designs on his daughter, he might forbid me to see Jacca, much less journey with her."

Nina smiled at the young man's fluster. "My brother has sired many a daughter and many a son during his long residence in the Hills. He must be considered an expert, by now, in reading the signs of young love. I can promise you, Wolfram: Master Galen knows where your affections lie. He must also know that you are the only man—and the only *wysard*—for a thousand miles in any direction who is worthy to be Jacca's 'escort'." Nina reached up to give Wolfe's shoulder a squeeze. "I have assured my brother that you are a gentleman. I've told Galen that I come by the knowledge from personal experience ... having journeyed with you myself, and occasionally, unthinkingly, peeled off a few items of clothing in front of you, when I thought you only a wolf."

Wolfram blushed crimson, and Nina laughed. But then she sobered.

"I trust that you will not make a liar out of me," she murmured, dropping her hand from his shoulder. "Bear in mind, young sir, that your lady love is fifteen. Give Jacca a little more time to grow up. She's still learning her craft, and she's still learning who she is."

Wolfram was so red in the face, Nina worried he would burst a blood vessel. In sympathy, she turned away from the embarrassed young man and renewed her attentions to the horses. Each got a parting rub of the ears, with an extra pat on the neck for Thorn to reinforce their connection. Then Nina headed back through the pine grove, following her nose toward the mouthwatering aroma of supper roasting on a campfire.

"Don't tarry long," she said, tossing the comment over her shoulder. "Jacca might think you don't like her cooking."

* * *

Nina and Galen rested for two days at the campsite that Jacca and Wolfram had established in the narrow width of the South Trail. They cooked on a fire dead-center in the rocky path, confident that they need not make way for any traveler, because the trail was seldom used in normal times, and these times were not normal.

Much higher up the path, amidst scattered pines along a ridge of bare rock, and just north of where the trail crested the slopes and disappeared down the other side, an uneasy glow continued to smudge the sky. By day, the glow was a pale blur emanating from a source that lay hidden under the peaks. After sundown, the light appeared more sharply defined, brighter and less blurry at its edges.

Unmissable though its radiance was at every hour of the day, the glow in the peaks came under focused scrutiny each evening when Jacca made the short climb to her lookout above their tree-sheltered camp. Every member of the party accompanied the girl, and all stood transfixed when she summoned magical rainclouds to the valley far below, in answer to the prearranged signal of a lit torch along the river. Jacca's weather-working was a graceful dance, the girl making her magic with elegant movements of her arms and hands.

Nina caught Wolfram looking on in wordless rapture, his hazel eyes filled with such hunger and longing that Galen would surely have stepped across to block Wolfe's view, had he noticed the look on the young man's face. But Galen was himself entranced, watching his fiery daughter conjure gentle waves of rain in direct contradiction to the girl's essential nature. Jacca had all of her father's talent for summoning flames so hot, they could melt platinum. Under the tutelage of her wizardly cousins, however, the girl had also learned to call together the humid vapors of the air and make of them a cloudburst.

A sense of pride again flashed upon Nina as she recalled what Jacca had said about taking inspiration from the "water-lady's" elemental magic. *That's a formidable combination, fire and water working in concert,* Nina mused.

When she had the rainclouds in place down below, blanketing the river in mist and drizzle, Jacca ceased her magian dance and turned her back on the valley. Slowly, her audience emerged from the spell they had been under while watching the girl. Nina and the two men also swiveled around, directing their gazes upward now, away from the valley and toward the high peaks where the ominous glow lit the night sky.

Seen from this perspective, the radiance contained clear spots of unevenness. The glow's upper reaches were uniformly bright and mostly steady, wavering only slightly as the four magicians looked on. At its base, however, the light flickered, blinking off and on through the distant straggle of trees that grew, wind-twisted, near the mountain summit. Irregular flashes of light outlined tall spires and pinnacles of black rock, the formations thrusting upward like giant fingers of stone. A sickly yellow tinged some of the flashes. Others appeared reddish. Just above the treetops and pinnacles, all color faded into a general wash of white radiance.

"It seems ...," Nina began but trailed off as she stood with her hands on her hips, studying the glow that brought disquiet to all of their upturned faces. After a considering moment, she continued. "It seems that we might peer into the heart of that fiends'-fire, but from a prudent distance, were we to ride on up to the top of the trail." She turned to Galen. "You know this country, brother. Can we get up there high enough on horseback but stay out of sight while we search for whatever is making that unholy glimmer? I'd rather ride than walk, since we've got the horses with us now."

Galen rubbed his ear. "The trail can take us near enough—to the doorstep of the enemy's camp, I judge, by the look of that balefire in the sky. But perhaps we'll not approach without being seen. I think it necessary, however, that we attempt to spy out the threat, its nature and its size, before we commit to a direct assault upon our adversary."

Wolfram stepped forward, his mouth open to speak as he overcame his habitual reticence around the fire-mage—the *wysard* he hoped would someday be his father-in-law. "I shall accompany you, sir," Wolfe declared. "All my powers and the strength of my limbs are yours to command, as is my Gift of transformation. A wolf moves more stealthily than a horse."

Galen shot a look at the young man, a look Nina could not interpret, although Wolfram read enough in it to step back and clam up.

"You will stay with Jacca," Galen snapped at the shapeshifter. "The two of you will remain here below, but with your horses saddled and ready to ride. At the first hint of danger, you will flee down the trail. Any rumbling from the heights, any sparks in the air, the slightest flaring of flames in the sky—you are to get Jacca away from here. Your duty is to my daughter. Keep her safe, for you should never have let her come up from the valley. You understand me, boy?"

Wolfram gave a brusque nod. In silence, he bowed stiffly to Galen and then to Nina, and then stalked away. Long strides took him down the ridge and into the trees below. Wolfe disappeared from sight like a silent shadow in a dark forest.

Jacca had said nothing during any of this. The girl had not spoken since ascending to the overlook, except to whisper inaudibly to herself as she summoned her rain magic. Now Jacca scowled at her father, her lips pressed tightly together. Then she, too, climbed down from the lookout and followed her young man into the shadows beyond the campfire.

A rebellion is brewing, Nina wagered silently. *Two powerful young adepts will not allow themselves to be shunted aside or dismissed like children from the grown-ups' table.*

Chapter Twelve

A t their sheltered camp, they rested, and Nina got reacquainted with her niece. The two of them spent hours together beside the mountain stream, watching the horses and lulled by the burble of running water. Jacca told the story of her last seven years, from ages eight to fifteen, and waxed enthusiastic on all that she had learned. The girl had studied fire-craft with her father, been tutored by her cousins in a great many wizardly disciplines, and also had absorbed an impressive knowledge of herb-lore at the knee of Mother Labéht.

More than once, Nina steered the conversation toward womanly matters, inviting every awkward question that Jacca might have hesitated to broach with her father. In the absence of a mother in the family home, Nina wondered how much guidance the girl had received as she grew from child to young woman.

But Nina found she had no cause for concern. Jacca had been taken under the wing of every woman in the girl's life, from Labéht to the female cousins amongst Vivienne's brood, and even the shrewd shopkeeper who minded the till at Galen's smithery. This coterie of strong, sensible women had prepared Jacca to manage the dark of her moon when the time came for leaving childhood behind. They'd shown her how to ease the discomfort and inconvenience of her monthly cycles, and given her herbs for stemming the flow of the female humors when travel or other circumstances demanded expediency.

Furthermore, Jacca had a thorough—if still theoretical—understanding of baby-making and how to prevent conception. She spoke of such matters with the relaxed openness of a girl who had been forthrightly instructed by independent, confident women. Jacca recognized the fragrance of the steaming tea that Nina brewed, the herbal mixture to forestall pregnancy which Nina, in widowhood, had made her habitual evening drink. The girl knew the herbs and their uses but she expressed no interest in partaking of them. To Nina's blunt question about whether she needed them, or anticipated the need to avoid impregnation anytime soon, Jacca made answer with candid innocence: she'd been with no man.

Which was not to say, the young woman added, that she hadn't thought about it with Wolfram. But he had never suggested intimacy between them, had never pressed her or hinted or even joked about it.

"I'm not sure he even likes me in that way," Jacca complained, looking pouty with her lower lip stuck out. "We're alone together a *lot*, with him riding beside me every time I leave home, even if I'm only going to Mother Labéht. If he liked me, wouldn't he at least try to kiss me?"

"Oh, girl," Nina murmured, then stopped, unsure how to continue. The first thought that sprang to her mind was hardly appropriate: *If Wolfram let himself kiss you, young lady, there'd be no stopping at kissing. You'd find yourself on your back in a haystack rising vigorously to the occasion, the two of you howling your pleasure.*

Nina cast about for a less provocative response, words to assure the girl of Wolfe's affections without encouraging her to seduce the young man.

"Wolfram respects you, Jacca," she finally said, and reached to brush back a strand of the girl's hair, its rich chestnut gleaming with copper tints. "He holds you in the highest regard, and he would never do anything to betray the trust that your father has placed in him. You must realize how furious your father would be, were Wolfram to stray from his duty and ... make eyes at you." Nina uttered a soft *Tah!* at the weakness of the euphemism, but she pressed on in the absence of anything better. "You must give both of them time. You're fifteen, with at least three years left in your apprenticeship. Those numbers hold sway with your father and your 'escort'."

"Numbers I wish to leave behind," Jacca muttered, still pouting but listening intently. "Mother Labéht says I'm at the awkward age—old enough to notice a handsome man but too young to know what he's good for." She cracked a sudden grin. "But Mother Labéht is wrong. I do know what men are good for. Or I've got a fair idea of it, at least."

Nina laughed. "You may think you know, but you should listen to Labéht, for she is wise. As we go through life, we women may find that men are 'good for' different things at different times. Often a handsome fellow will offer nothing except a night or two of sweaty pleasure. But then there are the men who are good for a lifetime—the special ones we want to marry and wrap in our love forever." As she spoke, Nina thought of the only three men she had ever bedded: her husband Makani, the Earthly mortal with whom she had spent blissful decades ... Odhrán the *wysard*, tall, blond and muscular, adept in the magian arts of lovemaking but 'good for' only a brief affair ... and Corlis, the desert nomad who had settled in Nina's heart like sand in an oyster, becoming precious in her memory.

"Wolfe is good for me," Jacca declared. The girl's simple statement brought Nina back to the present, to the streamside where she sat dabbling her fingers in cold, clear water. "He is the man I want for a lifetime. But I'm not sure he wants me."

"Drisha's bollocks!" Nina exclaimed with such vehemence that Jacca's pouty expression changed to one of surprise. "This evening when you summon rainclouds to the valley, spare a glance for Wolfram. Dance for him and look into his eyes. What you see there will dispel any doubts about what he wants."

Jacca's gaze widened, and she gave a little gasp. Color rose in the girl's cheeks, a blush of delight, not discomfiture.

Nina snatched the moment to also voice a warning.

"I suspect that Master Galen will not release you from your apprenticeship before you're eighteen, at a minimum," she said, leaning toward her niece for emphasis. "Ten years is the typical length of an apprenticeship contract. And I would remind you, Jacca, that you *did* sign a contract. I witnessed it, don't forget. By wizardly law and custom, the terms of that agreement bind you to your master—an obligation only deepened by the fact that Galen is also your father." Nina raised an admonitory finger. "Don't be thinking you'll run off and get married without your father's consent."

As Jacca pondered this, Nina hastened to add another caution, belatedly trying to keep a lid on the flames of ardor she had fanned between the two young people. "I beg you will not flirt with Wolfram," she said, holding Jacca's gaze. "I have told that young man to keep his hands off you." Nina gave her niece the most severe look she could muster. "Do not make me regret dispelling your doubts about Wolfe's feelings for you. My heart ached to see you moping and uncertain. But now I fear that you'll flutter those lovely eyelashes of yours and make Wolfe's life a torment, teasing him with forbidden fruit."

"That's not my way, Aunt Nina." Jacca sat up straight, her fingers laced demurely in her lap. "I am filled with joy by what you have told me. With gratitude, also, for your advice." She smiled. "Waiting and wondering has been hard. If I may now be sure of Wolfram's affections, things between us will be easier. When he chooses not to speak, I will understand his silence. In my heart, I will hear the words he does not say." Jacca raised a hand from her lap and curled her fist tight against her breast, and a dreamy look drifted over her face.

Drisha's balls, Nina swore silently. She'd earlier seen the same wistfulness in Wolfram's expression. What hope had anyone of keeping those two apart now that Nina had cracked open a door which Galen wanted locked and barred? All good intentions aside, and all of her admonishments notwithstanding—and despite the couple's attempts at self-denial, if such could be expected of them—youthful passions would entwine the two, sooner rather than later. Nina resolved to dose the girl with herbal preventatives: the daily cup of dark tea that Jacca had earlier declined. At least there need not be a pregnancy to complicate matters. For that, at least, Nina must take responsibility.

And when the explosion came—when Galen learned how Nina had poured oil on the smoldering heat between his daughter and Wolfram—she must draw his anger to herself alone, and away from the young couple.

I will reap what I have sown, in time, she thought. With an inward sigh of resignation, Nina leaned back and gazed up at a scattering of white clouds in a brassy sky. The wispy streaks over the desert mountains recalled to her mind Jacca's newly developed talent for summoning rain—a magian aptitude that might prove lifesaving in any blistering battles yet to be fought. Also whispering in Nina's head was Galen's declaration, made when Jacca was only eight, that the girl possessed an extraordinary gift for fire. Nina had herself seen flames blaze from the young adept's fingertips as though Jacca's hands were blow-torches.

Galen's thunderbolts and my waves of water have preserved us this far, she mused. *But to assault the arsonist's stronghold in the peaks, we might need more. Sheets of rain drenching the battlefield for hours would not go amiss. And what possible force could stand against Jacca side-by-side with her father, the girl's flamethrowers annihilating any threat that made it past Galen's firebolts?*

Nina straightened and looked around the glade where she and Jacca had spent the afternoon, talking. The men of the party were not in sight. It would be good, Nina thought, if Galen were taking this opportunity for a heart-to-heart with his future son-in-law. The goldsmith's attitude toward Wolfram seemed too cool, oddly distant and abrupt, given the trust that Galen obviously placed in the young man. Nina meant to get to the bottom of their tense relationship, but that was a conversation to be had with Galen, later. Right now, she wanted to test her assumption that neither Jacca nor Wolfram intended to be left behind when their elders rode higher to scout the fires that smoldered in the peaks.

"I couldn't help noticing," Nina said, turning back to her niece, "that you and Wolfe looked unhappy with your father's plan to leave you here in camp, while he and I go check out that weird glow. You must be curious to see what's up there."

"It's not fair!" Jacca exclaimed, her words exactly what Nina had thought the girl would say. "Wolfram is a fully trained *wysard*." Jacca fumed, no longer looking dreamy, but outraged. "Father should not dismiss him like a mere apprentice who can't do anything except babysit." The girl's lower lip stuck out again. She wore an expression of frustrated displeasure. "As we've been discussing all afternoon, Aunt Nina, I'm not a child anymore, and I refuse to be babysat like one. You know I can make fire as hot as my father's flamework. I can smelt ores and reduce to liquid every metal that he uses in his smithcraft."

Jacca pointed at a melon-sized boulder that rested on the opposite streambank. Nina flinched, expecting the boulder to shatter, sending shards flying. But under the touch of Jacca's perfectly controlled finger-fires, the stone melted into a shimmering pool at the water's edge. The molten rock dripped into the stream, each drop crystallizing as it touched the chill water. The girl's magical fires had transformed a dull, flint-colored lump into a heap of glassy beads that glittered every color of the rainbow: red and orange, yellow, blue and purple, and some that shone as green as Jacca's emerald eyes.

"Well done!" Nina exclaimed. She waded the shallow, fast-running stream, to crouch over the mound and pick out the brightest of the green beads. "I'm giving these to your father." She looked across at Jacca. "He will want to mount such beautiful gems in the finest rings and brooches that he makes."

Jacca looked pleased by the praise. But swiftly the girl descended again into resentful indignation.

"He can't stop us," she muttered. "As soon as he rides away with you, Wolfram and I will follow. Wolfe knows how to keep out of sight. We'll hang back in the trees beside the trail. By the time we're high enough that there are hardly any trees, we'll be up where we can see what you and Father see."

Nina nodded, satisfied. "Don't tell your father this, but I am glad you're determined to go up there. If a firestorm comes roaring at us, we'll want a cloudburst to extinguish it. You *must* stay back, however, out of danger. Conjure rain from a distance, the same as you do for the valley. Promise me?"

Jacca nodded vigorously. A happy smile replaced her frown.

"Thank you, Aunt Nina. Wolfe and I won't get in your way. I can call rain from far off, and Wolfe can keep watch to tell me where and when to make it fall."

"Your uncle Dalton would be proud of you," Nina said as she continued to toy with the bright beads in the stream. "You know, do you not, that you're the second skilled weather-worker in the family? Your father and I have a younger brother who calls the rain to the fields at home, and he raises brisk winds to get him where he's going at sea."

Jacca pushed a strand of hair behind one ear, using the same fingers that had spouted flames only moments before. "Father has told me about Captain Dalton. I hope to meet him some day. Can he really make it snow and whip the flakes into a blizzard?" Jacca's eyes grew wide at the thought. "Conjuring warm rain is easy for me. I often make it warmer than people would like. Cool showers are pleasant, after all, on hot days." The girl tilted her head wonderingly. "It's all I can do to withhold my fires so that my rain is only warm and not scalding when it falls from the clouds. How I would love for Uncle Dalton to teach me the magic of snow!"

"Snow," Nina repeated softly. She lifted her gaze from the stream to peer over the treetops toward the glowing peaks high above.

Was it coincidence that sparks had come down from the mountains in the hottest days of a desert summer, to burn farms and smallholdings? Or had the maker of those malevolent fires timed the attacks to avoid winter snows, when mountain summits lay draped in white, and blizzards howled amongst pinnacles of black stone?

At home in Ruain, Dalton could summon snow with a flick of his wrist. More than that, he could freeze a flood into solid ice. Nina, however, might count on the fingers of one hand the times she had successfully constrained her element, liquid water, and forced it to take frozen form. The spellcraft required for such a transformation was difficult and demanding. And yet, her brother Dalton worked the magic routinely, with seeming ease when he froze ponds to entertain ice-skaters in his native province, or when he conjured frosty cubes to chill drinks at the captain's table when the famous weather-mage was out at sea.

"Jacca, my girl," Nina said with a fond glance at her niece, "you're not only gifted and beautiful, you're brilliant. Dalton is exactly what we need. I want him here with his snow and his blizzards. Making plenty of ice."

"All the way from Ruain?" Jacca looked excited but skeptical. "My father says that Uncle Dalton has never, ever been to the Ore Hills. Though he *could* sail most of the way here, if the captain wanted to."

"That is what I'm counting on," Nina said. "I've seen maps. The Southern Seas crest upon the desert coast very near here. His ship could drop anchor due east of these mountains. Then he'd have only a narrow neck of packed sand to cross on foot. Or in the saddle, if he brought horses with him."

"But how can you ask Uncle Dalton to come?" Jacca's puzzlement showed plain on her face. "A messenger would need weeks to ride to Ruain. And if the captain chanced to be at sea when the rider reached Weyrrock, months could pass before he received your letter." The girl shook her head. "Getting him here could take a year—if he even consented to the journey."

"He'll consent," Nina muttered. "Or he'll suffer the wrath of his elder sister, when next I see him." She marked the progress of the westering sun. The orb would soon be in position, low over the mountaintops, dimming to the quality of light that she needed.

"As for sending Dalton a message: I know a quick way," Nina added. "With your help, Jacca, I believe I can make it work. Give me a moment to prepare."

Nina had not ceased toying with the colorful beads that Jacca's touch of fire had dropped into the cold stream. The feel of water on her hands was pleasant after the endless dry grit of the pilgrimage path she had lately traversed. Without conscious intent, merely as a result of her picking idly through the heaped beads, selecting the ones she wanted Galen to have, Nina had hollowed the mound into the shape of a wide-mouthed cup like a beaker. Lined with the glittering gems of Jacca's spellcraft, the beaker practically begged to be filled with water-bucket magic.

"Conjure a cloud, Jacca," Nina said as she glanced again at the sun. "A small one, thin and high, without rain in it. I need a curtain, gauzy, nearly sheer, between us and the sun to soften its light."

Jacca leapt to her feet. With a graceful flick of her slender wrist, the girl summoned the requested cloud and hung it in the sky as Nina directed. Then she jumped the creek to stand looking over her aunt's shoulder, down into the glistening beaker.

Nina took Jacca's hand and held it. The combined sum of their talents would raise the odds of getting through to Dalton. She hoped to find the captain already at sea, sailing upon the broad reaches of Nina's oceanic element. Jacca's cloud-conjuring—source of the tenuous shade that enveloped them—would resonate with Dalton's own weather magic. The low angle of the sun now favored this distaff alchemy. The gauze of Jacca's curtain-cloud dimmed the orb's rays until they mimicked the light of the full moon. All was as propitious as Nina could make it.

She leaned over the streambank to peer straight down into the beaker. Nina pictured Dalton on the foredeck of his flagship, summoning winds to fill his sails and speed him onward to his next port of call. She built a picture in her mind of her middle brother, his white-blond hair streaming in the wind like a blizzard, its paleness contrasting with his suntanned skin. Years of riding Ruain border-to-border, when he wasn't sailing the Eastern Sea, had bronzed Dalton's complexion.

"Dalton!" Nina called sharply into the water-filled beaker, keeping her mental picture distinct in her thoughts. "I need you."

"*Sister!*"

His answering cry rose amidst fog. The vapors cleared to reveal Dalton's face staring up from the beaker's center.

"Nina, have you *drowned?*" he demanded, looking shocked.

"Far from it," she exclaimed. "I'm in Galen's desert, in the mountains opposite the Ore Hills. I need you here. No time to explain. There's danger. Are you at sea?"

"Coming up on Easthaven. You sure you're not in the ocean? That's what I'm seeing."

Nina shook her head impatiently. "This is water-bucket magic like Aunt Megella's. Only way I knew to reach you. Skip Easthaven. Sail down to Seawood and stop there just long enough to pick up Legary. I want him, too," she added on impulse. "Galen and I have a situation. Come on around the south coast, quick as you can, and make your way to the Hills. Ask for Mother Labéht. She'll tell you where we are and what's happening."

"On my way!" Dalton replied with all the enthusiasm Nina could have wished for. "I've never sailed the Southern Seas. 'Bout time I did."

"Past time. You've got a flame-throwing, weather-working niece here who wants to meet you." Nina gestured for Jacca to lean in close, taking care that the girl not block the last slanting rays of the sun, for that would break the connection. In a rush, Nina made the introductions. "Jacca summons rain but hasn't mastered snow. I command water but not ice. Come help us, brother. We need your gifts, quickly. But don't leave Seawood without Legary," she added. "We might need him to seal up a mountain."

"I'm intrigued," Dalton said, flinging his hair out of his eyes. "I'll get us there on the fastest winds I've ever conjured."

"Not at risk of shipwreck!" Nina yelled into the beaker. But the sun had dipped behind the mountains, and the link was severed.

"How marvelous," Jacca murmured. "Not even in the enchanted city of my cousins is such magic commonly made. Will you teach me?"

"If I can." Nina leaned back, relaxing from her tense pose over the streambank. "You have already learned the rudiments of conversing by water bucket. You need water and light." She gestured at the stream and then at the sky, which was streaked golden now as the day moved toward dusk. "Most of the rest is luck and determination, or maybe desperation. Aunt Megella used to say that 'teacup tidings' would never fail a woman who really, *really* wanted to talk."

Jacca laughed. "Then certainly I must learn it, for I desperately wish to speak with any member of House Verek who will deign to speak with me."

"Master the trick," Nina murmured, "and they'll clamor for the privilege. You're a prodigy."

Jacca seemed not to hear. The look on the girl's face approached awe as she leaned to stare again into the beaker that Nina had shaped from the young adept's beadwork. "Captain Dalton is coming *here?*" she marveled. "And Master Legary with him? I can hardly believe I shall at last meet my honored uncles."

Then Jacca frowned as she spotted the flaw in Nina's plan. "But how will Uncle Legary know that he is to travel to the coast and take ship with his brother? Have you used this same magic to talk with the stonemason?"

Nina shook her head. "I have not. I doubt it would work with Legary. There's not enough water in the grasslands where he is. I suspect we only reached Dalton because the captain was at sea with water all around." Nina tapped her teeth with her thumbnail, taking a moment to examine the sudden impulse that had made her include her youngest brother in her plan.

"Your father will have to send word to Legary," she continued then. "Galen has told me of using bedrock, a vein deep in a gold mine, to send messages to the stonemason. It seems Legary's house sits on the same vein, but with endless miles of merciless desert between here and there." Nina leaned to drink from the cold, clear stream, feeling a spontaneous thirst as she recalled her badlands journey with Corlis, the many hot days they had spent together, winding through mostly waterless canyons.

Nina stood up and stretched. "Time for supper. Let's throw something together ... and see what the men are up to. They've been conspicuously absent all afternoon, haven't they."

Chapter Thirteen

The men, it was discovered, had gone hunting. Their efforts made for a fine goat-roast that evening.

Before they settled to the meal, Jacca climbed to her usual lookout and did not see the torchlight that would signal a request for rain. Nevertheless, the girl danced the magic of her weather-working for an appreciative audience of two. Galen had stayed below at the fire, tending the goat, but Wolfram and Nina followed the girl to her performance on the ridgetop. Standing aside from the young people, Nina nonetheless felt a sizzle in the air when Jacca danced close to Wolfe and locked gazes with him—emboldened, obviously, by Nina's encouragement. The look that passed between them must have left Jacca in no doubt about Wolfram's feelings.

Thank the Powers Galen isn't seeing this, Nina thought. Half regretful though she was for what she'd said to Jacca, Nina also felt relieved. It would have been tragic, after all, if Jacca had ended up spurning Wolfram because of a simple misunderstanding about the reasons for the young man's reticence.

After supper, Nina drew Galen aside, determined to learn why her brother seemed unable to accord Wolfram the frank respect and affection the shapeshifting *wysard* merited.

"Wolfe showed me the beautiful pendant you made for him, to give him safe passage into Ruain," Nina began, opening with a reminder of the special trust that Galen had placed in the young adept. She chuckled. "I wish I'd been there to see how our father greeted his unexpected visitor. Lord Verek must have been amazed—I daresay staggered—to stand in the presence of the first shapeshifter to appear in this world in five thousand years. But of course, he would show to Wolfram no shock or fluster. I expect he was stern with the boy."

Galen scratched the unkempt growth of beard on his chin. "I believe our father did give Wolfram 'the look'," he muttered, "... that same withering gaze you display upon occasion, Nina, when you wish to be particularly intimidating. Like our formidable sire, you can terrify when you choose."

Nina tipped her head in acknowledgment, a smugly satisfied smile on her lips. "I have long been grateful for the gaze I inherited. A woman who travels alone, as I so often do, benefits from possessing a 'look' that can freeze men's blood."

She shifted on the blanket where they sat beside the stream. Away on the creek's far side, Jacca and Wolfram moved among the horses, ostensibly grooming the animals, checking their feet, ensuring readiness for tomorrow's ride to the top of the trail. Nina noticed, however—as Galen must do—that the two were never far apart ... saying little, never touching, but staying within arm's reach of each other.

"You must know, brother," Nina said, opting now for bluntness, "that Wolfram will be your son-in-law. His love for Jacca is obvious to anyone who possesses a beating heart and a particle of feeling. And yet, I do not see you embracing the lad. You seem a mite standoffish around Wolfe, even while you charge him with your daughter's safe-keeping. Why is that? Has the young man offended you in some way? If he has erred in his manners, I'm sure he's eager to make amends, if you will but tell him how he may do so."

Galen left off scratching his chin and instead rubbed the back of his neck, his telltale gesture of tension. He sighed.

"How do I say this, sister? I know you rode far with the boy when he was locked in wolf shape. You grew comfortable in the presence of ... the beast."

Very comfortable, Nina silently agreed. *So much at my ease, in fact, that from time to time I stripped down in front of those unblinking hazel eyes. No* need to share the details with Galen, however. From the way he'd said *beast,* Nina already had a disagreeable sense of where her brother's thoughts were tending. She had to fight to keep from frowning at him.

"Have you seen the lad take the shape of the wolf?" she asked instead. "It's spectacular magic. I was privileged to witness Wolfram's restoration to his natural form. He *is* a man, if that's what troubles you, brother. He is *not* the beast."

"I keep telling myself that," Galen replied with another sigh. "But I can't help wondering. In a moment of passion, might the wolf within him be unleashed? Might he hurt my girl?" Galen grimaced. He gave his head a hard shake, as if to banish an unwanted mental image. "May the Powers forgive me, but I keep imagining my daughter on her wedding night being ravaged by a wolf."

"Oh, Galen," Nina murmured. She reached for his hand. "Wolfram is incapable of hurting Jacca. He adores her. And aren't you forgetting? He is not an apprentice, nor inexperienced. Wolfe is a trained *wysard.* His shapeshifting is entirely under his control. It's true, of course, that the boy was stuck in wolf form when I first met him. He'd come down from the mountains with a master *wysard,* and they were practicing his shifting when brigands sprang upon them and killed the Old One." A flush of anger rose in Nina at the senselessness of that old murder. "Wolfe was then a novice, not yet proficient in the difficult magic of transformation. But an Elder of the craft subsequently took him in hand and taught him the deep secrets of the ancient shapeshifters. That Elder—Gelgeis by name—would not have released Wolfram from apprenticeship if he were not satisfied that the man had control of the wolf."

Galen made no reply to this, but he squeezed Nina's hand as if in gratitude for her reassurance. He did not look at her, but kept his gaze on the shapeshifter who was barely visible now in the deepening dusk across the stream.

Nina glanced in that direction, then back at Galen. "Wolfe is a gentle soul," she continued when the smith did not speak. "Even as the boy who ran on four legs, he displayed great gentleness toward me. And respect, too, as he respects Jacca. That young man holds your daughter in the highest regard. I say again: Wolfram isn't capable of hurting the girl."

She hesitated, weighing her next words, and then cast tact to the winds. "Those two are lusting for each other, more every day from what I've seen, and you won't keep them apart, Galen. Why not embrace the inevitable and give Wolfram your blessing? You have given him your trust all the way to Ruain and back, so why not your approval? You'll avoid another scandal if you get them married before they go where the fire in their blood takes them."

Galen turned sharply to Nina. She expected anger from him, but his response, when it came, was one of grudging resignation.

"I accept the truth of everything you've said," he grumbled through gritted teeth. "I only hope their children are not ... furry."

Nina stared at him. Then she burst out laughing.

"Any cub of such parents can't help but be born with a luxuriant mane—copper-streaked like their grandsire, of course." She tousled Galen's uncombed ginger hair, though he grimaced and tried to bat her hand away. "I further predict," Nina added in a tone less teasing, "that the offspring of a fire-mage and a shapeshifter will possess a vastness of talent that has never been seen in this world. What wizardly gifts such children will have! The envy of the ages. They will make you proud, Galen."

He smoothed his hair and muttered something acerbic about having always wanted a "pack" of grandchildren. But Nina's attention was called away by the patter of rain falling on a clump of low-growing cedars. The rain fell nowhere else, only on the screen of trees at the far edge of the streamside glade. It was Jacca having a shower before bed.

Nina envied the girl's ability to conjure up a hot bath whenever she wanted one. After arriving dust-coated and sweaty from her "pilgrimage" along the skyway trail, Nina had reveled in the magical shower Jacca had summoned for her. She wondered that the men did not also avail themselves of the warm rains that Jacca could call with a wrist-flick.

But then in the gathering dark, Nina saw Wolfram in the stream, stripped to his waist and splashing ice-cold water on his face and torso. She had to smile at the young man's willpower. *Wysards*, after all, were creatures of Nature, possessed of elemental passions. Young adepts, especially, were notably amorous, not given to abstinence. And Wolfe's night vision was keen. He'd see the girl standing naked and dripping.

Abruptly, Nina shifted to a new subject to get Galen's mind—and her own—off of "puppy love" and lusty young wolves.

"I talked to Dalton this afternoon," she said. "He's coming to help us."

"*What?*" Galen exclaimed, jerking his head to stare at her. "How? When?"

"As soon as he can sail the Southern Seas on magical winds of his making." Nina described the water-bucket magic she had performed with Jacca's help. She laid out the plan for Dalton to drop anchor just long enough to pick up Legary.

"That's where you come in, brother," she added. "Tomorrow, after we've crested the trail and seen what there is to see, you must hasten to the bedrock that carries your voice to Legary." Nina rubbed her forehead, trying to recall what she knew of the conduit for messages that linked the brothers through their shared affinity for rock. The metalsmith of the hills mined ore for the raw materials of his craft, and down in one such mine Galen had devised a direct link to Legary, the worker in stone. "Is it far from here, your special rock?" Nina inquired. "I know you do not wish to be gone long, but you must go. You must tell Legary to head for the coast as soon as possible."

Galen gaped at her, momentarily lost for words. Then he found plenty.

"Absolutely not, Nina. Drisha's knuckles!" he swore. "I will *not* leave you and Jacca up here alone with whatever is lurking in the heights." He jerked his thumb at the summit that rose above them, where the fiends'-fire glow wreathed bare stone spires. "You've lost your mind if you think I would even *consider* leaving you up here on your own."

"Must I remind you again," Nina responded with more patience than she felt, "that we are not alone? We have Wolfram with us."

"What use is a shapeshifter against *that?*" Galen demanded with another jerk of his thumb toward the menace above. "Do you expect the wolf to pounce on a firestorm and snap sparks out of the air with his bare jaws?" Galen scoffed. "He'd burn his tongue and singe his fur."

"Your prejudice is showing, brother, and it's not pretty," Nina retorted. "Wolfram might lack our skills for fighting fire, but he'll make a far more capable spy than either of us will. Think of it: the wolf slipping unseen among rocks and trees, gliding on silent feet to the farthest corner of our adversary's stronghold. Whatever you and I may behold from the trail tomorrow, Wolfram will see more from the cover of pines and pinnacles."

Galen subsided, thinking this over.

"Maybe you're right," he muttered after a time. "But I'm still not leaving. If Dalton is already on his way, I will welcome him here with open arms. Perhaps our brother can raise a wind strong enough to snuff out hellfire. But I'm not going all the way down to the valley just to send a message to Legary." Galen's scowl deepened. "What could a stonemason do here anyway, that the rest of us cannot?"

"Carve the heart out of the mountain, maybe, and entomb a demon within?"

As she spoke, Nina offered Galen a frown of her own, displeased at the way he dismissed the considerable wizardly powers of their baby brother. Legary the master mason had been known to raise colossal blocks of stone from deep underground, throw impossibly thick slabs of rock up on end to make towering walls, and even bespell boulders for sending into battle like soldiers. From the moment that Nina had thought to tell Dalton to bring the stonecrafter with him, the conviction had grown within her that Legary's magian talents would be indispensable in whatever battles lay ahead.

"Call it woman's intuition," she snapped at the still-resisting Galen. "Call it the wisdom of the firstborn. I don't care what you call it, only do as I ask."

"Hunh," Galen grunted, a sullen sound, unwilling, but halfway toward acquiescence. "Get some sleep, Nina," he said as he rose from the streambank, still wearing a scowl. "We ride out early."

Chapter Fourteen

Before a glimmer of dawn had brightened the foothills that lay behind and below them, they were on the trail, Galen leading. As they climbed steeply toward the summit, Nina craned her neck to keep sight of the glow that rose a short way north of where the trail topped the crest. The radiance strengthened as they drew nearer, but the character of the glow did not visibly alter. Nina was on watch for any threatening movement, any rush of sparks or surge of fire. All remained quiet, however.

Almost too quiet. In the silence of the morning as day broke and the air warmed, sounds reached Nina from the two riders who followed at a cautious distance back down the trail. As Jacca had sworn they would, she and Wolfram were tagging along in defiance of her father's orders.

The pair had nearly been sent packing last night, when a tremendous noise of rumbling shook them all out of their blankets. Galen came awake shouting for Jacca and Wolfram to flee. Nina's eyes flew open to fix upon the glow in the peaks. It had not changed, but directly to the north of her location she saw roiling clouds of dust. They boiled up into the night sky, climbing to such heights that the dust caught and reflected the uncanny glow, sending it back to dimly illuminate the mountain slopes above the pilgrimage path.

"Rockslide!" Nina shouted as the rumble came again and she sensed movement in the direction of the dust. "Over there." She grabbed

Galen's sleeve and made him look where she pointed. "I'm glad we're off the Sky Trail, brother, because I think the mountain just buried it—that last bit of it, anyway, what we walked after I took a chunk out of the middle."

"Drisha's bones!" Galen swore as he stared at the towering clouds of dust and felt a final shudder under his and Nina's feet. The slide crunched to a stop, the noise of it fading into the distance.

No one slept much for the rest of the night, although not from worries about a similar rockfall crashing down upon their sheltered camp. The slopes directly above them were thickly wooded and the ground was firm, not riddled with cracks such as the long fracture that had carried a rushing river of lava down the mountainside. The rocks above the Sky Trail, perpetually unstable but holding together as though willed in place by generations of pilgrims, had been overstressed by that torrent of lava. So Galen said, and Nina agreed, for it deflected blame from the damage her water wizardry had done in that same place. She did not agree, however, that the segment of the pilgrimage path close by their camp needed inspecting that night. Sunrise would show more. But Galen went anyway, his steps illuminated by an orb of conjured witchlight.

Within an hour, he returned, glum-faced. The path was gone—sheared from the mountainside. Where once there had been a stone ledge, wide enough in places to pitch a tent, nothing now appeared except empty space under a cliff so steep, only birds could gain a foothold.

"You and I ... we were the last to ever walk it," he muttered to Nina, impressing her with a sense of loss that was out of proportion to her own slight experience of journeying on that path. But she could feel Galen's sadness, his regret for the loss of a tradition with deep roots in his beloved hills.

Morning of the new day found him restless, tightlipped and preoccupied. Nina dreaded the blow to Galen's already dark mood when Jacca's disobedience came to light. Nonetheless, she wanted the girl and her escort to maintain their stealthy approach and stay unseen and unheard until all had reached the summit. If battle were joined, she would want Jacca's cloudbursts reinforcing her walls of water.

Galen's strategy of reconnoitering early in the day, however, proved sound. Previous attacks had favored the night hours, whether directed at the valley-dwellers below, or against Galen and Nina after they'd climbed into the mountains to bring the fight to the enemy. Now as they stood together at the top of the sun-dappled South Trail, peering through scattered, wind-bent trees, they could look upon the enemy stronghold without fending off a storm of sparks or a river of fire.

But those would come. Nina felt the certitude like a knot in her belly as she surveyed a scene of devastation.

The glow that wrapped the peaks in demon fire arose from a basin that was tucked like a vast bowl beneath the mountain summit. In a narrow band along the bowl's rim, tree trunks smoldered, evidence that the basin had once been a sheltered, green oasis supporting pine-woods and cedars. Now, all stood blackened and charred. Farther be-low the rim, the walls of the bowl showed nothing but bare rock, every surface scorched and lifeless, for in the depths of the bowl, in a massive sinkhole with sheer sides of black stone, molten rock churned—a seemingly bottomless lake of lava.

Nina had been expecting fire, but not such a witch's cauldron as this. The lake bubbled like a pot of vomitous hot stew, thick with chunks of bloody red and livid orange, and streamers of bilious yellow. As Nina watched the "stew" splash high up the sides of the bowl, coating them with flaming gobbets, she felt like holding her nose in anticipation of a stench that would match the foul appearance of the huge stewpot.

The odor that rose from the pot, however, was a different kind of stink. The hot, acrid, sulphur-stink of the lava was the same smell as from the attack on the skyway, when a river of molten rock had streamed down the mountainside. As Nina ran her gaze around the bowl's rim, she detected a notch in its northeastern edge. The angle and position were unmistakable: that sharp dip opened outward into the rock chimney down which the molten river had flowed. She had previously stood at the bottom of the crack where it met the now nonexistent Sky Trail. Now she was looking across at the top of it but from high up, and from the other side. The inside.

"Look there," Nina muttered, directing Galen's attention. "If this lake were to boil up higher, lava would spill out through that notch and straight down into the valley. There's nothing to stop it." She rubbed her lower lip as she thought how her flood had plummeted down the same way. The torrent had undoubtedly done damage, but nothing like the ruin that would result if all this lava poured into the valley. Homes, farms, meadows, even people and their animals would burn if they couldn't flee. Molten rock would destroy everything in its path, until it reached the river. There, it would likely create a dam, and the river that had previously been the valley's lifeblood would drown the charred remains of a wasteland, and with it a people's way of life.

"Nothing to stop it?" Galen echoed as he looked where Nina pointed. "Has your water magic found its limits, sister?"

"I'm afraid so." Nina tilted her head, mentally measuring the distance, and frowned to realize it was too great to bridge with her magic. She would not be able to drop a wall of water on it from this far away, to cool the lava enough to stop it flowing beyond that point. "I'm glad Jacca has come up here with us," she said before she thought. "That girl may conjure a rainstorm where no wave of mine will reach."

"What?"

As Galen rounded on Nina, protesting and sputtering with confusion, he spotted Jacca standing not far behind them. He had been so intent on surveying the lava lake and the fire-blackened bowl that held it, he had not noticed the girl and Wolfram ride silently up and dismount at the top of the trail. Now the metalsmith directed a severe scowl at his rebellious daughter, his face flushing red beneath his shock of copper hair.

"Don't be angry with her," Nina said, intervening before Galen could vent his ire. "I encouraged Jacca to follow us up here, and Wolfe, too. As I've said more than once, I believe we need the skills that both of these young adepts bring to this fight." As she spoke, Nina moved to stand with Wolfram and Jacca. Together, the three presented a united front in the face of Galen's dark displeasure.

The smith threw up his hands and let out a long, fuming sigh. Then he trained his gaze on Wolfram.

"Remember what I said, boy," Galen snapped. "Get Jacca out of here if we are attacked. Even if Nina and I are losing the battle. Do not try to help us, just get my daughter to safety." Galen eyed the big, plodding horse that had brought Jacca up the trail, and which the girl would surely insist on riding back down, even if fiends of hellfire were at "Bobby's" heels. "Drag her off that damned old plowhorse, kicking and screaming if you have to, and toss her over your saddle, if that's what it takes for a quick escape." Galen shook a finger at Wolfram. "Do whatever you must to get Jacca out of harm's way. Do you understand me?"

Wolfe, his head high, locked gazes with Galen, the look in his golden hazel eyes piercingly direct. "Rely on me," he said in a voice lower and more restrained than the goldsmith's. "I will keep Jacca safe ... *always*."

As each man tried to stare the other down, Nina noticed for the first time that Wolfram stood a head taller than Galen. The smith, however, was more muscular, with powerful shoulders and bulging biceps. Wolfe, many years younger than Galen, had the lean and sinewy build of his shapeshifting alter ego. Nina wouldn't care to wager on which one would prevail in a fistfight. Although Wolfram could tip the odds decidedly in his favor, should the young *wysard* take the form of a snarling beast.

Jacca seemed to think that such a fight might be imminent. The girl bounced nervously on her toes, her gaze darting from one stern visage to the other.

"Forgive me, Honored Father," Jacca said, her tone respectful, and with an undernote of pleading. "I talked Wolfe into bringing me up here. I wanted to see *that*." Jacca pointed at the bowl of roiling, bubbling lava.

Nina did not follow the girl's gesture. She kept her eyes on the men, ready with a summoning of water to drench them both if their tempers brought them to blows. But not looking at the lava made her more conscious of the sounds that emanated from the lake. The molten stew sizzled and crackled, and occasionally hissed like a gigantic snake as gas escaped from deep in the cauldron.

Galen shot a look at his daughter but made no answer to Jacca's plea. Instead, the smith advanced a step, took Nina by the arm, and pulled her away from the young people. Galen marched Nina out to a tree-screened overlook above the flaming pit, beyond the hearing of the two who had defied his orders to stay clear of this place.

Uh-oh, Nina thought. *Here it comes.*

She expected Galen to unload on her for encouraging rebellion in the young adepts. What the smith had to say, however, was entirely unanticipated.

"That friend of yours from the east," Galen muttered, "that giant who threw himself into the abyss ... Are you certain he's well-disposed toward those who live in the surface world?" Galen had released her arm. With both hands, he combed his fingers stiffly through his hair, his movements tense. "I read the letter you wrote to Legary. Remember? You said I could read it, and you wanted me to talk about it with Legary."

Galen dropped one hand and jerked a thumb over his shoulder, indicating the molten lake that steamed and gurgled below the overlook. "I can't help but think that your 'king of the underworld' must have something to do with that hellhole. Doesn't he rule the realm, down in the bowels of the world, where fire burns in darkness and solid rock melts? Have you considered, Nina, that the creature who jumped into the abyss might have returned to the surface, here in these mountains—and he's returned with a vengeance?"

"No!" Nina stared at her brother, dumbfounded by such a suggestion. "You couldn't think such a thing, Galen, if you had ever met Grog. He's the soul of gentleness."

"Faugh! Like that wolf standing over there with Jacca? Nothing but a gentle little puppy dog?" Galen glared, his eyes like green ice. "That's what you said of Wolfram, but I mistrust your notion of 'gentleness.' I had occasion, just now, to meet the glance of the shapeshifter, and what I saw in the depths, below the countenance of a man, was the savagery of a beast. The hair rose on my head." Galen spat and cursed.

"What you find 'gentle,' Lady Karenina—mistress of strange oceans upon distant worlds—would strike many in Ladrehdin as terrifying."

Nina gaped, finding no word of response other than another indignant, "No!"

Galen brushed it aside with an angry gesture. "Having gone against my wishes and enticed my daughter to approach the gates of *farsinchia*"—again he pointed at the fiery lake—"you cannot now expect me to leave you alone up here with Jacca, poised on the brink. I have not forgotten your request, but I most certainly will *not* descend to the valley to summon Legary."

"You must!" Nina exclaimed, continuing at a loss in the face of Galen's anger. She had never seen her favorite brother in such a cold fury.

She cast about for an argument that could thaw and sway him. Nina's glimpse of the crack in the cauldron's rim had evoked uneasy memories of lying helpless below it, facing death from her own magic. She would have perished if Galen hadn't been there to drag her out of the way of the bone-crushing torrent of water that had cascaded down and into the valley below, carrying huge boulders with it. Legary, with his legendary talents for raising massive slabs of rock straight up from the ground, could have plugged that spillway and held the lava back with a permanent barrier of stone, not the short-lived, stopgap wall of water that Nina had conjured.

Stone.

That was it. In a word, Nina had found her best argument for persuading Galen.

She pointed at the glowing lava where red and yellow flames flickered, low over the lake's surface. "If you think it's the king of the underworld who has wedged open this door to hell and released the fires of *farsinchia*, then brother, you need a *wysard* who can slam the door shut and roll a great stone in front of it. You need Legary the stonemason."

Nina jerked her head in a vaguely easterly direction. "On the plains halfway to the ocean, when my friend Grog threw himself into the abyss, I saw him turn to stone. Can you understand what that means,

Galen? In his essential nature, Grog *is* stone. He's made of it, the same way it makes his kingdom in the underworld, deep at the roots of mountains and continents." Again Nina indicated the sluggishly roiling lava. "This witch's brew is thick with stone—rocks and boulders so hot, they're melted."

She started to reach for Galen's hand, but the memory of his anger stopped her. If he knocked her hand aside, something would change in the love they bore each other, the deep affection they had felt since babyhood when barely a year separated second-born Galen from his big sister Nina.

Instead, she dropped her hand and closed her argument, offering it with a plea. "Is not a stonemason best equipped to battle a man of stone?" Nina studied Galen's frosty expression. "Can you not see that Legary is our best weapon—and perhaps our only way of safely sealing yon break in the cauldron's rim?" She tipped her head in that direction. "If you would not have this pot of death overflowing its bounds, spilling down the mountainside and burying the valley below, then go summon Legary quick as you can. We need a master mason to plug the hole in this particular stone wall. In fact, we may need him to rebuild this mountain. The whole side of it might be ready to give way, after last night's rockslide dropped a fair bit of it on the valley floor."

Galen was wavering. Nina had wedged a crack in her brother's resolve. Only his concern for his daughter was keeping him from assenting to her request.

"I won't let anything happen to Jacca," Nina murmured, now allowing herself to take Galen's hand. "Between that girl's fire-magic and her weather-working, your daughter can protect herself quite well. But if I need to get us down this mountain quickly, I will conjure a flood and we'll surf my magical waves all the way to the valley." She gave him a mischievous grin. "You ever been surfing, brother? I have, and I'm good at it."

"I'll bet you are." He let slip a ghost of the lopsided smile that had marked Galen's acquiescence to Nina's demands ever since they were toddlers. "How could a sea goddess be otherwise?"

He sighed heavily, then stomped down from the overlook where they had stood together arguing. Threading his way through scattered cedars, Galen headed for the trail where their horses waited.

"Two nights," he snapped as he swung into the saddle. "I won't be gone longer than that. The mineshaft that carries to Legary is in the hills south of the river shallows." Galen paused as Jacca approached him and placed her hand on his boot where it rested in the stirrup. He gazed down at the girl, trying to look stern but ending with an expression of fond pride. "Take care of yourself, daughter," he murmured. "Use your powers well and wisely."

"I will, Father." Jacca smiled at him. "Thank you for not being too mad at me. This is where I need to be."

Galen sat silent for a moment, considering his daughter's words, and perhaps concluding, as Nina already had, that Jacca was indeed the best judge of where she ought to be in this time of trouble. He gave her a nod, then reined his horse down the South Trail, urging the animal to a quick jog.

He spared no glance for Wolfram. Ignoring the existence of a fellow *wysard*, especially one as renowned in magian circles as was Wolfram the shapeshifter, constituted a breach of courtesy that drew disappointed sighs from Jacca and Nina.

Wolfe reacted only with silence. He watched the metalsmith ride away, his expression impassive. Then he turned on his heel and disappeared among rocks and trees off the side of the trail. A short time later, Nina spotted a large, brown-and-tan wolf padding surefooted along the knife-edged upper rim of the mountain basin. The creature headed toward the gap, the distant notch in the rim that made a spout through which the lava lake might be emptied with deadly consequences for many lives below.

Wolfram, too, knows his business in this matter, Nina thought, watching approvingly as the beast slipped from view amongst pinnacles of stone.

* * *

The afternoon edged toward dusk, prompting Nina and Jacca to make what camp they could. In a gully off the side of the trail, they found water for the horses and refilled their canteens. They left the animals tethered in a green patch beside the water. The low ravine would not serve the three remaining riders as a nighttime camp, for those adepts needed to be where they could observe any change in the lake of lava. With Jacca at her heels, Nina returned to a spot near the tree-screened overlook where she had argued with Galen.

They made no fire, but ate dried meat and waybread from their packs. At Nina's insistence, however, Jacca snapped heat into a pot of water, bringing it to a simmer with the ease of a practiced magician. Nina brewed tea, and Jacca made no demur when she was offered a cup. She accepted Nina's special blend with a nod and a soft smile.

In the absence of both men, the two women stripped and enjoyed warm showers under the isolated raincloud that Jacca conjured on demand. When they'd dried off and got dressed, Nina sat the girl down and gave her firm instructions.

"Wake me as soon as Wolfram returns from his scouting expedition," she said, holding Jacca's gaze. "I know you will wait up for him, however late he stays out. I know you will wish to be alone with him while I sleep. But you must wake me." Nina gave the young woman her most severe look. "The swarms and storms of fire that your father and I battled on our way up the mountain came upon us generally after midnight. I must hear what Wolfram has seen out there"—Nina gestured at the far rim of the bubbling lake—"in order that I may judge how we can best defend ourselves against storms yet to come. Last night after the rockslide, I slept little. I will sleep now, while I can, and leave you on watch. But you must wake me when Wolfe returns, or if any change comes upon the lake of fire. Promise?"

Jacca sighed, sadly frustrated in her hopes for romance tonight. But the girl nodded.

"Rely on me, Aunt Nina. I shall do as you say."

Chapter Fifteen

Hours later, it was Wolfram himself shaking her awake. "Firebirds, my lady," he whispered. "Come see."

Nina sprang up from the blanket upon which she lay uncovered by anything other than her clothes. Even this high in the mountains, the air and ground were warm from the lava that bubbled below the overlook. Following Wolfram's lead, Nina crept cautiously to the exposed edge and peered over.

She caught her breath at the sight. In the dark night, the roiling lava was mesmerizing as it fizzed and simmered in its cauldron of rock. Brilliant ropes of red and orange writhed across the darker surface of the boiling "stew," and flames of incandescent yellow licked at the cauldron's sides.

Clinging to those sides, like glittering white birds perched on outthrust boulders, were swarms of dazzling sparks. Nina watched with uneasy fascination as each clump of sparks briefly broke up, then swirled back together in a shape that suggested the head, wings, and talons of a mythical phoenix.

"Firebirds, indeed," Nina whispered.

She gestured for her companions to retreat from the overlook's edge. Jacca had joined her and Wolfram in peering over, and when all were back behind the screen of trees, they huddled together, softly talking.

"Now you have seen what attacked Master Galen and myself down the mountain, before we joined up with you," Nina muttered. "Except we met with ill-defined masses of sparks—loose clouds and shapeless swarms." She rubbed her forehead. "These 'firebirds' are something new, and they alarm me. I wonder: how far might they travel? Could they wing their way the length of the valley and along the foothills?" Nina paused as another possibility occurred. "Perhaps they might even fly into the mountains and forests of the north country where we have family."

"Let me drown them," Jacca said. "Right now, while they're perched on the rocks, let me summon rain and snuff out every spark."

Nina studied the young adept. Should she allow Jacca to make the attempt? Without doubt, the girl could conjure a cloudburst sufficient to span the cauldron. Nina had seen her cloak the entire lower valley in rain.

But might a sudden downpour upon the fiery lake trigger such an explosion of steam as to knock all three of them off the mountain, their scalded flesh peeled away and their eyes burned blind? As Nina mentally pictured that gruesome possibility, she also imagined the force of the explosion blasting through the cauldron's rim. The notch at the rim's weak point might be blown open, allowing the cauldron's burning contents to race down the mountainside and flood the valley in a river of death.

"No, Jacca," Nina finally answered the girl. "Not yet. I have every confidence in your ability to extinguish those uncanny creatures." She gestured toward the firebirds that clung to the cauldron's inner walls. Some of them flapped their wings as though testing their strength, like nestlings making ready for their maiden flights. "I suspect you will be called upon to conjure endless rain, in days to come," Nina added, returning her gaze to the girl. "But we cannot now risk an attack. We must wait until our force is at full strength. Your father will soon return, and I trust that your uncles will not be far behind him. Then we shall be six, not three—each of us wielding our own special magicks." Nina nodded, her decision made.

Jacca looked disappointed but she bowed to her aunt's wishes. Nina seemed to be succeeding better than Galen, when it came to commanding the girl's obedience. Rebellion remained at the ready, however. Nina saw it in Jacca's glances and expression. To forestall it, she sent the girl back to bed. The time was well past midnight, and for all of them the day had begun in the dim predawn after a disturbed night.

Nina tried persuading Wolfram to get some rest, too. But the *wysard* hunkered down, awake, between Nina and the overlook, much as the wolf had maintained a nightly vigil when the two had traveled a different road, the young apprentice then trapped in his beast form.

The night seemed to expand as Jacca drifted into sleep nearby, and Nina sat silent under twisted cedars, studying Wolfram's back. She mused on how far the young man had come in seven years. He had completed his apprenticeship under a master, an Elder of the craft who was the only Old One remaining in the whole of Ladrehdin who could have taught a youthful shapeshifter how to employ and control such a formidable power of magic. Wolfram had battled brigands in the Rum Ridges, carried messages to Ruain, and safeguarded a granddaughter of House Verek on visits to her wizardly cousins in their own semi-remote lands.

In many ways, Wolfe had become indispensable to House Verek—a state of affairs that pleased Nina, but not Galen.

That narrow-minded brother of mine, came Nina's unspoken, unwelcome thought. She frowned as she mulled the defect in Galen's character that she would never have guessed existed. *He must be rid of his bigotry.*

For it wouldn't be long before Wolfe married into the family. If Galen didn't accept his new son-in-law, and treat the shapeshifter with the respect due a *wysard* of power and skill, he risked losing his daughter. Nina had few doubts that Jacca would cleave to Wolfram and abandon Galen, if the older man forced such a decision upon her.

As Nina pondered, with her gaze trained on Wolfram's back, she realized she had not yet received his report on the scouting mission that he'd undertaken before sundown. Nina started to rise and join the young man at his sentinel's post. But Wolfram's head was nodding.

The demands of this long day had finally forced sleep upon that strong young fellow. Wolfe sank to the ground and was, in a moment, dead to the world.

No matter. His report could wait for the morrow.

Alone with her thoughts, Nina crept to the overlook's edge and peered down at the ceaselessly boiling stew of angry red and lurid yellow. Though she found its appearance revolting, the restless movement of color and flame held her entranced. Nina watched the firebirds lift and flap their wings of gleaming sparks. One of the figures detached itself from the cauldron's inner wall and flew low over the lava's bubbling surface. Sparks trailed away from it and vanished into the burning lake, without visible detriment to the "bird." The flier reached the opposite side of the firepit and latched onto the rocky sidewall like a searingly white vulture coming to roost.

A cold chill ran through Nina despite the heat that crackled upward from the boiling, molten mass.

She watched for hours, prepared to conjure her magical walls of water against the glowing flock. Regardless of what she had said to Jacca, Nina resolved to drown the firebirds if they showed signs of leaving the cauldron and heading out over mountains and hills. She could not allow them to get loose and lay waste to the countryside, even if it meant unleashing a mountain-shattering explosion of steam, and possibly being caught in that explosion.

Nina wondered whether the creator of the firebirds knew she was watching. She and the young people—and Galen too, before he took the trail to the valley—had attempted to stay hidden behind trees and rocks. The smith had ventured a spell of concealment upon himself and Nina when they'd initially approached the cauldron, but she doubted its effectiveness. Neither of them had mastered that spellcraft when they were young apprentices learning at the knee of their old tutor, Welwyn. Nina suspected that Welwyn had deliberately shortchanged their training in that particular wizardry, to stop his impish pupils disappearing from under his watchful eye.

She thought it likely, therefore, that their adversary—the mysterious "arsonist"—was fully aware of their presence. Whatever kind of fiend it was, it could probably sense their footsteps anywhere on these mountain slopes. Long before she and Galen had completed their pilgrimage on the lost skyway, and subsequently made their way up the South Trail to look down upon the fiery stew in the big rock cauldron, they had been subject to random spark attacks. Every mile of their progress had been noted, Nina thought. Almost certainly, the enemy had eyes on her now, where she lay at the edge of the overlook.

Deliberately, she held up her fist with the middle finger raised—a gesture of defiance that Nina had learned on the ocean world. The people of that place called it "flipping the bird."

Seemingly in response, a figure of sparks lifted its birdlike wings and flapped them in her direction. A gust of hot air ruffled a loose strand of Nina's hair. The urge came upon her to drown the creature. She resisted.

* * *

To the question of whether their adversary was aware of them camped at the top of the trail, an answer came next day in the early afternoon. Nina saw nothing in the dazzling mountain sunlight, but she felt an oncoming rush of heat as if a furnace door had been blown open. In less than a heartbeat, her instinct for self-preservation raised a watery curtain to block the blistering attack.

"Rain, Jacca!" she shouted. "On us, not the cauldron."

The girl's reaction was nearly as quick as Nina's. One flick of Jacca's wrist, and they stood in a downpour, soaked to their skin and impervious to fire. With no more need of her hastily conjured wavelet, Nina let it collapse off the overlook's edge. The thin trickle steamed briefly as it dribbled onto the hot rocks below.

"Our opponent has changed tactics," Nina muttered, backing away with her companions as Jacca's warm, magical rain streamed down their faces. "This is the first spark attack that I have experienced in daytime. Did either of you see anything?"

Jacca shook her head. Wolfram, however, stared out over the cauldron toward its opposite rim. "I believe I did," he said, his hazel eyes bright and alert. "Only a glimpse, but I think a firebird flew at us."

"Drisha's breath!" Nina swore. She squinted into the white glare of the afternoon sky. All around them, everywhere except immediately under Jacca's compact raincloud, the summer sun bathed the heights in shimmering brilliance. Nina frowned. "On such a bright day, those winged fires are indistinguishable from the sun itself. We need darkness lest we be caught unawares again."

She tapped her thumbnail on her teeth, pondering the problem. Then, with a smile, she pushed a strand of wet hair off Jacca's face.

"Blanket the sky. Not with rain," Nina said, "but with clouds so thick and dark, they block the sun and bring night to this mountain. Can you do that?"

Jacca nodded eagerly. "Easy. Just tell me when to stop."

The youthful weather-worker dismissed the drizzle with another quick wrist-flick. Her two hands raised skyward, Jacca commenced piling up thunderheads. Murky clouds filled the sky over the cauldron, turning day to night. As a final flourish—or conceit—the girl conjured a single bolt of lightning. It streaked through the black clouds, and the mountain peaks rang with thunder.

"Oh no!" Jacca cried when a thin sheet of rain showered down upon the far wall of the lava pit, triggered by her show-offish thunderbolt. "I messed up." The girl shot Nina a shamefaced look.

Nina barely noticed her but stood transfixed, staring at scorched rock that glistened with moisture—an impossibility in the lava lake's intense heat. Not only had the brief shower extinguished the only roosting firebird it touched, raindrops continued to trickle wetly down the cauldron's sizzling-hot wall, retaining their liquid form.

"How?" Nina breathed the question to no one in particular as she tried to understand. How could water exist in that inferno without vaporizing—flashing to steam?

"Do that again, Jacca," Nina instructed with no glance at the girl. She could not peel her gaze off the still-moist cauldron wall. "Leave off with the thunder for now, but splash a little light rain on those rocks where the firebirds cling just above the lava." In the gloom imposed by Jacca's conjured clouds, several brilliant figures of flame were visible. Nina motioned for Wolfram to move up alongside herself and the girl. "Watch with me, Wolfe, with your sharp eyes. Look for any wisp of steam."

Jacca summoned another shower, and three more firebirds perished as rainwater dripped upon scalding rocks and trickled into the burning lake. Not a single drop appeared to be lost to steam. Defying all the long years of Nina's experience with water-magic and the inevitable results when water met fire, Jacca's conjured rain remained liquid. The extreme heat within the cauldron had no power to boil it away.

"Extraordinary!" Nina exclaimed. She put her arm around the girl's shoulder and gave her a hug. "What other hidden powers have you yet to reveal, Jacca? I do not understand how your conjured rain can absorb such vast quantities of heat without bursting into billows of steam." Nina shook her head in wonderment. "I think this world has never seen such magic. By the Powers! I had not considered, until now, the full range of possibilities that could open to a fire-mage who is also a weather-worker. Hot rain, indeed!"

Nina stood contemplating her niece. Then she stepped back and waved her arm at the boiling lake.

"Drown it, Jacca. Snuff it out. Kill every spark, and harden that lava to cold, dead rock."

* * *

An hour passed in a tempest of slashing rain, jagged lightning, and booming thunder. From Jacca's blanket of clouds, rain bucketed down upon the flaming lava but left the surrounding rimrock mostly dry. From the overlook where the three adepts now stood in the open, no longer troubling with concealment, Nina and Wolfram watched the girl work her unique spellcraft. The sensual dance of Jacca's magic rendered Wolfe slack-jawed. The young man's gaze burned with desire.

Both he and Nina had sent up a cheer initially, when firebirds vanished all around the cauldron under the first drops of what became a deluge. As the downpour continued, however, Nina took worried note of the lava's undiminished glow. The molten rock remained red-hot. It showed no signs of cooling or darkening under the flood that Jacca loosed upon it. If anything, the lava seemed to bubble with heightened vigor, its garish colors bright in the darkness of Jacca's rainstorm, the restless flicker from the cauldron reflecting off the clouds.

"Stop!" Nina finally shouted. She lunged to catch the girl's arm and halt her in the middle of a dance step. "Leave off for now, Jacca. I'm not sure this is succeeding as we had hoped."

The girl sagged with weariness when she ceased her spellwork, and Nina felt a pang of guilt. She should not have allowed the young adept to expend her powers with such intensity over so long a time. Learning to be thrifty with one's magical gifts was a basic principle in the education of any novice *wysard*.

"Is it just me," Nina muttered as she rubbed Jacca's tired shoulders, "or does it seem like the lake has risen?" She gestured with a nod of her head at the gap in the basin's rim, the notch where it opened outward to the valley side of the mountain. "I've been watching that low place, and I swear the lava has crept up nearer. It's closer to spilling out."

Wolfram tore his gaze from the lightly perspiring Jacca and the damp ringlets of copper hair that framed the girl's delicate face. He turned to scan the rim and the lava that bubbled below it.

"You are correct, my lady," Wolfe said after a moment's study. "When I made the circuit last night, I got as close to that gap as I could without burning my feet. Nearly at the notch, there's a bulge below, in the pit's inner wall—like the sheer face of the wall has been bumped out by something underneath. You can barely see it from here, but I got a good look, much closer." A frown creased Wolfram's brow. "It's like the rock has grown a tumor in that spot. Anyway, I saw lava splashing halfway up to the lump last night. Now it's splashing higher. The level is unquestionably above what it was yesterday."

"Drisha's busted knuckles!" Nina swore. "Did the rain do that?" Was the lava floating high on all the rainwater that she had encouraged Jacca to dump into the cauldron?

Nina bit her lip as she studied the molten lake. There was no sheen of water upon its roiling surface. So where *had* the inundation gone? The deluge had not escaped as steam.

No steam, no water visible as either liquid or vapor ... Nina could only conclude—in defiance of all reason and Nature—that Jacca's rainwater flood had settled to the bottom of the cauldron and now existed as impossibly hot water beneath a cap of flaming lava.

Far from being rendered cold and impotent, the lake was now gorged, swollen, its peril creeping nearer ... closer to bursting its bounds.

It seemed to have gained not only depth, but also strength from Jacca's hot rain. As Nina scowled at the bubbling lake, the heat that rose from the lava prickled her skin, noticeably more intense than before the cloudburst. Had the molten mass absorbed magical heat from Jacca's spellwork?

"Let the clouds go," Nina murmured as she massaged the girl's strained muscles. "Don't wear yourself out, shading the lake. Sunset's not far off. Once it gets dark tonight, we can see firebirds if they revive."

"Do you think they'll come back?" Jacca asked, surprised. "I'm sure I doused them all."

"I know you did. You were magnificent. But we must expect any number of unpleasant surprises to bubble up from that hellhole." Nina gestured at the pit. "You've done well today, Jacca. I've never seen a more beautiful or more powerful storm of magic. What a Gift you have! Get something to eat," she added, "then sleep. You've earned your rest. I'll watch."

* * *

The night was far advanced, more than halfway to dawn, and Nina the only one still awake when the crunch of boots on pebbly grit alerted her to a hiker ascending toward the overlook. She shot to her feet, the spell of stone at her fingertips, ready to petrify the newcomer.

"Steady, Nina," came Galen's voice from out of the darkness. "It's me."

"Where's your horse?" she exclaimed as the goldsmith limped toward her. "What happened?"

With a tired sigh, Galen slumped to the ground under a twisted pine.

"The useless creature threw me. One crack of thunder from that spectacular rainstorm, and I was down with a twisted ankle. I've walked miles on it." As he spoke, Galen struggled to unlace his boot and yank it off. Nina pushed him back against the tree and took over, gently tugging the leather over his swollen foot and ankle. "I expect my horse didn't stop running before it reached the river," Galen grumped, "unless the fool animal broke its damned leg. That trail's too steep for running."

"I'm sorry," Nina murmured. "As you probably guessed, the spectacular storm was your daughter's doing. But I put her up to it."

As Nina bandaged Galen's wrenched ankle, wrapping it tight to counter the swelling, she caught him up on all that had happened at the lava pit in his absence. Galen frowned at Nina's description of fire-birds, and he muttered a coarse oath when told of the daylight attack by sparks that hid in the bright sun. He listened speechless when Nina talked of magical rain that fell upon scorched rock and neither dried on contact nor flashed to steam, but endured as liquid that filtered down through boiling hot lava. She gave him her supposition, supported by the bloated state of the lake, that the rainwater Jacca had conjured had pooled in the bottom of the cauldron. The lava now floated upon it, riding high. Incredible though it seemed, Jacca's hot rain could absorb the heat of hellfire and remain liquid.

"By what strange alchemy has your daughter's fire-magic melded with her rainmaking?" Nina pondered aloud without expecting an answer. "I have never heard of fire and water joining together as they seem to have done in Jacca. The two elements are too different, diametrically opposed, incapable of coexisting without the one extinguishing the other."

Galen rubbed his neck, his characteristic response to tension. After a moment he pushed up to his feet and hobbled to the edge of the overlook to stare into the pit. Then he turned to study the notch in the rim. The fiery glow of the lava bathed the flanks of the gap in restless, flickering light.

"You put Jacca up to it?" he finally muttered. "That rainstorm?"

Nina nodded, wondering what Galen was thinking but not saying. "You would have been proud to watch her work that magic. Her spellcraft is without equal. The results, however, are as you see." Nina gestured at the swollen, vigorously boiling lake. "I miscalculated."

Galen sank to the ground and gripped his injured ankle. He tried to rub it through the binding, but winced at the pain.

"I wish you were better at conjuring ice," he grumbled. "I could use some."

"Another reason we need Dalton here," Nina said. "He could pack your ankle in snow. But I've got something that will help."

She dug through the medicine kit that Wolfram had produced from their stock of supplies. The young man had brought it to her earlier when she'd wished for a pain-reliever to ease the ache in Jacca's overtaxed muscles. Nina pulled out the same packet of dried willow bark, and poured water in a tin mug for Galen to heat with a snap of his fingers. While the tea brewed, she asked the fire-mage about his errand down a mineshaft on the other side of the valley. Had he reached Legary?

He had.

"Our baby brother was waiting to hear from me," Galen related. "The bedrock under his house has been trembling for days. He knew something was stirring out this way. He had his bag packed and his chariot ready to roll."

"Chariot?"

Galen managed a grin despite his pain. "I think it's a wagon with big stone wheels. Legary ensorcelled the wheels to turn on their own, no horses needed. From what he said, his enchanted chariot will get him to the port at Seawood in a matter of hours, not days."

"In good time to sail with Dalton," Nina enthused. "It lightens my heart, brother, to know they're on their way."

"But with neither of them having more than an inkling of what awaits them here." Galen gestured at the hellfire pit. "Legary did not seem to need or want details. All he heard was that you had commanded him to be here, and that was enough to have him out the door and barreling away."

Nina breathed a soft, contented sigh. She closed her eyes and sent silent thanks to the Elementals who had restored Legary's gift of magic. At her last meeting with her youngest brother, he had mourned the loss of his powers. Legary was an artist in stone and a painstaking builder, but pride had led him into ostentation and excess. His wizardry had been stripped from him as punishment for his arrogance. For years, Legary had been filled with remorse, and now Nina had confirmation that the Powers had heard and shown mercy.

It hadn't hurt, she thought, that she'd sent up a plea on the stonemason's behalf on her previous journey through the south country. Every night of her life since her "grand tour," Nina had offered obeisance to the Elementals, unfailing in her gratitude for the Gifts they had bestowed upon herself and all the children of House Verek—gifts she was counting on to freeze the fires of *farsinchia* and shut the gates of hell.

Nina turned back to Galen, and indulged her ever-present impulse to tease him. "Our baby brother comes when I call, no questions asked, because he has learned to show me the proper respect." She assumed a lofty bearing, her nose in the air as she handed the goldsmith a steaming cup of willow tea. "You, sir," she decreed in stilted tones, "must take a lesson from Legary and never again argue with your big sister, for I *am* the firstborn. I always know best."

Galen snorted. "You *think* you know best. But now and again, I see your mistakes." He indicated the swollen lake of lava, and Nina's lighthearted moment evaporated. "I've decided you're right, though, about

Dalton and Legary," he grudgingly admitted. "We need what they can bring to this fight. It's bigger than you and me."

"Even with Jacca and Wolfram to help." Nina glanced at the sleeping pair. The young people lay fully dressed except for their boots, both of them curled on their sides and half screened by low-branching cedars, almost but not quite within reach of each other.

Galen followed Nina's glance, and frowned. At the sight of his scowl, she heaved a mental sigh.

"Have you been awake all night, sister?" Galen demanded with a sharpness that suggested he would have found her derelict in her auntly duties, had Nina failed to properly chaperone the pair through the dark hours.

But when she wearily nodded, Galen banished her to her own blankets. "Sleep. I'll take the watch. Ankle's hurting too much for me to doze off. Before you turn in," he added, "give me the brandywine. I saw the bottle in your kit."

"It's not for drinking," Nina protested, but she pulled out the brandy and handed it over. "It's medicinal."

"This *is* medicinal." Galen pointed at his bound ankle. "I'm an injured man. You can't deny me a tonic, oh great wayfarer who has seen the stars of a distant world and thinks she knows everything."

* * *

An air-shattering thunderbolt and a brilliant flash jolted Nina awake at the next day's dawn. She sprang up and rushed from the cedar grove alongside the young people, all of them drawn to the sound of battle.

It was Jacca who reached Galen first, out on the overlook where he stood cursing his ankle, his hangover, and the firebirds that swirled high above the cauldron, glittering in dense swarms. Sparks exploded as Galen blasted the figures out of the air. Glowing embers fell like bright rain into the lava below.

Nina skidded to a halt, well clear of the pit, where she could keep watch over father and daughter and backstop their fiery magic as required. Alone, Galen might have been overwhelmed by the furious rush of winged sparks. But Jacca matched her father's wizardry. The young adept threw lightning bolts as hot as Galen's, and with all of his speed and accuracy.

In the east behind Nina, sunrise touched the Ore Hills with clear, strong light, but Jacca gave the firebirds no chance to hide in the glare of the new day. The girl paused her flamethrowing long enough to summon clouds. The heavy overcast darkened the sky without rain or storm, but imposed a gloom that revealed every flickering spark of the figures that flew endlessly from the pit.

With no visible sun by which to judge the time, the hours passed unnoted. Morning gave way to midday, and the onslaught did not slacken. Jacca and her father stood shoulder to shoulder, slinging thunderbolts. Firebirds died in showers of sparks, but only to be reborn in the heat of the mountain crucible. Sweat dripped down both their faces, but the two fire-mages gave no ground as they sheared the wings from firebirds and knocked the figures out of the sky before the oncoming sparks could burn them.

Nina lent support with small waves of water, every ripple tightly controlled and precisely thrown, but only where she could reach the sparks when they flew low, down close to the lava, not up near the overlook where the defenders made their stand. She would not risk catching Galen and Jacca in a scalding cloud of steam. Everywhere that Nina's conjured wavelets overtook firebirds, white vapor billowed until masses of steam filled the cauldron, obscuring the field of battle.

"Stop with the water!" Galen shouted. "I can't see."

Before she could warn him, Galen had cast a lightning bolt down through the vapors, in an attempt to burn away the haze. The fiery streak hit molten rock and exploded. Boulder-sized gobbets of lava splattered high into the cloudy sky.

"Umbrella, Galen!" Nina screamed.

He reacted with magian reflex before Nina got his name out. A canopy of white flame unfurled above their heads only seconds before blobs of red-hot lava rained down upon them. Every gobbet that hit the umbrella burned instantly to ash.

Down below, however, the lava lake roiled furiously, as if it had absorbed heat and potency from Galen's thunderbolt. From underneath his conjured canopy, the fire-mage found himself more hard-pressed than ever, forced to redouble his efforts to knock swirling sparks out of the air. Firebirds flocked from the cauldron in such numbers, their brightness lit the sky and reflected off the low clouds of Jacca's conjuration.

"My mistake!" Galen shouted over his shoulder, hardly able to catch his breath as he fended off a stream of attackers. "Not what I expected."

"It feeds on heat," Nina shouted back. "Hit it with fire, and it only gets stronger."

She was busy off to the side, a few steps from the overlook, raising walls of water to extinguish the firebirds that were now starting to get past Galen and Jacca. Winged figures soared out of the cauldron and attempted to glide downslope on the valley side of the mountain. Nina drowned each fugitive firebird before it could escape, and watched her conjured waves soak harmlessly into the mountainside's dry soil. No troublesome steam rose from the bare outer slopes that rimmed the lava-filled basin.

"Drisha take the hindmost!" Nina swore. "This is intolerable." She spared a quick glance for the two defenders on the front lines ... she saw Jacca and Galen bathed in sweat ... saw the wobble in their stances ... and glimpsed the umbrella crumple above their heads. Galen could not sustain the canopy of protective white flames while also battling a ceaseless onslaught of firebirds. Tottering on his wrenched ankle, he was about to collapse from physical and magian exhaustion.

Seeing no other recourse, Nina gambled with chance. "Take cover!" she yelled. Her warning encompassed Wolfram as well as the two fire-mages. The young man stood nearby holding the fire-resistant tarpaulins of felted wool that Warthog had provided early on, down in the valley. Nina pointed at the tarps. "Get under those, *now*. I'm making lots of scalding steam. Protect your eyes."

So saying, Nina summoned water. With a violent, two-handed beckoning, she raised a tidal wave. Water slammed into the soaring firebirds and killed every spark. A cold flood cascaded down into the cauldron, where it hit hot lava.

Steam exploded. The mountain shook. Flaming lumps of molten rock flew high.

Nina hit the ground, jolted off her feet. She curled up in a ball, her arms shielding her head and neck. With her eyes clenched shut, she awaited the burn of skin-peeling steam, wondering if it might not be a mercy to die first under a skull-crushing weight of falling lava.

Neither fate befell her. Gradually the mountain ceased to tremble. Half fearing to breathe, Nina listened as blobs of hot lava smacked the ground, the thumps sounding at a little distance. Closer, she heard a shower of rain, and she smelled rain's fresh scent through the acrid stink of burning rock.

Nina opened her eyes and uncurled her body. She blinked up at a restored canopy of white fire—a newly conjured umbrella that had protected her from falling gobbets of sizzling-hot lava. Nearby, spanning the overlook but not extending beyond its edge, rain fell in a thin sheet. No blistering steam from the explosion in the cauldron made it past that curtain. The rain blocked the vapor and washed it from the air.

"Well done, family! All of you," Nina exclaimed. She scrambled to her feet and went to help Galen disentangle from one of the wool tarps. The heavy fabric had been tossed Galen's way haphazardly. Wolfram had taken more care in spreading the second tarpaulin over Jacca and himself. Only gradually did those two come out now from under their shared shelter, with the sweaty girl giggling, and Wolfram trying hard not to grin.

"More warning next time, if you please!" Galen growled as Nina tried to get the tarp off him while using it to block his view of the flirting pair. "I barely kept us all from getting buried alive." He glanced up, looking for airborne lava. But no more blobs rained down. The splatter had ended. Galen closed his magical umbrella.

"I hope there won't be a next time," Nina muttered as she gathered the tarp and stepped across to Wolfram. She pushed the bundle into the young man's chest so hard that Wolfe had to back up. As a space opened between him and Jacca, Nina slipped between the two and put her arm around the girl's waist.

"No master *wysard* could have done better," she murmured, hugging Jacca close. "Your rain curtain saved my skin. I thought I was cooked." Above the cauldron, the air had cleared, no longer choked with steam from the elemental collision of floodwater and fire. "Cease your summoning now, and let's see if anything has changed down there."

With a one-handed wave, Jacca swept aside the sheet of magical rain. Nina walked with the girl to the overlook's edge, and together they peered into the pit. No firebirds perched on the charred walls or winged upward on scorched air. Down in the cauldron, however, lava churned and crackled. Tongues of fire licked the molten surface. The seething reds and yellows gave an impression of barely repressed rage.

Nina's shoulders slumped, and she fought a wave of hopelessness. All the water-magic that was hers to invoke, she had thrown into that flood. But it had not been enough. The lake of fire yet burned. She had won them nothing except a little time, a brief respite.

Not even that, perhaps. Nina pried her gaze from the boiling lava and stared across at the rim-wall notch. The gap was wider now, deeper and more pronounced.

"Again I have failed," she muttered when Galen hobbled on his sprained ankle to stand with her and Jacca. "My magic does not quench this fiends'-fire, and I dare not risk the steam it spawns. That blast nearly blew the side out of the mountain."

Galen scratched his ear and heaved a weary sigh. "It does seem, sister, that the forces you wield are not best suited to our present needs." He laid a hand on her shoulder, and then on Jacca's. "But we must find a way to end this. My daughter and I will do our best for as long as we are able, but we cannot fight this battle indefinitely." He glanced into the cauldron. The pit remained empty except for the relentless bubbling of molten rock. "At least you drowned the firebirds."

"For now," Nina muttered. "I expect they'll be back." She scanned the cauldron's black walls, seeking any glimmer that would betray a re-emergence of the figures. The day was far advanced, the late-afternoon sun ablaze in the sky above. But streamers remained of the heavy dark clouds that Jacca had earlier conjured, enough to shadow the cauldron's interior and reassure Nina, for the moment, that all remained dark and motionless upon its walls.

She waved Galen and Jacca away from the edge. "Go sleep, both of you," Nina ordered them. "You're done in and ready to drop. I'll take the watch."

"No, my lady."

Wolfram spoke clear-voiced and decisive as he stepped up from where he'd been standing, listening, off to the side. "You must rest," he said. "Though you may be denied the working of your greatest magic, your water wizardry remains unrivaled, and its value is fathomless in this present circumstance. All here need you to be strong ... especially your honored niece and myself." Wolfe looked at Jacca, who smiled at his glance and blushed prettily as she pushed perspiration-soaked strands of chestnut hair off her face. The young man's gaze lingered upon the girl's. Then he looked back at Nina, pointedly ignoring Galen. "I will be the watchman. You know from our past journey together, my lady, that I see and hear what others cannot."

Nina studied him, then nodded. "We are in your debt, Master Shapeshifter," she said with a formal nod of respect, extending to Wolfram the courtesy owed to a fellow *wysard*—the courtesy noticeably lacking in Galen's behavior toward him. As Nina took the hand that Wolfram offered to help her down from the overlook, she stepped close and gave her young friend a hug.

"Thank you," she whispered. "I'm not sure how long any of us can keep this up. The Powers may have no limits, but *wysards* do." Nina looked over Wolfram's shoulder in the direction of the mountain trail they had climbed to this uncanny battlefield. "Keep an eye open for my brothers. I believe those two magicians may be our only chance of winning this fight."

Chapter Sixteen

T hey did keep it up. Through the hot days and the bleary nights, they fought on. In a haze of mounting exhaustion, each found ways to use their strengths while avoiding previous errors.

Jacca summoned downpours to protect them all, even the horses, against the firebirds' blistering attacks. Mindful, however, that her hot rain would deepen and swell the lake of lava, the girl kept her cloud-bursts far enough from the cauldron's lip that no shower trickled down into the pit.

Galen was similarly cautious with the lightning bolts that he flung into swarms of firebirds, only blasting the figures when they rose high in the air. He did not again allow the molten mass, blazing down below, to gain strength by absorbing heat from his own considerable powers of fire.

For her part, Nina held the ground behind the two frontline fighters and raised water-walls to drown any sparks that escaped the net woven by Galen and his cloud-conjuring, flame-throwing daughter. During lulls, when firebirds ceased to fly and the lava subsided to a low simmer, Nina and Wolfram took turns watching while the others rested. Wolfe's shapeshifting instincts—his understanding of how one thing could become another—gave him an insight that Nina had missed: He perceived that the figures of fire arose directly from the intense, shimmering heat that burned the very air, deep in the cauldron. Hatched from that heat, the firebirds were scorched air made tangible.

It followed, then, that lowering the heat would discourage fire from taking wing. From time to time, Nina ventured to slip a slow-rolling wave down the cauldron's inner surface, aiming to cool the roasted rocks and slow the birth of firebirds. Inevitably, her small incursions produced steam, but only in puffs, not billows. The cauldron hissed and lava seethed, but there came no mountain-shaking explosion to strike at the foundations of the damaged rim-wall. Evanescent though they were, Nina's gentle splashes provided enough of a quick, cold soak to hinder the hatching of new firebirds. She looked with satisfaction upon this ephemeral but advantageous use of her native element, glad for a way to lighten the burden on Galen and Jacca, and pleased with Wolfram for identifying a chink in their adversary's armor.

That young man had made himself indispensable in ways that went beyond his role as their principal watchman. Wolfram prepared their daily meals, and went regularly to check on the horses. The three animals had broken their tethers and fled down the ravine when Galen and Nina had earlier succumbed to wizardly foolhardiness that resulted in flaming gobs of lava arcing through the sky. Too loyal to run far, the horses had sensibly avoided the danger, and had then settled farther down the ravine. Wolfram found them grazing peacefully in a gully the other side of the South Trail.

He gathered what the animals had carried of gear and supplies, lugged it up to their makeshift camp at the top of the trail, and dug in for the duration. Wolfe threw together surprisingly tasty meals from the meager foodstuffs in their packs, and even managed to bring in fresh meat. He seemed embarrassed to have caught only rabbits, but his companions devoured the meat and picked the bones clean.

A week into their siege, all were showing the strain of nearly constant battle against swirling sparks and flocks of firebirds. Nina could only slow, not stop, the hatching of new threats. With a series of well-placed splashes down the cauldron's inner walls, delivered in quick succession but kept small to avoid the ground-quaking release of steam, she bought the fighters an evening's reprieve. Nina ordered them all to rest, including Wolfram, who seemed not to have slept for days.

While those three collapsed in a moon-shadowed cedar grove, Nina sat on the overlook and gazed into the pit. As always, the steady bubbling of molten rock held her half entranced. She had learned to judge its mood by the rhythm of its motions and the sounds it made. A fast, roiling boil would produce swarms of firebirds. But a slow simmer such as the lava now exhibited meant fewer hatchings.

Wrapped up in the moment of relative quiet, Nina contemplated the bizarre situation that had embroiled herself and her loved ones. The lake of lava seemed alive, a thing capable of calculated cunning. Did it mean to keep them here until all were too exhausted to hold it in check? Was it hoping that fatigue would lead to careless steps too close to the cauldron's rim? Perhaps the lake aspired to claim their bodies. If any among them slipped and fell in, death would be quick but torturous: skin burnt to ash ... flesh seared from bone.

As Nina shot a glance at her sleeping companions, she toyed with the idea of stepping away entirely, all four of them together. She could not shake the feeling that they'd been lured to this place. If their adversary wanted them here, making this stand on the edge of the lava lake where it could feed on their strength and largely neutralize their powers, then perhaps they should back away with all haste.

But if they withdrew, firebirds in unchecked numbers could ravage the countryside. What had begun as the defense of a thinly populated valley, had now become a battle to preserve vast tracts of land from being laid waste by an unknown enemy. If they did not stop its fires here in this rock-rimmed basin high in the mountains, their adversary might burn every village, farmstead, and settlement from the Ore Hills to the Plain of Imlen. Such a wide swath of ruin would not spare the lands of Nina's magical relatives in the home those *wysards* had made between the Ore Hills and Ruain.

In her mind's eye, Nina could picture the firestorm advancing northward up the river valley, flames leaping from haystack to rooftop, carried onward by ravaging flights of firebirds. Cloudbursts both natural and magian might drown the first swarms of uncanny sparks. But as long as this cauldron kept hatching out new ones, firebirds would continue the assault, unless or until their adversary got its fill of destruction and sank back down to whatever demonic realm had spawned it.

Nina's roving thoughts touched on Galen's suspicion that her old friend Grog, the shapeshifter from the down-below, had something to do with this gout of fire and lava erupting from the bowels of the world. "Impossible," she muttered to herself. "Wherever Grog is right now, I hope he stays far away from this hellhole. There's danger here even for a man of stone."

Nina stared into the glowing lava, and flinched as she imagined her blocky-shouldered friend perishing in that molten mass. For an instant she seemed to see Grog's head sticking up out of the lava. His head was round and bald, and sat on his neck like a boulder. The giant's enormous blue eyes showed no expression as his head melted in the heat of the cauldron, the man of stone swallowed up and ebbing out of existence in the molten rock.

But no: the blue she had glimpsed was only the lava itself, glowing eerily in the night as the sulphur inside it burst into flames of purple and azure. Nina blinked away the ghastly vision. She'd been sitting here too long, gazing into the pit, mesmerized. The murmur of the lava's ceaseless bubbling had become her adversary's voice. Ancient and angry, it muttered in her ear, filling her mind with despairing thoughts as hypnotic patterns and colors played across the lake's surface.

To break its hold on her, Nina summoned water and flung a wave upon the lava. She barely managed to curb her instinct to dump another flood down the cauldron's throat. Mindful, however, of the weakened gap in the rim-wall, she held back, stymied by the restraints upon her powers in this battle of water against fire—a battle her element was losing as she had never known it to lose before. The enemy had her at a disadvantage, having rendered Nina's great magian Gift too dangerous to fully unleash.

The wave she'd risked, although modest, released copious amounts of steam. Nina scrambled up from her seat on the overlook and spun away. As she turned, she covered her face with her hands and took long steps away from the edge, avoiding the hot steam that hissed from the cauldron.

Her quick whirl brought her long raven braid swinging around, over her shoulder. Nina glimpsed the ribbon with which she customarily tied her hair. It was only a strip of fabric, bedraggled with the steam, rain, and sweat that had soaked her these past many days. But to Nina, the scrap of cloth was a precious memento of Grog. Her friend had once worn the fabric. Though most of the material had been lost at the time of their separation, each had retained a tatter as a symbol of their bond.

As Nina fingered the limp ribbon, she thought of how she'd swished it in the water when her leap across the void landed her in the hot-spring pool on Galen's hillside property. She winced, wishing with all her heart that she had not sent that hello, had not attempted to inform Grog of her return. Haunted by the specter of his destruction in the lava pit, she wanted her friend nowhere near this place.

The steam-fog from Nina's latest act of frustrated defiance was still thick, but beginning to clear. She fanned at the vapor, preparing to return to her watch-post on the overlook. But a familiar male voice brought her head snapping around.

"This miasma reminds me of those billowing storms, those tempests you inflicted upon my flagship, dear sister, when you sailed with me to Easthaven," the voice complained with a low chuckle. "What mischief have you now summoned to Galen's desert? And how may I serve the firstborn daughter of House Verek? I will always come at your call, Lady Karenina, but I *would* like to know what's making that stink."

Chapter Seventeen

D alton!"

Nina couldn't stop the tears rising in her eyes. In two steps she was in her brother's arms, holding him tight and almost shaking from the sudden release of her tension.

"Thank the Powers you're here!" she cried. "But don't be asking what mischief *I've* summoned. I'm only trying to keep Galen's desert from burning even more crispy than it already is." She released Dalton from her bearhug but continued to grip his arms as she looked past him, searching for their youngest brother. "Is Legary with you?"

"I am," the stonemason answered. Legary's dark hair was the first thing Nina saw of him as he approached through the steamy haze. "I've long wanted to visit these hills and tour the mines, but that blasted desert stood in the way. When Dalton offered me a berth on his ship, I jumped at the chance to come by sea." Legary tipped a nod at Nina. "Good to see you again, sister. I didn't expect a reunion this soon."

"Nor did I." Nina gave Legary a one-armed hug while keeping firm grip on Dalton with her other hand. They were standing too near the overlook's edge for her comfort, particularly with neither newcomer aware of the danger below. Magian steam still shrouded the view in a moonlit sea of white. "We're on the brink of *farsinchia*," she warned, holding the men back. "Conjure a breeze, Dalton, and clear the air so you can see hell a-burning. You've smelled it already."

The weather-mage eyed Nina quizzically, but he did as she asked. A quick wave of Dalton's free hand raised a light wind. The remnants of Nina's steam-cloud wafted away on the breeze. Both men inhaled sharply as the mountain basin came into view, the lake of lava bubbling at the bottom of the rocky bowl, a stinking stew in a devil's kettle.

Dalton's conjured breeze acted upon the lake like a bellows in a blacksmith's forge. The lava boiled furiously. High near the rim, three firebirds hatched in the intensified heat, a trio so luminous they outshone the moon and every star that glittered in the clear night sky.

"Snow!" Nina entreated with a sharp tug on Dalton's arm. "Smother them before they burn us."

His eyebrows shot up, but he gave her a quick nod of comprehension. As Nina loosed her restraining grip, Dalton raised both hands and conjured a miniature blizzard. Snow—heavy and wet—flew from the fingertips of one hand. With a flick of his other wrist, the weather-mage called forth a hard puff of wind and slammed the snow into the attacking firebirds. Every spark vanished in a flurry of thin, ephemeral steam.

"That was brilliant!" came a girlish squeal from behind Nina. "How did you do that? Teach me!"

Nina whirled, the two men turning with her, to discover Jacca staring wide-eyed, enraptured to have viewed a species of magic the girl longed to learn. Nina made quick introductions, mindful that Jacca and her uncles knew each other by name and reputation but had never before met face-to-face. Then she redirected the attention of all to the bubbling cauldron, wary of fresh attacks by new-hatched firebirds.

The lava had again subsided, however, to a low, simmering boil, quelled by the snow. Was their enemy intimidated by the arrival on-scene of a master weather-mage? If so, Nina could give it even more to worry about.

"Look there," she said, and pulled Legary around to see where she pointed, at the gap in the rimrock where the crevice opened to the outer slope. "I'll be asking Dalton to freeze the flames of hell," she said with a wry smile at the expression that came over Dalton's face when he glanced up, startled, from his study of the bubbling lake. "But first,

Legary, we need you to shore up that long crack in the mountainside. It's threatening to give way. If this lake spills out, it'll flow down into the valley and burn everything in its path."

The stonemason peered across at the notch, straining to see by moonlight and the lava's lurid glow. He shook his head.

"Can't really see the problem from here. I must get closer. But if I'm understanding you, there's a weak seam in the rock, and you want it mended before Dalton freezes that mess." Legary gestured at the roiling lava. "Rocks heave and stone shatters in frosty weather. You want me to make sure that crack doesn't split wide open when Dalton brings the frost. Right?"

Nina nodded vigorously. "That's the idea. But you mustn't get too close." She pointed at the steep rim-wall where it narrowed precipitously toward the top. "Wolfram has been out on the rim, and he says it's treacherous."

"All but impassable," the shapeshifter put in.

Wolfe had quietly joined the group, drawn from sleep by the sound of strangers' voices in the night. He stood behind Jacca with his alert and serious gaze fixed upon the two newly arrived *wysards*.

At a wave from Nina, the young man stepped forward to greet his elders with formal bows as she made the introductions.

"I can guide you," Wolfe said with a nod at Legary. "I have scouted a route nearly to that crack. Been meaning to go back and take another look at the pit-wall where it drops sheer from the rim, straight down to the lava." Wolfram cocked his head, looking perplexed. "That wall bears a strange lump." Briefly, he described what he had seen of a protuberance, a tumor-like swelling in the stone. "It does not look natural. I've been trying to keep an eye on it from here. Just never found time, these last days, for another run out that way."

"No, indeed," Nina said with a grateful glance at her young friend. "We've all been hard put to knock down firebirds before they incinerate us." Nina gave her brothers a summary of recent events, explaining how her powers and Jacca's had been largely nullified. Between Nina's floods and Jacca's rainstorms, they might have succeeded by now in drowning the lava, burying it cold and dead under their combined water-magic, if not for the overriding need to protect the valley from a river of molten rock spilling down an unstable mountainside.

"I believe that's my hint to get going," Legary said with a jaunty air as Nina finished her account. The stonemason clapped Wolfram on the shoulder. "Lead on, friend. Show me the way. I'll take it from there."

"Not so fast," came Galen's indignant growl from the direction of the cedars where he'd been napping in the night. The fire-mage rubbed sleep from his eyes as he limped up to the others, favoring his sprained ankle. "Did no one think to inform me that my brothers have come at last to the land I call home? I've been trying to get them here for years. My invitations lack the power of our sister's summons, obviously. One word from her, and you fly to this place."

Nina started to stammer something out, partly to apologize for neglecting Galen in the excitement of their brothers' arrival. But mostly she gestured at the cauldron, indicating its quiescent state and their need to act before it started spitting sparks at them again.

"I'm as ready as you, sister, to put the new arrivals to work," Galen said. He gave her the lopsided smile that meant he was mostly joking, but serious underneath. "I've had my fill of blasting thunderbolts at firebirds. But give me a moment, pray, to greet these long-lost brothers of mine."

A round of hugs and backslapping followed, the three men reveling in their reunion. Though as Galen pointed out, this was his first face-to-face meeting with his youngest brother.

"Chief Steward Dalton, I know from our years together in Ruain," Galen said as he clapped Legary on the shoulder. "But you, Master Mason, would be a stranger to me if not for our talks down the mineshaft."

"Talks that I have welcomed," Legary replied. "I look forward to visiting that mine and learning its secrets. But first ..." He jerked a thumb over his shoulder, indicating the notch in the rim-wall.

Galen nodded. "Go plug that damned crack. Then all of us together will snuff out this hellhole."

He limped to the edge of the overlook and hawked a wad of spit down at the lava. The scorched air in the cauldron took the spittle without so much as a puff of steam.

* * *

Galen was left on his own to watch for threats arising from the depths of the pit. All the others had their eyes on Wolfram and Legary as those two made their careful way along the cauldron's outer rim.

"Look where you step," Wolfe warned the mason. "It's narrow and steep, and there's a lot of loose rock along the edge. If you slip, it's a long way down."

"With a fiery plunge on this side ...," Legary muttered as he peered down at the glowing lava.

"... and nothing to break your fall on the front slope," Nina added from where she'd followed the two *wysards* a short way out onto the rim. "The valley side of this mountain has already been weakened by a rockslide," she cautioned, recalling the ground-shaking event that had sheared away the old Sky Trail several nights ago. "Don't heave any boulders out that way, or you might start another slide."

"Point taken," Legary called over his shoulder, and Nina heard the tension in his voice. "Now back away, please, all of you. I've got this."

She nodded, and turned wordlessly to retrace her steps through the coarse, pebbly shingle that topped the rim-wall. On her way back to the overlook, Nina squeezed past Jacca, who had also trailed the men outward for a short way. The girl had planted herself in a spot that afforded a good view of Wolfe and Legary's slow progress toward the notch in the rim. The shapeshifter in the lead had now taken wolf form: the animal's clawed feet got better purchase on the loose rocks. Nina caught her breath as she watched Legary skid and stumble his way along the knife-edged rim.

Time seemed to hang suspended when she'd rejoined Galen at the overlook, and Dalton stepped up beside her. She listened, half attentive, while the captain told of sailing the southern coast on waters unknown to him. He grew animated as he described the howling winds that he had summoned to fill his sails and send his ship flying over the waves.

"My fastest trip ever, on any sea I've ever crossed," Dalton boasted. "Given your reputation, sister, for making mischief when you're with Galen, I expected to find you amidst turmoil and trouble. But I must confess, this is more than I anticipated." He clicked his tongue as he smoothed his white-blond hair. "Why has a water-sylph climbed a dry desert mountain to get herself charbroiled at hell's front gate?"

Absently, Nina started to explain about the false accusations that had swirled around Jacca's fire-magic. She was drawing out her amulet of ocean waves, intending to show Dalton how Galen had managed to reach her in her island world. But Nina broke off in the middle of a word when a tremendous crash sounded from the direction of the notch.

"Look!" she yelled, and pointed. "I can't see Legary, but something big just dropped into that gap."

They had no time to admire or celebrate the stonecrafter's wizardry, for the mountain shook, and the cauldron exploded. Lava splattered high in the air.

Galen, wobbly on his swollen ankle, threw up his hands and conjured a canopy of fire: the white-hot fire he had invoked before. Bright masses of flaming lava streaked through the night sky and showered down like meteors. Those that struck the canopy burned to ash. But south of the overlook where Nina hunkered with Galen and Dalton, red fire erupted in the pine trees.

She summoned water and drenched the groves to the crest of the trail and beyond, out as far as her conjured waves could reach.

With a feeling of horror then, Nina whirled the other way to look for Jacca. Had the girl been caught in the rain of molten rock?

No. Jacca's reflexes were as quick as her father's. The girl was indeed standing in a downpour, but not a rain of fire. The young weatherworker had summoned a cloudburst. From a sky gone suddenly overcast, rain fell in sheets, but only at Jacca's location and thence past her, out along the rim-wall where Wolfe and Legary had made their way into what had been a moonlit night.

The moon was behind the clouds now, and the only light came from the furiously boiling lava that splashed high up the walls of the pit, and from the fiery remnants of ejected rock that continued to blaze through the sky.

"Shoot those down, Galen!" Nina grabbed the fire-mage's arm, steadying his wobble as she pointed at airborne blobs that were arcing toward Jacca. The lumps of lava would cool as they pelted the girl's streaming downpour, but that would not end the danger. Cold lava, rock-hard, could kill just as surely.

Before Galen could loose a thunderbolt, however, his daughter unleashed her own fire-magic. Jacca thrust out her hand, her fingers stiff, and sighted down her arm as she tracked the incoming blobs. Flames spouted from her fingertips, and the blackened lumps went up in smoke—smoke that was lost in the spray of the rainstorm the girl had summoned. The warm drops of her conjuration continued to fall, the magic seemingly effortless and unattended. The rain quenched any fire that tried to catch in the sparse vegetation that grew, wind-beaten, amongst the rocks and pinnacles of the rim-wall.

"Impressive," Dalton muttered from where he still stood at Nina's side. The captain had his hands on his hips, alert to all that was happening. But apart from the small blizzard he'd summoned against three firebirds, Dalton had yet to join the battle. His siblings and his niece were doing fine without him, or so it appeared.

The weather-mage's time, however, was fast approaching. Nina had nearly forgotten Dalton's presence in her worry for Jacca. Now she was consumed with anxiety for Legary and Wolfram. She peered into the rainy night, trying but failing to glimpse either of them in the direction of the notch. Thumps sounded in the far distance, which Nina interpreted as the sound of Legary continuing to mend the weak seam in the rim's outer slope. By the glow of the violently boiling lava, which had now bubbled up the cauldron's black walls to within spitting distance of the notch, she could see that Legary had successfully plugged the top of the crack. He must now be working to seal the crevice all the way down from the rim to where it had once met the mountain ledge—

the erstwhile pilgrimage path that she and Galen had walked and then seen destroyed.

Nina was peering intently at the newly rock-filled notch when she saw movement almost directly below it … movement that made her doubt the seeing. She gasped, her gaze fastening upon the bulge in the cauldron wall—the swelling like a tumor that Wolfram had noticed on his first circuit of the rim. That lump was squirming—twisting in the rock.

"Drisha's mercy," Nina muttered so softly that neither Dalton nor Galen heard. The latter was still occupied with his canopy of fire, ensuring that the white flames consumed every last gobbet of sky-borne lava that might yet fall in their direction. Dalton's attention was on Jacca and the girl's spontaneous shaping of a rainstorm that wet the rim but did not trickle into the pit nor spill down the valley side of the mountain slope. In all the weather-mage's travels, by land and by sea, he had never encountered an adept who had such fine control as this young woman did. His niece's elemental gifts held him bemused.

But Nina, suddenly remembering that he was there, grabbed Dalton's arm and almost jerked him off his feet. "Look at that!" she exclaimed. "See where the notch was? Where Legary filled the gap? Just below it, the rock is wriggling like—"

A bag of worms, she would have said. But Nina never got the words out, for the "bag" exploded. Fire boiled from the tumor, a colossal, roaring storm of flame. A rim-hugging stand of dead pine trees went up like torches. Unbearable heat scorched the overlook where Nina and her brothers stood. It enveloped them as if they had been flung bodily into the burning belly of a furnace.

All three cried out in pain, and Galen went down. Unsupported on his injured ankle, he hit the ground perilously close to the overlook's edge. Dalton and Nina, although staggered by the force of the fire-blast, kept their feet and their magian reflexes. Acting by instinct, un-heedful of the consequences, Nina flung up her hands and summoned forth the immensity of her powers. For an instant that could not be measured in time, two walls of water hung suspended, towering as high as the mountain peak that rose above the basin. Then the water crashed down into the cauldron—

—Except it was no longer water. With a flick of his wrist, Dalton froze every drop. What hit the lava's surface was ice—such a great thickness of ice that it filled the basin nearly to the brim.

Frosty air gusted from the now frozen lake, bringing such relief to the three scalded *wysards* that again they cried out. But their relief was short-lived. The vast weight of the ice was more than the mountain's outer slope could bear, where it had been weakened by the earlier rockslide. Now, with a deafening noise of rock splitting and stone grinding, the front slope began to crumble.

"*No!*" Nina shrieked. She watched in horror as the outer rim-wall gave way. The overlook where she stood with her brothers—where Dalton was now hauling Galen back from the edge—shook beneath their feet but remained intact. Beyond that mantel of safety, however, boulders broke loose from the rim and tumbled down the valley side. The pinnacles of bare rock that had jutted fingerlike from the cauldron's lip shattered to pieces. Dust rose in a choking cloud as rubble, stone, and soil slipped down the mountainside.

"Jacca!" Nina screamed. "Where are you?" In the suddenly dark night, she could see nothing of the girl. Had the young adept been swept off the mountain? Was she buried in rubble? The rim had collapsed where Jacca had stood to watch Wolfram and Legary teeter toward the stonemason's task at the notch.

Which begged a further question: Where were those two *wysards*? In the fleeting moment between the tumor spouting flame and Nina summoning water to keep from burning alive in that hellfire, she had glimpsed a molten upwelling that overtopped the rim near the notch. Had Legary and Wolfe been caught in that rising surge? Nina strained to see but could not pierce the gloom. Billowing dust and high clouds obscured the moon, and Dalton's ice-cap threw the lava pit into inky blackness.

"Light!" Nina yelled. "Galen, bring light!"

The fire-mage was a step ahead of her. Even as Nina drew breath to shout her plea, Galen was remaking his magical umbrella. The canopy opened wide, high above their heads, dancing now with cool blue flames. There was no longer any need for a sheet of white-hot fire that could burn lava-splatter to ash. The lake of molten rock lay frozen under Dalton's ice.

By the canopy's sky-blue light, Nina searched frantically for any sign of the missing trio. She started to leap down from the overlook, to carry the search onto the tottering rim, on foot.

A new and violent shaking knocked her off stride. Nina threw out her arms, struggling to keep her balance, and gaped amazed as slabs of rock thrust upward along the rim. Like massive low walls, the slabs displaced the rubble and rebuilt the long, narrow edge that had tumbled down the mountainside.

"Legary?" Nina called into the night. But her voice was lost in the deep groan of the uplift as stone slabs crunched and scraped their way out of the bedrock below.

Whether it was her stonecrafter brother who raised those ramparts of rock, Nina had no time to discover. Dalton's shout in her ear brought her head around. She looked where he pointed, and saw crimson fire. It blazed once again from the uncanny tumor that bulged from the cauldron's inner wall like an inflamed, diseased growth. Though the fire lacked the explosive force of its first appearance, it streamed from the pulsing tumor like hot blood from a beating heart. Where it flowed onto the ice, the fire melted the top layers, creating an ever-widening puddle of water that glistened gory red atop the otherwise frozen lake.

"This time we'll kill it dead and cold," Nina vowed as she raised her hand in the beckoning motion that would summon the waves of her magic. "Ready, Dalton?"

"Keep the water coming, sister, and leave the rest to me," the weather-mage replied.

If asked for an accounting, Nina could not have said, later, how many walls of water she flung at that fiends'-fire, every drop of every wave frozen as it fell by Dalton's mastery. She gloried in the wizardry the two of them worked together, the harmony of their combined spellcraft. And yet, the tumor continued to blaze, showing a sullen red under layers of ice, then bursting out again with blistering tongues of fire that melted holes in the glacier which pressed heavily upon it.

After a time, Dalton shifted from ice to snow. Nina shot him a puzzled glance, and lost her magian elation when she saw the strain on his face. From her own experience, she knew the difficulty of turning water into ice. It was serious, demanding magic—spellcraft that she herself had worked successfully only a few times in her life. And here she'd been expecting Dalton to keep it up indefinitely—an expectation that was both unfair and unrealistic, she now saw.

He voiced no complaint, however, only motioned for more when Nina slacked off in supplying him with moisture to freeze. In his weather-working aboard ship, out on the ocean, Dalton needed no assistance: there, he had plenty of damp to transform into mist, cloud, rain, or snow. Here in the desert mountains, however, he relied on Nina's power to summon water to a dry landscape. She kept it coming, and Dalton dumped a blizzard on the relentless eruption of fire.

Over her shoulder, Nina cast an anxious glance at the rebuilt rim-wall that groaned out of the bedrock. Would it hold against the mounting weight of all the water, ice, and snow that she and Dalton were hurling into the cauldron as they tried to quench the demon flames? Was Legary below on the lower slope, out of their sight and hearing but struggling to raise that wall and hold it in place?

And where—*where* in the name of all that was good and merciful— were Jacca and Wolfram?

The answer to one of those questions came just then, streaking off the rim, out of a ruined heap of shattered stone spires. A wolf—its fur dark against the snow—raced down the cauldron's inner slope and leapt onto the frozen lake. The creature struggled to keep its footing on the slick ice that lay under a deepening blanket of snow.

"Stop!" Nina shouted, not at the wolf but at Dalton. She grabbed her brother's arm, interrupting the weather-mage's conjurations, and pointed at the wolf that floundered in the snow. The moon had finally broken through the remnants of Jacca's rainclouds: it added its white glow to the blue of Galen's canopy and the red blaze of the burst tumor. In the weirdly flickering light that filled the mountain basin, the wolf was so plainly visible that Nina could see its injuries. A strip of flesh and fur hung from the creature's side.

"Wolfram!" Nina screamed from the overlook. For another agonized moment, she watched the shapeshifter's painful progress through the snow.

Then she was sprinting out along the rebuilt rim, her boots clattering on loose rock until she reached the ruined spires and followed Wolfe's path in a mad dash down to the ice-filled cauldron. But the moment she skidded onto the frozen lake, Nina's feet went out from under her. Under its snowy mantle, the surface of the ice was mirror smooth. Nina fell heavily and lay still, the breath knocked out of her.

Then Dalton was there with her, crouched on the pebbly slope at her back. Nina's head swam as he caught her under the arms and pulled her off the ice, her body sliding frictionless over the uncannily smooth surface. He lifted her onto the snow-dusted rocks beside him, and helped her to sit up.

"Look," Dalton murmured, and pointed to where Wolfram had paused his advance out on the ice. "That's not something you'll see every day."

"No, indeed," Nina managed in a hoarse whisper, still laboring for breath.

As her head began to clear, she stared in awestruck wonder at the shapeshifter who stood bathed in blue-tinged moonlight. Over and over, Wolfram metamorphosed: from beast, to man, then back again. It was a power of wizardry unseen in the world for five thousand years until this young man appeared and shocked his magian Elders by displaying a Gift they had thought lost. Even now, with Wolfram having completed his apprenticeship and taken his place among the masters of magic, hardly anyone had witnessed the spectacle of his transformations.

Early in her friendship with the young adept, Nina had been privileged to see him be "unstuck" from wolf form and returned to his true human shape. But in recent days in these mountains, in all the time they had worked together to quench the fires of *farsinchia*, Nina had never directly observed the shapeshifter's transfiguration. She'd seen him walk as a man into the shadows of a cedar grove, and then reemerge as the wolf. Hours ago tonight, she'd noticed the way Wolfram chose his moment. He had waited until he passed among standing spires of rock, and only when screened from view had he taken the form of a wolf to lead Legary on toward the rim-wall notch.

Now, however, Wolfram shifted in full sight of every watching *wysard*. Nina and Dalton gaped from the edge of the frozen lake, and Galen stared down fixedly from the overlook above. A tremor of shock ran through all three of them, and they gasped as one when they finally understood why Wolfram had ignored his wounds to race in panicked, four-footed haste to one particular spot on the ice. When he gained that spot, he fell on his knees, a man once again, and naked in the night.

Jacca lay out there in the snow, her body limp and unmoving.

Chapter Eighteen

Wolfram brushed snow from Jacca's face and pressed his mouth to hers. He forced breath into the girl's lungs, pinched her nose shut, and repeated the breath. He centered his hands on Jacca's chest and pressed hard. Four times Wolfram did these things.

When he paused with his ear turned to Jacca's lips in an attitude of listening, his three watchers hung in mortal suspense with him. Nina and her brothers exhaled pent-up breaths when Wolfram raised his head and lifted his hands in a gesture of thanksgiving. As they gazed upon him, the man became a wolf that tossed up its head and howled at the moon, a song of joy.

Despite these positive signs, anxiety gnawed at Nina's heart as the wolf tugged the girl out of the snow and attempted to drag her over the ice, its fangs locked in the fabric of Jacca's shirt. The claws of the beast could get no firm purchase on the glassy surface. But Wolfram fared even worse when he shifted back to man-shape and took Jacca in his arms. His feet went out from under him, and he sprawled as Nina had on the mirror-slick ice.

"Wait!" came Galen's bellow from the overlook.

Wolfram jerked his head toward the sound, startled by the smith's voice. Nina also snapped a look at the fire-mage, for Galen's shout had carried so clearly in the night, it made her aware that near-silence had arisen behind her. The sustained, subterranean noise of grinding and groaning had subsided to a barely audible rumble. Nina threw a look over her shoulder, up toward the newly buttressed section of rim-wall, and exclaimed in a questioning voice: *"Legary?"*

The stonemason did not answer, and Nina detected no movement in that direction.

But out on the ice in front of her, magic was happening. Galen had crawled to within inches of the overlook's edge, and from that vantage point he threw down a ray of pale fire. The ray struck the ice some distance from where Nina waited with Dalton at the edge of the frozen lake. The fire hit about midway between her location and Wolfram's, out where he huddled on the slick ice, hugging Jacca close. From the point of impact, white flames shot in both directions, dancing over the ice in a straight line outward to Wolfram and in toward Nina. As the low flames neared her position on the pebbly edge, Nina felt a welcomed warmth. She'd been sitting long enough to absorb the cold from Dalton's conjured snow.

More importantly, however, the flames roughened the surface of the frozen lake. They scraped a path through the snow and scuffed the ice, and then died away at each end of the narrow track the magic had etched in the glassy surface.

Wolfram launched himself onto that track. With Jacca enfolded in his arms, he made the crossing surefooted on the ribbon of abraded ice. In moments he was huddling with Nina among rocks at the cauldron's edge.

"She's frozen," he gasped, shivering so hard he could barely speak.

"Allow me," Dalton murmured as he doffed his seaman's topcoat and flung it around Wolfe's shoulders, covering the young man's nakedness. With another quick gesture of casting, the weather-mage wrapped all four of them in a circle of warmth, invisible, but closing around them like a balmy bubble of summer.

"Thank you," Nina said without looking up. She was absorbed in trying to chafe heat into Jacca's icy flesh and rigid muscles. The girl was breathing but unconscious, and dangerously cold.

Nina cursed herself for allowing Jacca to venture onto the exposed rim-wall. The girl had gone out too far as she watched for Wolfram, anxious for his safe return from the notch. Her devotion had cost her. She'd had no shelter from her weather-working, nor from Dalton's. The girl's own conjured rain had soaked her to the skin. And then she'd ended up on the frozen lake—knocked off the rim and onto the ice, Nina surmised, by the massive buttressing that had shored up the rim after it partly gave way.

How long had Jacca lain out there, insensible to all that was happening around her, while Nina flung water at the fire-spouting tumor, and Dalton changed that water to ice? The girl had not been in the direct line of attack—Nina would have seen her. But sprays of water and endless showers of snow must have heaped upon Jacca's damp body as the girl lay sprawled on the ice. If Wolfram had reached her any later, she would have frozen to death.

"Thank the Powers you saw her," Nina muttered to the young man who kneeled on the rocks at her side, endeavoring with her to rub life into the girl's cold body and get Jacca's blood moving. "I never caught a glimpse. But the sharp eyes of the wolf saw what I could not." Nina brushed crystals of frost out of Jacca's hair, and ran her gaze over the girl's light clothing—the typical Ore Hills costume of desert-pale, summer-weight fabric. Dressed as she was, with ice collecting in her chestnut hair, Jacca would have been invisible to any mortal, and to most *wysards*. Only a shapeshifter possessed of a carnivore's keen vision could have spotted the girl out on the frozen lake.

As Nina worked to revive Jacca, she was aware of Dalton moving a little aside. Briefly he stepped out of her line of sight, and then returned.

"We have a problem," he whispered as he leaned over her shoulder. "Take a look."

"What now?" Nina exclaimed. "Is it Legary? Do you see him?"

She got clumsily to her feet, braced on Dalton's shoulder and wincing at the pain in her hip. She'd hurt it in her fall on the ice. As Nina limped around to glance where Dalton pointed, her chest tightened with renewed worry for the missing stonemason. In the partial collapse of the rim-wall, Wolfram had sustained a bloody injury to his side: a long, ragged laceration that now lay hidden by the greatcoat

Dalton had draped over the young man. But what had become of Legary in that collapse? Had he been swept off the mountain?

"About our absent brother, I've no idea," Dalton said as he helped Nina stand. "More's the pity, because I think we could use his help against *that*."

Nina followed Dalton's finger-point, and nearly lost her footing again as she recoiled in horror. Across the frozen lake, the bulge near the notch had gushed fire all this time, with no one paying close attention to it in their concern for Jacca. Now, however, Nina could not look away. A vision from a demonic level of *farsinchia* riveted her gaze.

The swollen tumor had grown a taloned foot. Immensely long claws jutted out of the rock, hooked and curved like a vulture's. The claws opened and closed ... questing, it seemed, for prey. Fire streamed from the tip of every talon, liquid in appearance, flowing like hot blood—hellishly hot, red blood that puddled below the tumor and spread toward them over the surface of the frozen lake.

"It's melting the ice!" Nina cried. "Quick, Dalton—make more. I'll bring water." She raised her hands to summon a flood, but Dalton stopped her.

"I'm done in," he muttered, and shot Nina an anguished look. "I can keep those two warm"—he jerked his head at Wolfram and the still-unconscious Jacca—"or I can make a little more ice. I can't do both at once ... and I don't know how much longer I'll be able to conjure ice." Stiffly, he cracked his knuckles. "Maybe I make it look easy, but it's not."

"I know," Nina whispered after a brief, dismayed pause. She laid her hand on Dalton's arm. "I know how hard it is. I can barely do it at all ... and you've done it all night."

She glanced again at Jacca and the shapeshifter, saw Wolfram's state of shivering, nervous distress, and studied the girl who lay in his arms as cold and limp as a jellyfish. *Turn up the heat*, Nina started to say, but she broke off at another bellow from Galen. His shout did not come from the overlook this time, but from a high point considerably nearer.

Nina jerked her head around and saw him up on the rim-wall, limping toward them, making what speed he could on his wrenched ankle.

He had reinjured it—of that, Nina was certain from the way he moved. Pain showed in every step.

"Stay there," she yelled at him. "You'll fall if you try to come down."

"Bring me Jacca!" he thundered. Galen stopped where he was and dropped heavily to the broken, stony ground. "Wolfe," he shouted, "bring her to me."

Against the jumbled black rock of the rim-wall, Galen showed up clearly, for he was wrapped in sapphire light. Around him swirled an aura of magian flame—an aura reminiscent of a scene Nina had beheld before, back when she traveled with Galen and Jacca from the Ore Hills to the mountain crossroads northward. In his rippling magic, Nina saw Galen's purpose: this fire-master was bringing the warmth of his wizardry to wrap his daughter in its elemental power.

At Nina's feet, Wolfram struggled to stand. A grunt of pain escaped the young man as Dalton helped him up. Wolfe wobbled on shaky legs, his breath coming in gasps. Nina remembered the physical toll that shapeshifting had wrung from the adept when she'd first known him. As a teenager, Wolfe had been rendered almost helpless every time he shifted, so great was the drain on his bodily reserves. He'd been rail-thin when the Old One, Gelgeis, restored him to his true shape, despite all the wild game Nina had fed the boy during the weeks of their journey together, when Wolfram had walked on four legs. Though the boy had become a man, and a trained master of his craft, no longer a youthful apprentice still learning the art, a shapeshifter could not help but be physically depleted with every change of form. It was the price demanded of those who were given such a powerful magian Gift.

Only minutes ago, Wolfram had changed repeatedly, in rapid succession, seeking the shape he required to save the girl he loved. He was drained to the dregs now, but he heaved a labored breath, gathered Jacca to his chest, and lurched, stumbling, up the slope. Nina watched him lay the girl in Galen's arms, and then collapse alongside. Wolfram sprawled on the rough ground with his head against the mage's shoulder. He, like Jacca, was fully enclosed in Galen's swirling wizardry of warmth.

Assured of the trio's immediate safety, Nina released the breath she hadn't been aware she was holding. She hobbled around on her sore hip to resume her study of the erupting tumor. The clawed foot had withdrawn, disappearing into the liquid fire that continued to spurt from the rock.

What took the foot's place, however, was an appendage even more monstrous. A wing stretched forth—broad, heavy-boned, and covered in scales that reflected firelight and moonlight, with a touch of blue from Galen's aura on the rim-wall. The wing flapped once, stiffly, and sent a thick spray of molten fire arcing toward Dalton and Nina.

She wreathed the fire in a curl of water, and steam billowed high, a scalding white fog that rolled through the cauldron.

With a sweep of his hand, Dalton froze the steam into snow. He packed the crystals into a glittering mass and hurled a blizzard at the tumor. Steam swirled again as snow met fiends'-fire, and again Dalton chilled the vapor, capturing and transforming it. The weather-mage continued until every flake had fallen, and the last wispy puffs of steam drifted away through the moonlight, thinning to invisibility.

In the wake of his magic, the night air had a crystalline quality, as clear and still as glass. Nina smelled no sulphur, no acrid stink of burning, none of the noxious odors that had assailed her nostrils since her arrival at the lava pit.

From the burst tumor, however, fire continued to drip, no longer running like a river but trickling steadily. The clarity of the air sharpened Nina's vision. Although the rock of the tumor was lost in darkness, the stone backdrop only a featureless black wall obscured in the glare of the oozing fire, she immediately detected the immense wing. The scaly appendage was still there, but now it pressed close against the rock, folded at its bony joints, not extended like a wing that would take flight.

"See how it's tucked up and clenched hard?" Nina said, directing Dalton's gaze. "Whatever that abomination is, I think it doesn't like cold and snow."

She'd hardly voiced this hope before the wing began to straighten again. Across the frozen lake came a noise like the clattering of innumerable metal pots. The wing's heavy scales clinked and rattled, and a series of concussive pops hammered Nina's eardrums as the bony joints snapped open and locked back in place.

"Drisha's mercy!" Nina swore. From Dalton came a low but heartfelt, "Breath and blood." They stood together, still battle ready with their hands raised, prepared to call upon their overworked powers. But for a long moment they could only stare at the wing that protruded from the oozing tumor. It flexed and stretched, tightened and relaxed, in the manner of an avian creature exercising flight muscles.

As they watched, the wing pitched upward. Down below it, the clawed foot reappeared. The foot did not stick straight out from the tumor as it had before. Now its curved talons sought downward for a foothold upon the rock. When the claws locked on in a secure grip, the wing stretched tight, high in the air. It flapped once in a powerful sweep, through an arc that cleared the rim-wall at its apex. Then the wingtip rushed downward to strike the surface of the ice—a surface that was mushy below the eruption, partly melted in the heat of the uncanny fire that dribbled from the tumor.

The wingtip caught a little mushy ice, but a great deal more liquid fire. As it soared upward again, back to the top of its arc, the wing flung blazing droplets at Nina and Dalton. It proceeded to flap furiously, spraying them with fiends'-fire.

The two *wysards* fought back. Nina summoned water that met fire in the inevitable cloud of steam, and out of that blistering vapor came Dalton's blizzards of snow. A thick mist filled the cauldron, and through it they caught only glimpses of their adversary.

But every glance deepened the feeling of hopelessness that had crept upon Nina. Her brother's snowstorms were weakening until they were hardly more than flurries, and her own walls of water were thinning. Her conjured waves struck with less force and weight, and they did not reach far enough to fall full upon the creature that was struggling to pull itself out of the rock.

Every glimpse through the steam and the flurries showed Nina a little more of the monstrous shape that was gradually emerging from the burst tumor. *Not a tumor*, she silently corrected herself. She'd been thinking of it that way ever since Wolfram had used the word in his first mention of the lump. But now she knew: that swelling in the rock was an egg.

"We're witnessing a birth," she gasped to Dalton during a lull in the tumorous delivery. "But what kind of creature is born of rock and fire ... with wings like a gigantic, scaly bat?"

"A devil straight from hell, I'd say," Dalton muttered. He lowered to the ground and sat with his hands on his knees, his fingers curled in pain. "I can do no more, Nina. I'm spent. There's nothing left in these." With a weary nod, he indicated his bent hands.

Nina touched his shoulder. "I'm sorry I got you into this," she murmured. "You and Legary both. In my wizardly arrogance, I thought all of us together—my brothers and myself—could face any threat and defeat any foe. But I never imagined a foe like *that*."

She jerked her chin at the winged monstrosity that continued to squeeze out through the cracked face of the rocky egg. This was a sideways birth: One foot and one wing were in the clear, and now the creature's breastbone was showing. Under a glittering coat of scales, its powerful chest muscles rippled.

Nina flicked a wave toward it, but the wave collapsed short of the mark. Water sloshed onto the lake's surface, raising no steam but adding to the mushy, melting breakup of Dalton's formerly solid icecap.

"We can't stop it," she whispered. "It's going to break free."

"And then what happens?" Dalton murmured.

Then we die, Nina thought but did not say aloud. She gripped his shoulder, and Dalton understood. He raised a limp hand from his knee to touch her fingers in wordless acknowledgment.

For the first time in her life, Nina realized as her stomach clenched in a hard knot, she was afraid. She'd grown up supremely confident of her abilities, and that confidence had only grown over the decades of her sojourn across the void. In her island home, she had faced off against pirates and marauders, and restored peace to a shattered, lawless society. She'd had moments of anxiety, of course, both in that world and here in her native realm. She'd felt twinges of unease. But deep-in-the-gut fear? This feeling was new and unfamiliar, and Nina did not know what to do with it. She could only crouch with Dalton and watch as the birth progressed.

Amidst a great cracking noise across the lake, a rending of rock, part of the creature's neck became visible. Its neck was long and snake-like, and bent sharply sideways so that the head was still buried in the rock. But a few strong jerks of that muscular neck succeeded in yanking the head free of the enclosing "eggshell." And Nina found herself meeting the fiery gaze of a monster that should not exist except in legend.

"Death of my life!" exclaimed Dalton, uttering an antique oath whose origins were lost in time, but was generally heard only in moments of uttermost extremity.

Nina, by contrast, was rendered silent, stock-still, caught in the hypnotic gaze of red, reptilian eyes. She was vaguely aware of the horns that bristled from the creature's head, two to either side of a thick, bony crest. She saw the snout, long and tapered, and then she saw the fangs. They glistened a bony white when the creature opened its mouth and emitted a roar.

Rocks rattled behind her, shaken loose by that deep, rumbling voice of thunder. On the ground beside her, Dalton grunted, struck by a stone that rolled down from the rim-wall at their backs. But Nina did not look around. She'd felt a distant puff of the creature's hot breath on her face, and she knew enough mythology to know what came next. Painfully, she levered herself up from her crouch and squared her stance. With her arms raised, Nina stood ready with the last dregs of her strength—

—Ready for the fire that belched from the creature's open mouth, the flames arrowing toward her as if shot from an impossibly powerful Ladrehdinian longbow.

Nina flung up a wall of water, curtaining the air barely in time to intercept the fiery blast. Steam exploded, and she went down. Black spots danced before her eyes as she collapsed in a heap beside Dalton.

"Get up!" she managed to yell at him, her voice hoarsened by pain. "Move. The next firebolt will fry us if it catches us."

Nina struggled to regain her feet, in agony from her bruised hip. Dalton also had trouble rising: the falling rock had hurt his back. They tried to scramble up the steep rim-wall, desperate to reach some sort of cover before the next gout of fire caught them on the exposed rocks at the edge of the thawing lake. But loose pebbles and dislodged cobbles hampered their progress, and they were still in full view of the fire-breather when the cloud of steam dissipated.

The ground shook under them then, and they slid down with the loosened rocks, almost all the way back to their starting point. "It's out!" Nina gasped, certain in her own mind that the creature had jerked free of its stony egg, and in doing so had jolted the mountain. Her supposition was supported by an earsplitting screech that filled the final remnants of the night. The moon had dropped behind the western peaks, and a faint hint of dawn now showed in the eastern sky.

Nina quit trying to crawl up the unclimbable slope. She flopped over on her sore hip, wincing as she settled her backside into the loose scree. She would rather have died on her feet, but at least she would depart this life while facing her enemy, not turned tail and fleeing.

With the setting of the moon, the only light in the rimmed mountain basin came from Galen's sapphire-blue, magian flickers, and from the liquid fire that continued to drip out of the cracked, black-rock egg. In the relative dimness, Nina strained to see her opponent. She expected it to take wing and fly at her, exhaling fire.

But as another howl split the air, Nina realized that the creature had not yet fully hatched. Both wings were out of the egg, true. Yet it still had one foot stuck in the rock.

This was the final moment in which she could act. But how? With what?

Nina's weapons flitted to mind, but she dismissed the idea before it fully formed. She'd relied so heavily on a magical defense, she wore no weapon except the knife at her belt. Her bow was with her bedding in the cedar grove—she'd never retrieve it in time. And what use would an arrow be against a fire-breather that was covered in scales? If the arrow didn't flame to ash in flight, it would bounce off of the creature's armor.

Reflexively, responding not to thought but to ingrained muscle memory, Nina loosened the knife in its sheath while she made a second inventory, taking stock this time of what magic still remained in her arsenal. She could summon no more torrents: her water-wizardry was exhausted, spent. But her frantic riffling through the spellwork she had learned as a young adept turned up no other ensorcellments that had any chance of prevailing against a hellfire monster. Nina's childhood apprenticeship, after all, had lasted only eight years, from ages five to thirteen. She'd studied with Master Welwyn for less than the standard term of magian scholarship, for she'd been eager to jump the void and restore the Elemental balance to her ocean world of thundering spray and gossiping dolphins.

As a consequence of her youthful haste, there was much in the way of advanced spellcraft that Nina had never learned—a wizardly deficit that now promised to prove deadly.

But what about the spell of stone? whispered her quietly desperate inner voice.

Nina shook her head, impatient with the notion. That simple spell-craft was as easily broken as cast. And she doubted the enchantment would have any power to hold the creature if she attempted to cast the magic across the expanse of melting lake that lay between her and the fire-breather.

But: when the creature broke free and flew at her ... when it came close enough ... then the spell of petrification *might* slow it for an instant, and a spell of containment might then restrain it long enough for Nina to leap with the monster into the void, dragging it with her into nothingness.

The void: that vast emptiness which lay between this world and Nina's island home. Hurdling into that oblivion was magic she might just manage. The frozen lake held plenty of water to support the required spellcraft—especially since she would attempt no full crossing of an immensity that could not be measured. She needed only to enter the void, with no destination in mind and thus no exit within reach. Stranded there, she would drift until she perished—the fire-breather dying with her, if Nina gave it no way out of the nothing.

She struggled to her feet. Barely able to stand, unsteady on her injured hip, Nina drew her knife. She had no hope of piercing the creature's scaled armor. But in the instant when she took it into the void, she might have the advantage of surprise. She might get close enough to plunge the blade into the thing's eye. The red, staring orb that had fixed her with a murderous gaze was the creature's only vulnerability.

Nina stared across at the horn-spiked head, waiting for the "hatchling" to jerk its foot out of the last fragment of rock that held it. She had her free hand up, ready with spellcraft which, she knew in her heart, had only a fleeting chance of immobilizing the monster before its fires burned her to ash. But she had to try. She'd been so cocksure about trapping the "arsonist," she'd drawn her loved ones toward their deaths. If she succeeded in vaulting the fire-breather into oblivion with her, Nina would die, lost in the void for eternity. But those she loved would live. And her native world would be safe from whatever devil's spawn was now hatching, here at the gates of hell.

She tensed, the salt taste of cold sweat in her mouth as she readied for the moment when the creature pulled free and flew at her. Nina held her knife in a death grip, her gaze seeking the monster's red stare.

But the thing's head was flailing, denying her a glimpse of its eyes. It seemed not only angry now, but distressed. Nina gaped, not trusting her senses. She blinked to clear the sweat that beaded in her lashes. She looked again, and saw the reason for the creature's struggles:

An enormous stony hand held the monster by its throat.

Her breath caught. Slowly, Nina lowered her knife, her gaze riveted as another stony hand emerged from the pit-wall under the notch. This hand seized one of the creature's furiously fluttering wings and pressed it down, trapping the wing against the monster's body.

The creature shrieked in fury and tried to claw the hands away, raking them with the talons of its one available foot. In response, yet another hand emerged from the underlying stone and grabbed the thrashing claw.

The hand on the creature's throat limited the movement of its head, but it struggled madly to stab its restraints with the horns that crowned its brow. This gained it nothing, for a fourth hand wrapped stony fingers around the creature's head and pinned it motionless. A single fiery eye showed through the fingers, and it glared across at

Nina with baleful, red rage as a muffled roar escaped the creature's throat.

Only one wing remained unfettered, but not for long. A *fifth* hand stretched from the rock and smoothed the wing, tucking it tight against the creature's body.

The light of dawn had strengthened in the east, giving Nina a clear view of what happened next. Every hand kept a tight grip, and they moved as one to tug the creature straight down into the rimrock, and deeper still, into the heart of the mountain. The remains of the hatchling's eggshell crumbled, and rocky shards followed the creature on its downward path. Steam boiled as meltwater from Dalton's conjured ice flowed into the vertical shaft that was created by the fire-breather's forced removal from the upper world.

"By the Powers!" Nina swore, finding her voice after long moments of stunned silence. She pressed a hand to her aching hip and sank back down to the ground. "Dalton, are you seeing this?" she asked without taking her eyes off the column of steam that rose from the supernatural borehole.

"I'm seeing ... but not believing," came Dalton's hesitant reply from a short way above and behind her. "Galen never told me these desert mountains were *alive*. But I think that only living rock could sprout winged monsters and gigantic hands."

Living rock. The phrase lodged in Nina's mind, but she had no time to shape a thought around it, for Dalton cried out.

"Legary!" he shouted. "Over there, Nina. On the rim between us and the notch. See him?"

Nina looked where Dalton said, and gave a scream of relief as she spotted the stonecrafter. Legary was alive—limping, but alive. He stumbled toward the notch, the former weak place in the rim-wall. The mending he'd accomplished hours ago had held firm during all that had followed. What, therefore, could his purpose be in making his wobbly way back to that point?

"Where's he going?" Dalton asked, his perplexity an echo of Nina's.

"The borehole," she said. "That must be it. He's dug deep holes in his time, and maybe he can't resist dipping into that one."

Her focus was intense, her breath half held, as she followed Legary's laborious progress atop the treacherously rugged, narrow rim-wall. But Nina's gaze twitched suddenly aside as a huge boulder popped up farther along the wall, just past the repaired notch. The boulder had eyes: large, round, limpid blue. The eyes looked down at her.

Nina stared up at them ... and had to lift her gaze higher and higher as the boulder rose out of the rimrock, pushed upward on a short, squat neck of stone. Below the neck, blocky shoulders emerged from the underlying rock. Two arms appeared, each ending in a massive, five-fingered hand. The figure—the man of stone—continued to rise until he towered over the rim-wall, but still with only his upper body showing. From the waist down, the stone giant remained stuck in the rock.

Not 'stuck,' Nina corrected her first impression. *Immersed, in perfect unity with the mountain. He is the mountain.*

"Grog!" she shouted. "I'm overjoyed to see you."

Nina tried to stand again but couldn't manage it on her injured hip, with the loose rock clattering out from under her. Forced back on her butt, she could only wave two-handed at the colossal figure that had shot up into the cloudless sky, his smooth stone skin bathed in soft morning sunlight.

In acknowledgment of her greeting, Grog flattened his hands against the ground in front of him and bowed, a low bow to Nina that brought his head looming out over the rapidly melting ice in the mountain basin. She heard a gasp from Dalton as the huge boulder appeared to hang unsupported above the inner rim-slope. Nina smiled as Grog straightened and the boulder lifted back into place, his great round head balanced once again atop a squat, almost nonexistent neck.

"That fellow is *enormous,*" Dalton muttered at Nina's back, a touch of awe in his voice.

"He's grown," she admitted. "Grog was a giant among men when I traveled with him. But now he's truly mountain-sized."

"Legary seems to want him for something," Dalton said. "He's trying to catch your friend's eye."

Nina's gaze flitted over the rim-top and found the stonemason down on one knee, still a considerable distance from Grog. Legary was gesturing, drawing pictures in the air with his hands. She watched for a moment, then said, "I think he's asking Grog to seal the borehole. Maybe Legary meant to do it himself, but he's hurt and he's limping, and Grog is closer to where the mountain swallowed the monster."

Grog appeared to reach the same conclusion. He gave Legary a nod—a casual dip of the head that conveyed little of the formal respect he'd extended to Nina. With the ease of water streaming over glass, Grog flowed down into the rock under him, his body disappearing, absorbed into the substance of the rim-wall.

"By the Powers!" Dalton swore, softly. "How does he do that?"

"He's made of stone," Nina answered. "The bones of the mountain are his bones. The stuff of the world is the stuff of his body, for they are, in truth, the same. He is rock, but more than rock. He is also water and salt, metals and gemstones … he's everything. Whatever is found in the body of the world is also within him. The world is his flesh." Nina smiled, and shook her head. "I fear I'm not making sense, brother. I'm very tired, and I'm hungry and sore."

"So am I," Dalton muttered. "Now that we're not running for our lives, let's try again to get up this damned slope. I'll go save Legary from collapse, if my legs will carry me that far. The poor fellow looks like a house fell on him."

Chapter Nineteen

With Legary returned to them, more or less in one piece, the six *wysards* slept until late afternoon. They woke to a blazing campfire and to a whole pig roasting on a spit.

These comforts were provided by Mother Labéht, who had materialized amongst them while they lay exhausted and unconscious. She moved from one to another of the younger magicians, treating their more serious injuries. The Old One had stitched up the long tear in Wolfram's side and bound Galen's ankle, this time with the added protection of a splint. She'd poulticed Jacca's head where the girl had struck it a hard blow in her fall from the rim onto the frozen lake.

Other than a bruised noggin, the young adept seemed none the worse for her steep tumble and long, icy slide into insensibility. The warmth of Galen's fire-magic had restored the color to Jacca's face. And no one who observed Jacca with Wolfram could doubt the heat that smoldered in the girl's heart. Wolfe had saved her life, summoning the full powers of his spellcraft and pushing his body to its limits in his rapid changes from man to beast as he wrested her from a cold tomb. They belonged to each other now, and no power existed that would separate them.

Galen showed his gratitude for the young man's devotion, and at last his acceptance. Nina saw him pat Wolfram on the shoulder, and she heard the smith call the shapeshifter "son" when Galen limped past, on his way to sit with Legary.

The stonemason was in the roughest shape of any of them. Patches of skin were gone from Legary's arms and from his bruised face. He had bloody knuckles, torn clothes, scraped knees, and a hip joint that had nearly been wrenched from its socket. Labéht popped the joint back in place and strapped it tight. She salved Legary's various other wounds, and demanded to know how he had collected so much damage.

"I got up the mountain in time to see what was going on with all the rest of you," she said, darting a glance around the campfire, where everyone had settled to watch the pig roast. The meat turned, unattended, on a wooden spit—a small display of the Old One's magic. Labéht pointed at Legary and at Dalton, who had also gone to sit with his brother. "When those two boys appeared on my doorstep, seeking to know where they might find the Lady Karenina, I resolved to follow them up the South Trail. For it isn't every day that one may see four grown children of House Verek called to work spellcraft together. The spectacle was not to be missed."

"Was it worth the climb?" Nina inquired from her place next to Jacca and Wolfram. "What did you see?"

"Legendary things!" Labéht exclaimed. "I saw the power of the elements unleashed: water, fire, stone, wind and weather." She nodded at each adept in the circle as she named their particular gift. "I saw an ancient magic that I thought was gone from this world." With a graceful wave of her hand, Labéht saluted Wolfram. "Master Shapeshifter, you have the heart of a lion and the eyes of an eagle, wedded to the strength of the wolf."

"And every bit of him to be wedded to me, quite soon," Jacca murmured under her breath, too softly for anyone to hear except Nina—and of course Wolfram, who sat with Jacca's bandaged head resting on his shoulder. Nina smiled, but pretended that she hadn't caught the girl's whisper, or seen Wolfe's hand twitch on their shared blanket and his fingers move to caress the girl's thigh.

"I believe, however," Nina said, directing her remarks across to Labéht on the other side of the campfire, "that we all saw more legendary things than you have named. Will you share with us your thoughts,

Elder One, on the creature that hatched from rock, and the hands of stone that preserved us all from a fiery death? Are such things spoken of in the ancient lore of Ladrehdin?"

Mother Labéht tilted her head, then nodded. "I will tell you the stories that were recounted around the campfire many long years ago, when I was a girl about Jacca's age. I thought them fanciful then, but now I must believe those old tales held kernels of undeniable truth."

Labéht paused as if sifting through centuries of memories. Then the Old One began to describe a lost age, far back in the night of time, when giants contended for dominion in the world of Ladrehdin. They were creatures of stone and creatures of fire, and in the high mountain peaks they dwelled, not sharing the slopes peacefully together, but perpetually in conflict. For the fire-breathers laid waste to vast areas of mountain forest and filled the green valleys with lakes of molten rock. The destruction disturbed the tranquility of the stone-people. Through countless ages, they strove to drive the winged fire-spawn out of the mountains.

These great rivals, the stone-people and the fire-breathers, were creatures of primordial magic, and all suffered in the long, slow decline of Ladrehdin's natural potency. There came a time when the fire-breathers ceased to fly, and the blaze in their bellies cooled to cinders. They sank to the bottom of the molten lakes they had made, and thick crusts of cold rock spread above them, entombing them. Deep in their crypts of darkness and silence, the creatures slept, slumbering in a state not far removed from death.

The stone-people could not rejoice, however, for they also felt the ebbing of the world's magic. Their heads grew heavy, and when they could no longer raise up to see over the highest peaks, they laid themselves beneath the mountains and became bedrock.

"Bear in mind," Labéht said as she neared the end of her account, "that all of this happened in a world without *wysards* of the true Power, for our kind had not yet arisen. Furthermore, in that distant age, no mortal of Ladrehdin lived this far west. The river valley below the Ore Hills was a pristine wilderness, uninhabited, never glimpsed by human eyes. I think that might be why the first sparks of the reawakening burned only haystacks and roof-thatch, down in the valley. Upon stirring from its long sleep, and sensing an unfamiliar presence in its former territory, instinct drove the *savitar* first and foremost, to be rid of that strange presence."

"*Savitar!*" cried several voices together.

"A myth come to life!" exclaimed Dalton. "I remember my old tutor reading me bedtime stories about gallant heroes battling winged monsters. I never imagined the monsters could be real—or that I would someday see a *savitar* with my own eyes."

Nina did not join in the general hum of wonder and surprise, for she had heard those same stories during her own childhood in Ruain, and a scrap of memory had already put the name to the fire-breather that had defeated her water-magic. The *savitar* was close kin to a similar firedrake that figured in the legends of her island home across the void. In her idle moments on that ocean world, Nina had sometimes imagined herself going up against an Earthly dragon. She'd always prevailed, of course, in her fantasies. But reality had proved much different when she'd faced the dragon's Ladrehdinian counterpart. The ancient magic of fire had overpowered her water wizardry.

"Mother Labéht," Nina said as the startled hubbub subsided around the campfire, "if the *savitar* sensed—and resented—the presence of ordinary mortals in the valley below its lair, then it must also have detected a new power of magic abroad in the land. It must have been aware of the two magian fire-makers, Galen and his daughter. And I'm certain that it knew exactly where Galen and I were as we made our way up the mountain to confront it. The creature dropped sparks in front of us like breadcrumbs, luring us into its presence." Nina paused, and rubbed her lower lip. "But why?" she continued after a thoughtful moment. "Why did it draw us to its place of concealment? If it hadn't brought us to this high pit, it could have emerged from its 'egg' unopposed."

Labéht shrugged one shoulder. "Perhaps it was simply curious about you," she said as she casually bespelled the campfire to burn a little lower, to avoid charring the meat that continued to turn on its magical spit. "As you say, you embodied a new power of magic—a potency foreign to what the *savitar* had known when it soared through the ancient skies of a world very different from the world to which it awakened. Curiosity and perhaps puzzlement—colored by hubris—may have compelled the creature to draw you into its presence. If the *savitar* regarded you as a new challenger to its dominance, it might have wished to look upon the faces of its rivals and test you, before consigning you to its hellfires." Labéht waved a hand in airy dismissal of further speculation. "Whatever the creature's motives, it brought trouble upon itself to a far greater degree than it could have anticipated. For not only did it face six *wysards* of the true Power, it provoked its greatest and most ancient rival."

"Thank the Powers for Grog!" Nina exclaimed. "I believe all of us would have perished in hell's flames if my old friend hadn't come to our rescue."

From her spot in the campfire circle, Nina cast a glance around the top of the rim-wall. In the late-afternoon sun, she saw no trace of the colossus, and she felt a twinge of disappointment. Had he left without saying good-bye?

Nina pushed aside her vague sense of letdown, and looked back at Labéht. "I was collapsing with weariness, my magic spent by the time Grog arrived and took matters in hand. I might have been half delirious and seeing things by that point, but I swear I counted five hands that reached out of the rock to grab the *savitar*." Nina swept her gaze around the campfire circle, directing her question to all. "When Grog and I traveled together on the grasslands, he shook my hand on more than one occasion, so I can tell you with confidence that he had no more than the typical two. But here, I counted five. Did anyone else see the same?"

"I can shed light on that," came Legary's tired voice from the other side of the fire. "But first, I want a plate of roast pork, and with it I'd welcome another dose of painkiller." He cast a look of entreaty at Mother Labéht. "Whatever you gave me worked wonders, madam. But it's wearing off, and I can't tell my story if I'm screaming in pain."

* * *

Evening had closed in by the time they'd pulled the pig off the spit and all had eaten their fill of the tender, juicy roast. After his dinner, Legary fell soundly asleep, and most of the others drifted off as well. They'd be long recovering from supernatural battle against a mythological monster. Labéht moved among them, bestowing relief: a fresh poultice for Jacca's head, a change of bandages for Wolfram's laceration and Legary's abrasions, and deadeners dispensed to anyone who needed them. Nina, hobbled by her sore hip, accepted a small dose of painkiller. Then with a nod of gratitude for Labéht, she settled into her blankets, glad for the ancient herbalist to take charge of patients who would otherwise have fallen to Nina's care.

Through the night they all dozed and woke, conversing softly together when they roused enough to do so. Gradually, Legary's story came out.

He'd made a good start, he said, toward mending the weak seam in the northeastern slope. With his magian stonework, he had blocked up the gap at the top of the crevice. Then he'd proceeded down the crack on the outer slope, filling it as he went, sealing the chimney-like crevice and binding it with the same spellwork that he employed to repair cracked stone walls, back home in Granger. Legary was about halfway down when Grog suddenly stuck his head out of the solid rock alongside the fracture.

"I was so startled, I damn near fell off the mountain," Legary grumbled. He touched his arm, where Labéht's bandages covered a raw patch of missing skin. "That crack was lined with volcanic rock as jagged as broken glass, and down it I went sliding and jolting along. I'm lucky I lost nothing but skin. That rock was sharp enough to slice off a finger. I was trying to stop my slide, trying not to fall so far that I broke my neck, when a big chunk of stone slid out of the mountainside below me, and I slammed into it." Here, for emphasis, Legary rubbed his nearly dislocated hip. "I'm grateful to Grog for catching me. I don't know if that hunk of rock was his elbow, his shoulder, his knee, or something else. But when he shoved it into my path, he broke my fall and probably saved my life."

Grog had recognized him, Legary admitted, more readily than the stonemason had identified the big bodyguard who used to ride with a traveling merchant. The Grog of Legary's acquaintance had seemed massive, but the stone giant who stuck his boulder-like head out of the mountainside was a true colossus, a towering titan.

Grog grew up, Nina mused as she listened to Legary's account. She recalled the story the traveling merchant had told of his first meeting with the strange being who became his bodyguard. The merchant—Nimrod by name, but "Roddy" to Nina—had said Grog was like a lost infant, an innocent babe of enormous size. *Now the baby is grown*, Nina thought, *and he's strong enough to move mountains.*

She refocused on Legary as he described his shock upon comprehending the identity of the stone giant. The master mason of Granger had known Grog—the infant Grog—for many years. In his befuddled amazement, Legary found himself babbling, jabbering away with news of Grog's former employer. He told the giant all that he had seen or heard of Nimrod over the past several years, even tracing the merchant's travels along the man's old trade route through Granger, and mentioning a few new roads that Nimrod had ridden since Grog left the fellow behind.

"You'll forgive me, Nina," Legary said, calling to her across the low-burning campfire, "for chattering away about Nimrod and completely forgetting to inform the giant that you were only a short way up the mountain, dumping water on a diabolical fire. It quite slipped my mind that you'd traveled many a mile with the big fellow. I only ever saw him with Nimrod, never with you. You'd parted company from the giant before you came to visit me in Granger."

Nina nodded, and motioned for Legary to continue his story. "I do not begrudge your long visit with my friend," she said. "I only wish I could talk with Grog myself, now that we're no longer battling fiends'-fire. But please explain what happened when the front side of the rim gave way—under the weight, I fear, of all the water and ice that Dalton and I threw at the *savitar*. You were caught in that landslide, were you not?"

Legary confirmed that he was—as evidenced by the state of his face, his knuckles, and his clothes. Once again, Grog saved him. The slide swept past the man of stone, but it tumbled Legary farther down the slope. Grog caught and shielded him, and then the giant went to work buttressing the mountainside. The slabs of stone that thrust upward along the collapsing rim, crunching and scraping and groaning their way out of the underlying bedrock, were mostly Grog's doing. But when Legary had recovered some of the wits that the landslide had knocked out of him, he joined the giant in raising enormous stones to rebuild the upper front of the rim-wall.

"We were just finishing the job," Legary related, "when Grog froze. He went still as a ... well, I won't say still as a stone. That's too easy. But he halted in place, dead quiet as if listening, or sensing something that demanded his immediate attention. He looked right through me—through the mountain, it seemed. Then he flowed down into the slope below me and disappeared—leaving me in a predicament," Legary grumped. "I had a bad hip, skin was hanging off me in shreds, and my head was ringing from all the hits it took in the rockfall. But out of that rubble I managed to conjure a stone staircase. Up it I crawled, climbing to the rim-top and cursing Grog all the way. I felt abandoned by the big fellow."

Legary paused to accept a cup of medicinal tea from Labéht. He took several small sips to ease a throat that had gone dry and scratchy from all this talking, and also from the stone dust he'd inhaled in his ordeal on the outer slope.

"Like I say," Legary continued, his voice less husky as he lowered the cup, "I considered myself ill-used by Grog. But now I believe he had good reason to leave me hanging. I think he became aware of the *savitar* up here in the pit, out of sight though it was above us, and he went to get help."

"Help? You mean ... others of his kind?" Nina asked, remembering the five hands.

Legary shrugged. "Maybe his friends, maybe his family. For all I know, his vassals and retainers. After that remarkable event at Winfield when he leapt into the underworld, people took to calling him the king of the nether realms. Maybe he is."

And a king, Nina silently reflected, *has many demands on his time. He saw me. He greeted me. I shall be content. It is enough, if I do not speak with him again.*

"What do you suppose they'll do with the *savitar*?" asked Dalton in a drowsy voice. The weather-worker lay on his back, his blankets pulled up to his beardless chin. Nina wasn't sure how much of Legary's narrative Dalton had heard. His eyes kept closing, and he seemed perpetually on the verge of drifting off. Dalton's elemental powers had been depleted as thoroughly as Nina's had in their united effort to fend off the fire-breather. He must need to rest as badly as she did. But the ice-bringer had attended to enough of Legary's story to pose that one question, which he asked of the group at large.

"I hope they'll lock that monster in a deep, cold tomb for all of eternity," exclaimed Galen, who sat on Legary's other side, across from Dalton. "I don't want to go through this again. If the thing gets loose, 'King Grog' might not bring his stone-folk to rescue us again, just in the nick of time." Galen paused, then added, "If the *savitar* gets loose, there might not be an 'us' to rescue. The creature won't bother to scatter sparks along the river, burning haystacks to let us know it's back. I suspect its curiosity about humankind has been thoroughly satisfied. Next time, there will be no taunts or 'breadcrumbs' to lure us to its lair. The monster will rise in secret on those fearsome great wings, soar down the mountainside, and lay waste to everything in the valley and the hills."

Galen's words provoked a brief pause, during which Mother Labéht leaned to stir the campfire. In its flickering light, the face of the Old One looked decades younger. For an instant, Nina had the sense of looking upon a face she knew well, someone she'd known longer, and more intimately, than the recently met herbalist of the Ore Hills. Labéht straightened, drawing back into the darkness beyond the reach of firelight, and Nina was left pondering that brief flash of familiarity.

"I believe we can trust the legends," the Old One said in response to Galen, as she leaned back. "What I have witnessed here, with you, accords with the stories I learned in my youth. It seems the legends did not lie, nor even much exaggerate. The stone-people are the ancient enemies of the *savitar*, and only they have the strength to subdue the creatures. Perhaps I err, however," Labéht added, "in calling them enemies. From the way those rock-hard hands grasped the hatchling, ever so gently as they returned it to the fiery womb of the underworld, I wonder if perhaps the stone-folk are not more truly regarded as the custodians of the *savitar*. The creatures' shepherds, if you like."

"I saw no sane reason for their tender treatment of that thing," Galen muttered. "They ought to break the monster's snaky neck and bury the carcass far under this mountain."

Labéht tossed another stick of wood on the campfire. She kept to the shadows and gave Nina no further glimpse of the face that had seemed, for an instant, to be someone else's.

"Regardless," the Old One resumed, speaking out of the darkness, "I believe we can trust the stone-folk to be vigilant, going forward. How fortunate for the whole of Ladrehdin, that the people of stone awakened earliest from their long slumber. If the *savitar* had been the first to feel the renewal of magical potency in this world—if that race had been the first of the ancient enemies to rise to the surface—then humanity's fate would be as you have said, Galen of House Verek." The Elder paused, then added, "I doubt that even a regiment of master *wysards* could prevail against a fire-throated *savitar* with any greater success than the six of you have known on this mountain. The magic of those beings is too old, born of a time that far predates our own age of wizardry."

Nina shot a look at Legary, knowing the stonemason must be remembering, as she was, their long talks together in Granger. They had spoken of their legendary mother, Carin of Ruain, and what they'd been taught all their lives about the perils Carin had faced and overcome to renew the wellspring of magic in the world. Through that lady's courage and determination, a new magical vigor had spread from the heart of Ladrehdin to its highest mountaintop—a reinvigoration that was felt by every *wysard* in the land, but also by the slumbering stone-folk and, dangerously, by the fire-fiends.

On Nina's side of the campfire circle, the two younger adepts had sat silent during all of this talk. Jacca and Wolfram listened with rapt attention, absorbing each word uttered by the senior *wysards*. Nina glanced past the girl, and devoted a moment of study to the shapeshifter, Wolfram.

Different though he was from firedrakes and stone giants, Wolfe must be counted among their company. For his Gift of shapeshifting was also an ancient power of magic, an ability lost in this world for millennia until it reappeared in the form of this young man. Wolfe, a native son of the western mountains, had been abandoned in boyhood by parents who were known only to the two master *wysards* who had taken the youth into apprenticeship. One of those masters had confirmed to Nina what she'd suspected: Wolfram's gift arose directly from the same worldwide flood of reborn magic that had awakened Grog and his stone-folk, and after them the *savitar*.

The talk died down around the campfire as, one by one, her companions drifted off again. Nina watched Wolfram and Jacca snuggle under blankets beside her. The pair fell asleep in each other's arms.

As she looked on, Nina thought of the flippant way she'd teased Galen about the "wolf cub" grandchildren these two would soon give him. But in truth, the matter was not to be taken lightly. It needed serious consideration of the sort Nina now found herself mulling in the calm silence of the night, when only she remained awake.

In the veins of Jacca's children, the blood of House Verek would mix with the ancient magic of the shapeshifter. The girl's magian lineage was a noble one that went back millennia. Wolfram's gift, however, was far older: primeval, so the legends said, with mythical origins shrouded in the unknown night of time.

What would their union produce? What new power of magic would the young lovers bring into the world? Their offspring must possess a wizardly potential beyond anything ever before seen in Ladrehdin.

Nina's roving thoughts conjured a memory from her youth, something her father had once said: *A limitless gift needs boundaries.*

He'd been speaking of Nina herself, worrying over the heedless way she'd summoned her water-magic and thrown it around recklessly in her girlhood. She'd flooded the garden and even the hallways of her childhood home. And then, with the stubborn resolve of a six-year-old, Nina had flung herself to a distant world, riding high upon a wave of her own wild magic.

I was out of control, and so was my niece with her own element, Nina thought as she studied the sleeping Jacca. As an eight-year-old, Jacca had set the curtains on fire and burned herself painfully before the girl learned to control her fire-magic.

If history repeated itself, the next generation was going to need a firm hand: somebody who had the experience to impose and enforce boundaries. Jacca's children would require a governess. And who better than a water-*wysard* who could quench fire and command the respect of wolves? Especially a *wysard* of the true Power who counted the king of the underworld among her dearest friends.

You already have a family to look after, whispered an accusatory little voice in the back of Nina's mind. *You have generations of your own progeny waiting for you beyond the void.*

But did they really expect her to return? Had they even noticed she was gone?

Nina recalled a passing remark, offered by another widow, a much older woman with whom she had idly conversed when the two found themselves in the same patch of shade one hot, sleepy, island after-noon on her adopted world. "People have their own lives," the woman had commented, "and after a while those lives don't include you."

The old widow had been complaining, albeit fondly, about the way her children and grandchildren had neglected her lately. But the woman's words struck a chord with Nina. That chord rang loudly now, as she looked at Jacca and Wolfram entwined in their contented slum-ber.

Why should Nina return to the family she'd left behind? Her Earthly descendants had shown her, on her last brief visit, that they did not need her anymore. They took her for granted and barely saw her now, shunted aside as she was in the "granny flat." Nina's progeny had their inheritance, and it went far beyond the family home on the coral-sand beach of their ocean world. They had the magian vigor of their birthright.

But that faraway offshoot of House Verek would only decline in magical potency as each generation descended one degree farther from their magian matriarch. Here in her native world, however, Nina could nurture and guide a powerful new cohort of wizardly apprentices. She could train them as she herself had been trained, to use their powers wisely and in humble gratitude to the Elementals who bestowed the Gift upon the magicians of Ladrehdin.

I'll stay for a while, Nina temporized. *Just until my niece is wed and I have midwifed Jacca's first child into this world. The girl would want me here for that.*

If Nina *was* eventually missed, out across the void, so much the better. How had the poet phrased it, in that old verse she'd read on Earth?

Absence makes the heart grow fonder;
Isle of Beauty, fare thee well!

Chapter Twenty

Encamped at the top of the trail, they hung about for what became days as their bodies healed and their gifts replenished. All of them complained of sore hands and wrists, their fingers swollen and stiff from the endless snapping and flicking of powerful spellwork. Labéht rubbed an eye-wateringly hot liniment into their overtaxed joints, and ordered them to rest their hands until the swelling went down.

Dalton, too unacquainted with idleness to stay down for long, got back on his feet before any of the others. Except for his knotted fingers, he'd suffered no physical injury other than a bruised back from a tumbling stone. But alongside Nina he had drained his powers in the battle with the *savitar*. For a time after he was up and about, the weather-mage could not produce so much as a thin mist.

Even so, Jacca clamored for her uncle to teach her to summon snow and ice. The girl's cold burial had not dimmed her enthusiasm for "frosty magic," as she called it. Jacca's heart and breathing had been nearly undetectable when Wolfram carried the girl to her father. Galen's fire-magic had recalled the young woman from the brink of death, filling her veins with the warmth of their shared element, restoring the lifeblood to Jacca's limbs and heart and brain. Though she admitted to neither dizziness nor headache, Galen suspected she had suffered a concussion from her hard fall on the frozen lake.

But upon the advice of Mother Labéht, who said the mental exercise would be good for the girl's faculties, Galen permitted her an hour of daily lessons with Dalton. The weather-mage could only describe, not demonstrate the spellcraft, but still Jacca caught on quickly. Soon she progressed from hot rain to cool drizzle, and squealed with delight when she produced her first ephemeral snowflakes.

Wolfram was never far from the girl. Labéht cautioned him to protect the side of his body where she had stitched up the long, bloody tear that Wolfe had sustained in his frantic dash through broken rocks to reach Jacca on the ice. In his zeal, however, to impress his soon-to-be father-in-law, the young man ignored the healer's advice. Galen, still hobbled by his wrenched ankle, could only cast dark looks at the rim-wall and grumble that *somebody* needed to go out to the filled notch and make sure the *savitar* was really gone.

"All of you will head home after this," Galen said, frowning at his brothers and at Nina. "It won't be *your* lands that burn to cinders if the gates of *farsinchia* are again breached."

"For you, brother, we would always come back," Dalton replied, his manner irksomely unconcerned. "Besides, the Ore Hills will have its own snowmaker by the time I've finished teaching Jacca everything I know about 'frosty magic'." The weather-mage smiled at his niece. "The next time a firedrake dares to raise its ugly head in these parched mountains of yours, my protégé will freeze it solid."

Careful with the conceit, Dalton, Nina thought, scowling at him. *Overconfident wizards get their comeuppance.*

If the *savitar* came again, Jacca would be spirited out of harm's way as quickly as Galen could manage it, with Nina flinging Wolfram to safety on the girl's heels. And then she'd go down on her knees to beseech Grog to return with the firedrake's "shepherds." Labéht had said that only the stone-folk could subdue the monster, and recent events had borne out the evident truth of the Elder's words.

Whatever your brothers may do, Galen ... wherever they may choose to go when we get down from this mountain, Nina thought but did not say, *your big sister is sticking around.*

Dalton's brash remark had only hardened her resolve to remain on this side of the void. If there was to be any reappearance of the *savitar*, Nina needed to stay close to raise walls of water and make a fireproof escape corridor for the whole of the local population.

Besides, she mused as she glanced at the peaks that soared above their trailside camp, if she stayed in this land, she might yet enjoy a reunion with Grog. Was the giant up there somewhere? Would the king come if she requested an audience with him?

Preoccupied, Nina barely heard Wolfram's quiet aside to Galen, that he would do as the fire-mage wished and venture out upon the rim-rock, to search for any sign that their adversary might be able to resurface. She didn't notice when Wolfram slipped away into the cover of the trees. But a moment later, a howl of pain caught the attention of all within earshot, including Labéht.

"The young fool has ripped out his stitches. I *told* him not to shift until he'd healed." Muttering spicy profanities, the Old One gathered her needle and thread—and her spells of magical mending—and went to remedy the tear in the shapeshifter's wolfish hide. Jacca had already raced into the trees to find and comfort her beloved.

Galen watched the women go. Absently he scratched his ear, then turned to regard his remaining companions. His gaze lit upon Dalton, and his eyes narrowed.

"You're up," Galen said, peevishly insistent. "Go take a look and tell me how the land lies."

"Uh-uh." Dalton shook his head. "That rock is too loose and tricky for anything but a mountain goat. I'm not risking my neck."

Legary cut in. "I'll do it."

"You can't walk!" exclaimed his siblings, the three speaking with one voice.

"I *can* walk, if Dalton will find me a stick," Legary protested, as stubborn as Galen. "While I'm about it, I'll lay stepping-stones. And then all of you malingerers can stroll the rim in ease and comfort, when you finally decide to get off your butts."

There was truth in Legary's faultfinding, Nina had to concede, silently, as she watched Dalton snap a limb from a dead tree and fashion a crude crutch for his little brother. He got Legary up on his feet and supported him as the two worked their way slowly through the rubble atop the rim.

As they went, the stonecrafter magicked flat rocks into place. With seemingly no effort beyond two raised fingers, Legary levitated small stone slabs and laid them down in a solid, curving path all the way out to the notch that he had earlier sealed and brought nearly level with the surrounding brim of the mountain basin. Unlike his siblings, Legary's powers had not been exhausted by the battle with the *savitar*. He'd spent more time getting knocked around than working magic. The ease of his spellcraft hinted of great powers barely tapped. Nina smiled as she remembered the stories she'd heard, years ago, of Legary's prodigious feats of wizardry, his bespelling of bedrock throughout the southland from Granger to the coastal plains.

When he and Dalton were well out on the rim, no longer within ear-shot of their camp, Nina rose from her blankets and limped over to sit with Galen. As Legary had seemed to suspect, she was reasonably able to get around on her bruised hip. These last days, however, Nina had enjoyed her status as a patient under Labéht's care. It was a rare cir-cumstance, to find herself accepting the healing arts instead of dispensing them. She wondered if Galen, too, might not be favoring his injured ankle more than was strictly necessary.

"What's wrong, brother?" she asked him. "Are you in much pain? You seem out of sorts with everyone, even those who go out of their way to please you." Nina gestured at the two men who were now barely visible where they'd gone to inspect the former site of the tumor, or egg, or whatever it was that had hatched a mythical monster. "First Wolfram hurts himself, he's so eager to do your bidding, and now you've got Legary putting weight on a hip that he should be resting."

Galen sighed, and rubbed the back of his neck. "I guess because I'm miserable, I want everyone else to be, too," he muttered.

Nina fixed her gaze upon him, concerned as well as surprised. "Mis-erable, Galen? You should be rejoicing. The *savitar* is gone, the valley isn't burning, and all of us are alive. I don't mind telling you that I feared for your daughter when Jacca came off the ice. She was so cold,

I wasn't certain she would survive. It seemed the spark was gone out of her, that she'd lost the raging inferno of the fire-magic that I had seen within her when she was a child." Nina laid her hand on Galen's arm. "With your powers, you saved Jacca. Why are you not celebrating?"

Galen picked up a small stone and threw it at the banked campfire. Sparks scattered in all directions.

"I should never have allowed Jacca to come up here," he said, his tone vehement. "I should have sent her home the instant I discovered her presence, back down the trail. Instead, I placed the girl in danger and nearly got her killed." Galen huffed, a sound of self-disgust. "I've been slow to see my duty, but I know it now: I'm sending her north to Vivienne. Jacca will complete her apprenticeship in Ruain, far from these mountains and the terrors they spawn."

Jacca, under Vivienne's care?

Such an arrangement would not suit Nina's plans. She had it all worked out: She'd stay in the hills for the girl's marriage to Wolfram, midwife the couple's first child, and give them whatever help they needed, whether that be tending the newborn or summoning a tidal wave against a dragon.

"But I—" Nina began her protest. Galen cut her off, talking over her.

"Jacca is outgrowing me," he said. "I've watched her work with Dalton, I've seen how fast she is to learn new magic. It's been the same with her cousins up past the crossroads. Every summer she spends with them, Jacca comes home knowing spellcraft that I have never mastered. She needs a more accomplished teacher than I am. Fire is my element, and it's really the only thing I know. But I can't teach Jacca anything about fire that she doesn't already understand, instinctively." Galen ran his hands down his face. "She needs to study with Vivienne. You're water, I'm fire, and those two"—he gestured at Dalton and Legary—"are wind, weather, and stone. But Vivie does it all. Jacca has the potential to become one of the greatest *wysards* to ever walk this world. But she'll be stunted if she stays here. She must go to Ruain."

Nina became aware that her mouth was open, her tongue ready with arguments for keeping Jacca in the hills and entrusting the girl's further studies to herself and to Labéht. Galen had an Old One on his doorstep, after all. Who better to tutor Jacca in advanced spellcraft than an Elder whose knowledge of the *art magick* stretched back centuries?

Instead of arguing, however, Nina found herself agreeing.

"I don't know Vivienne as well as I would like," she said, her thoughts running back over her brief visits at home with Vivie and their parents. "But I'm told she is an excellent teacher. All those years she spent in the western mountains, training novice *wysards*, she gained a reputation that is admired to this day. When I visited our relatives beyond the crossroads, I met an Elder there who knew Vivienne from when she taught school at the foot of the mountains. He esteemed her greatly and complimented her manifold magian abilities. He said her mastery rivals that of the Ancients."

As she spoke, Nina experienced an unaccustomed emotion. For the first time in her life, she felt envious of her baby sister's multifaceted talents. Vivie was clearly best qualified to train a powerful young novice—far better suited to the job than either Galen or Nina. Galen could not do better than to send his remarkable daughter to Ruain, to learn from the gifted *wysard* who would someday succeed Lord Verek as the head of their ancient House.

"I'm sure our father will also take an interest in Jacca's schooling," Nina added, ruthlessly suppressing the unwanted and unpleasant wave of envy. "He'll be intrigued, to meet a granddaughter whose power of fire may exceed his own. And certainly he'll become the girl's weapons master, as he did with us." Nina laid a hand on the hilt of the knife at her belt. On her previous visit to the south country, she'd often called upon her skill with blade and bow. Such weapons, however, would not have served against the *savitar*. A sorcerous foe demanded a magian defense. But in a world where every man went armed, every independent young woman also needed to know how to handle weapons.

"I should already have sent Jacca north," Galen said, and in his words Nina heard both his regret and his resolve. "Our parents have asked me, more than once, to pack her off to Ruain and let them keep her for at least a year. They want her to soak up the magic of the place and to study in its great library, same as you and I did. I've been selfish, keeping her here on the edge of a wasteland. No more. She goes north as soon as we get off this mountain."

"Whoa!" Nina exclaimed. "I believe you're forgetting that your daughter is a strong-willed young woman who has a mind of her own. If you don't want her to dig in her heels, don't be giving her orders." Nina tilted her head, gazing shrewdly at her brother. "And unless you mean to personally escort Jacca to Ruain, then I suppose she'll make the journey accompanied by Wolfram. I can't imagine any circumstance, in fact—with or without you—in which Jacca would agree to be parted from the man she loves. That being the case, you best get the magistrate in, to see them properly wed before you send her off with Wolfe." Nina smiled at the expression on Galen's face. Pretending sympathy while she needled him, she added, "The wedding need not be large or elaborate. It can be a private family affair since we have Jacca's uncles here to stand up with Wolfram, while Labéht and I attend the bride."

"You've got it all worked out, don't you," Galen grumbled. "Given this some thought, haven't you."

Nina's grin widened. "A lot of thought. I've even been planning for the birth of Jacca's first child." Her smile faded as she added, "But Jacca will be in Ruain when that baby comes … and who knows where I'll be? Back across the void, perhaps."

Galen seemed poised to offer a testy reply, but he left his thoughts unspoken as Wolfram came limping back to their campsite. The young man's face was pinched with pain. His shirt was off and his chest wrapped in many thicknesses of linen bandage. The wrappings hid the ragged tear down his side. But below the white linen, blood darkened the waistband of Wolfe's trousers, evidence of the damage he'd done to himself when he foolishly tried to shift to his four-footed form while stitches held his human flesh together.

Nina pushed herself upright, intending to go to him. But he already had all the help he needed, with Labéht supporting him on one side, and Jacca on the other. Nina nodded approval as Galen heaved a remorseful sigh and held out his arm to the young man, inviting Wolfram to settle next to him.

She moved out of the way so Jacca could take her place at Galen's other elbow. On her way back around the campfire, Nina stirred up the embers and threw on a branch of desert-dry brushwood. The sun was westering toward the mountains, and it was time she got off her butt, as Legary had suggested. Mother Labéht had not seemed to mind having the care of half-a-dozen infirm *wysards*. The Old One had busied around their camp for days, passing out painkillers and preparing meals. This evening, however, Nina would do the cooking. Moving gingerly on her sore hip, she sorted through their dwindling supplies and came up with the makings of frybread to serve with the usual beans and tubers.

While she worked, Legary hobbled into camp, leaning heavily on Dalton's shoulder. The stonemason was too winded to speak, so it fell to the weather-mage to deliver their report. With his bright eyes looking out from a wind-burned, sun-bronzed face, Dalton gave an impression of breezy good humor, and Nina knew him to be slow to rile. He'd never snapped at her, even when she'd given him good cause to do so. Now, however, Dalton leveled a stern gaze at his brother Galen, and he spoke with a decided note of exasperation. His tone made it clear that he blamed Galen for inflicting unnecessary and painful wear and tear on Legary's nearly dislocated hip joint.

"You may cease your fretting, and stop pestering us all about that thrice-damned firedrake," Dalton said, biting off his words in a manner that recalled his sire, the famously short-tempered Theil Verek. "The creature left no trace." Dalton jerked his thumb to indicate the site of the burst tumor. "The borehole that swallowed the thing has disappeared entirely. Nothing can be seen at that spot except a plug of what appears to be solid granite. Your giant friend—'Grog,' as you call him, although I doubt that's the name his mother gave him—but regardless, your colossal friend has done a thorough job of sealing the monster in a bedrock tomb. In all good conscience, therefore, I will board my ship in a few days and sail home without a moment's worry that I have left my hillfolk brother to the mercy of a hellfire demon."

"A few days? You cannot leave so soon!" cried Jacca, who had pried herself from Wolfram and come to help Nina fix supper for seven. "Please, dear uncle. You must stay and teach me frost."

At this, Dalton's expression lost its severity. He smiled with his usual amiability, but shook his head. "I don't think there's much more I can show you, my splendidly gifted niece. You've made snowflakes already. With a little more practice, you'll have ice."

"Don't be troubled, Jacca," Nina chimed in, speaking to the girl but loudly enough that all would hear. "We'll keep your uncles hill-bound until Legary is back on his feet—without the aid of a crutch or a strong shoulder—and while Captain Dalton regains the use of his powers. He can't go sailing the Southern Seas, or all the way up the coast to Ruain, without his weather-magic at his fingertips."

"That's right!" Jacca exclaimed. With her arms outflung as if to embrace joy, she whirled in a graceful pirouette. "Both *must* stay until they're healed."

"There's sense in that, I suppose," Dalton replied, giving Nina a nod of acquiescence. "We might hit a storm on the way back, and I'll need to calm it down. Bad enough that Legary fell off a mountain and skinned his knee. I wouldn't want him seasick, too."

"I concur," the stonemason said. Having finally caught his breath, Legary tried to smile, but he winced with pain as he squeezed his aching, overworked hip. "Once I'm back in whatever you people call civilization here in this Drisha-forsaken corner of the world, I'm going to want a hot soak and several nights in a soft bed ... along with all the painkillers that you wisewomen will give me."

"You'll get plenty, brother," Nina promised him. "There's a good strong deadener that will get you down this mountain comfortably enough on horseback, if we double your dose. We just have to be careful not to stop your heart."

As she turned to Labéht to consult the herbalist on weights and measures for the mixture, Nina couldn't help thinking ahead to Jacca's wedding, which must be organized as soon as they were back in the hills with everyone recuperating. She shot a grin at the two brothers from the east, who as yet had no idea of the roles they were to play.

Legary looked faintly distressed now—alarmed, no doubt, by the suggestion that his quest for pain relief might end in a fatal overdose. Nina gave him a wink, which did nothing to assuage the stonemason's concerns. But she ended the day happy with her plans to include Dalton and Legary in their niece's imminent wedding. Though it might fall to Jacca's aunt Vivienne to midwife the newlywed's first child into the world, Nina would have the pleasure of seeing the young woman married to the man who was her perfect match.

But then where do I go? wondered a restless corner of Nina's mind. *Back to the granny hut?*

With a hard shake of her head, Nina quelled the thought, for it did not bear thinking about. In any event, it was a question for another day. She pushed it aside and returned to stirring the pot of beans and tubers, while visions of a wedding feast danced before her mind's eye.

Chapter Twenty-One

On the day they left the mountain, Nina was out of her blankets in the predawn. She moved freely on her bruised hip now, thanks to Mother Labéht's strong wintergreen liniment and a miniscule dose of the powerful painkiller the herbalist had prescribed for Legary.

With a witchlight orb to illuminate the path, Nina walked the perimeter of the rim-wall. The lip of the mountain basin was no longer treacherous underfoot. With his stonecraft, Legary had laid a broad walkway of rock slabs, flat and level. Nina followed the stepping-stones out to the notch the mason had plugged only moments before the *savitar* first thrust its talons out of a bulge in the pit-wall. She shuddered to think what would have happened if Legary had been standing on the rim when the creature's head came through that same protuberance. For all the strength of his wall-building magic, she doubted he would have survived the encounter.

The bulge—the tumor—was no more to be seen. The inner slope of the rim-wall dropped toward the floor of the basin in a series of smooth stone ripples, looking like ocean swells that had hardened to rock.

In the growing light of dawn, Nina extinguished her orb of Ercil's fire and sat on the rim, gazing into a lake of crystalline clarity. All of Dalton's conjured ice had long since melted in the heat of the desert summer. There was now no steam or mist or hovering curtain of rain, no such trace of the elemental battle that had been fought between fire and ice, pitting hell's heat against magical cold. Nothing now blocked Nina's view down through the pristine lake of her endless conjured waves. In her struggle against the *savitar*, she had summoned enough water to fill the mountain basin nearly to its brim.

Beneath the cold, clear lake lay a black crust of hardened lava. All of the heat had gone out of the once molten rock, and all of its fiery color. No red or orange or yellow flickered in the drowned mass. But where fire had once seethed, gemstones now gleamed, embedded in glassy ripples of obsidian black. Forged by magic, created in the collision of primordial forces, a treasure of diamonds, opals, emeralds, and ice-blue sapphires blazed from the depths.

The first rays of the rising sun picked out hints of green, not only from the emeralds that studded the lakebed, but also upon the upper slopes of the basin, where the mountainside had once been dotted with pine trees and cedars—trees that had burned and charred in the intense heat belched out by the formerly bubbling lava. Seedlings were springing up on the denuded slopes, bringing a promise of renewal to a landscape that supernatural fire had devastated.

"Hard to believe it's the same place," commented someone approaching along the rim-top trail. "When you flood the mouth of hell, Nina, you do it beautifully."

She looked over her shoulder to see Galen drawing near. He walked with a slight limp still, but Mother Labéht's remedies had put his ankle mostly to rights.

"Am I correct in thinking that this is now the biggest lake anywhere near the Ore Hills?" Nina asked, a sweep of her arm indicating the crystal-clear expanse. "I don't know how long it will last in the heat of your desert sun. But your neighbors need to hear of this extraordinary place. It's worth the climb to get a firsthand look."

"They'll hear of it," Galen said, "and they'll come in droves. Everyone west of the Rum Ridges will want to see where the *savitar* clawed its way out of the bowels of the world." Galen picked up a pebble from the loose rubble alongside the stepping-stone path. Idly he tossed it into the lake, sending ripples across the mirror-smooth surface. "Not everyone will believe the stories they hear," he added. "Six *wysards* battling a firedrake? Hands of stone enfolding the monster within the bosom of the mountain?" Galen laughed wryly. "I wouldn't believe it either, if I hadn't been here to see it. But the stories will spread, people will make their way to this lake, and the legend will grow with each telling." He gave Nina's shoulder a nudge. "Your name will be famous, sister."

"Why mine?" she demanded, surprised. "As you say, we are a company of six, and all fought as best we were able."

"But at the end of the battle, only the lake remains. People will marvel at the water-conjuring that created it. They will not think of what they cannot see—not the snow and ice, nor the magical rainstorms or thunderbolts that also fell upon this place. Those things will be forgotten."

Nina shook her head. "I believe Legary's stepping-stones must long outlast the water that I poured into this high bowl. Everyone who ventures up here will walk upon the stones as you and I have. But latecomers are likely to find only a deep, dry hole in the ground." She gestured at the morning sun, which was now high enough to hint of the glaring heat to come as it made the air shimmer, back along the rimrock toward their fast-disappearing camp. "Your arid southern summers will suck this lake dry."

"They'll lower it a little," Galen conceded as he reached to help Nina to her feet. "But we often get big snows in these mountains in wintertime. Meltwater will replace what the summer sun takes. I'm willing to bet you a good horse that in fifty years' time this lake of magic will be just as you see it now, only it'll have a green forest growing thick on the slopes above it."

Nina started to say that she could not match his wager because she did not own a horse, nor have the money to buy one. She'd arrived on Galen's doorstep with little more than the clothes she wore, and not a penny in her pocket. The horse Nina would ride today, down the South Trail to the valley, had only been lent to her. The animal belonged to Galen—or perhaps to the nomad, Corlis. Nina wasn't clear on whether

Galen had actually purchased the mare called Thorn, or he was really only looking after the animal until Corlis reclaimed it.

She'd not voiced any of this, however, before Galen was directing her attention to the bustle of activity that filled their former camp at the top of the trail. Wolfram and Dalton were bringing up all of the party's horses, along with Mother Labéht's sturdy mule. The Old One and Jacca were packing bags, gathering blankets, and lashing together cooking gear to tie onto various saddles. Legary braced against a rock, watching. He was so full of Labéht's painkillers that he wobbled when he walked, but he was walking—well enough, anyway, that the herbalist had deemed him fit to sit on a horse for today's departure down the mountain.

"I've got to figure out what I'm riding," Galen muttered as he walked with Nina back toward the others. "We're a horse short since that damned fool creature of mine threw me and disappeared." He snorted, a sound of disgust. "I suppose I'd better double up with Legary. He's not looking too steady."

"Jacca's big bobtail can carry you both, easy," Nina commented. "That horse has probably got the smoothest gait, anyway. Best for Legary's aches and pains."

Galen let out a sigh. "I've never been on that creature's back. Jacca's 'Bobby' is devoted to her, and she to him. But if I'm ever going to make the ride, this is the time to do it. She'll take that horse to Ruain with her ... and maybe it'll be a long time before I see either of them again."

Nina heard the hollow sadness in Galen's voice. She stopped beside him, gently taking his arm when he paused to watch from a distance as Jacca saddled the horse with the long-accustomed ease of a rider who had built trust with her mount since childhood. Galen glanced up briefly, at the cloudless sky that overspread the mountains, and then returned his gaze to his strong, confident daughter.

"If I kept her here," he murmured, "Jacca could conjure rainstorms over these peaks every summer, and then you'd know, sister, that your lake would always be full to the brim."

Nina inclined her head. "Let's leave that job to the winter snows. I'd never want to shackle Jacca's magic in service to mine. Bigger and better things await that daughter of yours, Galen." She paused, then added, "I think you've known it for years ... ever since Jacca first came home from time spent with her cousins, knowing the magic that you never mastered—spellcraft that's beyond me as well, I'll freely admit."

Slowly, he nodded. His hand came up to rub the back of his neck as if he'd cricked it.

"It's just that I'll be so terribly lonely without her," he whispered.

* * *

Jacca did not get the private family wedding that Nina had proposed. The event could not be kept a secret, for as soon as the *wysards* were off the mountain and back in the Ore Hills, Nina went rushing around to every sort of shop and merchant, ordering food and table linens, candles and flowers, ribbons and rosewater. She spent Galen's money liberally, which soon had tongues wagging. As word got around that the goldsmith's fiery daughter was getting married to her long-time escort, Wolfram of the West, everyone for miles around expected an invitation. Rather than a small ceremony witnessed only by family, the event would be a grand celebration, a festival for the whole of the Hills and most of the valley. The people were in the mood to make merry now that their roofs, barns, and haystacks were no longer going up in flames.

Jacca embraced her father and cried tears of happiness when informed that he had dropped his opposition to her union with Wolfram. He was now eager, in fact, that they be married immediately. She lost some of her joyful glow, however, when Galen explained the reason for the hastily arranged wedding.

"I will do as you ask, Father," Jacca said solemnly, taking Galen's hands in hers. "To study in Ruain is a great honor, and I am humbled by this chance you offer me, to complete my apprenticeship under the renowned teacher of magic, Lady Vivienne. I am awed to think that I shall meet her, and my noble grandparents as well. But you must come with us."

As Galen started to protest, Jacca rushed to add, "Ride with us at least as far as the land of my cousins. Every summer that I have spent with them, they have asked for news of you. You have not been to see them for a very long time, and they wish for a visit."

When this got a quiet nod of acquiescence from him, Jacca smiled and continued. "On our way to the mountain crossroads, we must of course call upon my mother and grandmother. I will wish to spend a few days with them, for I may not see them again for years if Aunt Vivienne holds me long in apprenticeship. I must say my good-byes."

At the prospect of reuniting, if only temporarily, with his old lover Taji, Galen brightened. "I shall certainly accompany you to the home of your mother," he said. "It is right and proper that you receive her blessing, not only mine, on your marriage."

"Good," commented Nina, who had stood listening to all of this. "Now that's settled, please get out of our way, Galen. We need nothing from you except your coin purse. Take your brothers and find somewhere to be while we scour the shops for satin and lace. We'll need musicians, too," Nina added in an aside to Jacca as she took the young woman by the hand and steered her briskly in the direction of the high street. "Who do you know that plays?"

* * *

Galen was only too glad to escape the bustle of wedding plans. He cleared out of his small cottage, leaving Nina to lodge with Jacca while he moved in with his brothers. For Legary's convalescence, Galen had rented a four-bedroom house on a back ridge of the Ore Hills, overlooking the river valley. When the bed rest, painkillers, and skin-scorching liniment prescribed by Mother Labéht had put the stonemason solidly on his feet, Galen took Legary and Dalton on a tour of the hills that he had called his home since he'd arrived here, so long ago, as a fourteen-year-old novice apprenticed to a master goldsmith.

A feature of the tour was the mineshaft where Galen had discovered a seam of bedrock that ran beneath the desert sands all the way to Legary's home in the grasslands. He had devised a means of tapping out messages that juddered through the rock and arrived in intelligible form, often shaking the foundations of Legary's cellars when Galen wished to communicate with him. When the three brothers went down the mineshaft—joined somewhat warily by Wolfram, who'd come along at Galen's firm invitation—Legary managed to get a message to his wife, Willow, who anxiously awaited the stonemason's return to their home in Granger.

"Soon," Legary assured her. "Right after I stand up with a wolf at his wedding." He drew Wolfram to him and gave the young man a hard clap on the back.

"You'll have to explain that, when you get home," Dalton muttered as the connection was lost and the four men began the long climb back to the surface.

Rambling onward, over the hills and across the river, the brothers caught up with each other's lives and got to know one another as they never had before. Dalton had not seen Galen since the goldsmith's last visit home to Ruain, which was many years ago when Dalton was newly appointed as the chief steward of that remote province. The captain occasionally met Legary on business at the deep-water port in Seawood, but before their swift voyage around the southern coast, they had not spent much time together.

Not as adults, anyway. When baby brother Legary had been still a boy, he had worked under Dalton's supervision, lending his stonecraft to the building of seaports on Ruain's eastern shoreline. As soon as he came of age, however, Legary had sailed south and settled in the farming village of Granger. He had never returned to Ruain afterward, not for even a brief visit.

Always impressed by Legary's magian gift for wrangling enormous rocks, Dalton now showered the mason with compliments for his spellcraft on the mountain, how he'd prevented the collapse of the front slope and thereby saved the lives of both Dalton and Nina. The two of them would have been borne down to their deaths if the rimwall had given way.

This talk led naturally to the rockslide that had weakened the slope before Dalton and Legary arrived on the scene. Before he knew it, the stonemason was back up the South Trail, not all the way to the top, but far enough to view the shattered remains of the sheared-off pilgrimage path. When Dalton expressed the opinion that little brother Legary could easily rebuild the hallowed skyway, Galen responded with skeptical disbelief.

That was all it took for Legary to throw himself into the task. While his brothers watched from a prudent distance, the stonecrafter swept aside rubble as if it were house dust, and then began to raise and hang slabs of solid rock. Laboring under the hot sun, Legary was soon sweating. But he didn't let Galen call him back to the shade beneath the trees until a wide stone ledge was projecting from the mountainside, expertly restored for almost a mile, back toward the rock chimney where Nina's vertical waterflood had smashed a gaping chunk out of the Sky Trail.

"You can work on it more tomorrow!" Galen exclaimed as he poured water over Legary's sunburned ears and neck. "You've convinced me you can do it. But not in a single afternoon."

The reconstruction so absorbed Legary's attention, and that of his brothers who kept him company day by day, Nina was obliged to send Wolfram up the trail to fetch them all down, only hours before the young man's marriage to Jacca. When the four men of the wedding party were all back in the rented house on the hilltop, Nina ordered them to scrub off the dirt and sweat, wash their hair and trim their beards, and otherwise make themselves presentable for the grand occasion. From her temporary post in the hallway outside the tub room, she directed maids and attendants to deliver soap and razors and well-starched clothes to the mildly grumbling men within.

Assured that they would be ready on time, Nina raced down the hill to help Jacca dress in a gorgeous gown of flame red. Its flowing lines accentuated the girl's graceful movements, and the color brought out the copper highlights in her hair like embers glowing against a rippling sheet of bronze. As befitted the daughter of a master goldsmith, Jacca wore a fortune in precious metals and gems. At her throat was a sunburst on a jeweled collar magnificently crafted of gleaming gold and red diamonds. Adorning her bare arms were all the bangles and bracelets that would fit. Among the silver, gold, and copper creations of her magically artistic father was the bracelet that Galen had gifted to Jacca when she was just a little girl, a seemingly ordinary child passed off by Maynor and his wife Taji as their legitimate daughter.

Nina doubted that anyone in the Ore Hills had believed the pretense. But whatever rumor had circulated behind closed doors, the people of the hills had chosen to play along, until Galen upset the applecart by publicly acknowledging Jacca as his out-of-wedlock child. Even then, the scandal might have been short-lived, if Maynor had salved his injured manhood in private. Over the last seven years, however, the cuckold had passed up no opportunity to vilify Galen and pillory Jacca.

All of that was now forgotten, left in the past by grateful townsfolk and valley dwellers. When Nina took her place in the wedding party as the bride's matron of honor, she spent a moment looking out over the great crowd that had gathered on the hillside to witness the nuptials. All of the shopkeepers and artisans were there, every merchant or maker with whom Nina had dealt in liberal fashion, spending Galen's wealth with no word of complaint from the goldsmith. Gathered at the edges of the crowd were valley farmers and smallholders, the people who owed the safety of their homesteads to Jacca's conjured rains and to the spellcraft of her wizardly family who stood with her and Wolfram before the magistrate.

The ceremony went off without a hitch, although Jacca had a hard time standing still. Even when the musicians paused to let the magistrate get on with things, the girl wanted to dance, and the grin never left her face. Nina detected no trace of wedding jitters in the young woman's voice when she rattled off her vows to love, cherish, and honor.

Indeed, only the magistrate seemed nervous. He did a lot of throat-clearing, and he kept glancing at Jacca's uncles, the pale-haired sea captain who bent the weather to his will, and the deep-voiced stonemason whose legendary status in the south country had grown with every new mile of Sky Trail that Legary restored. Like all dwellers in the Ore Hills, the magistrate was accustomed to *wysards* passing through, coming and going from secluded abodes in the western mountains. But it was fair to say the man had never before been face-to-face with so many members of a powerful magian dynasty. As soon as the ceremony concluded, the magistrate beelined to the beer keg and drew himself a tankard, full and frothy to the brim.

Not far from the keg skulked Maynor, dressed to the nines in a high-collared shirt and tight-fitting britches that showed his paunch. He had not been invited to his former stepdaughter's wedding, but he'd come anyway, to eat and drink free food and ale. He lurked off to the side, scowling, ignored by everyone except Warthog, who somehow managed to dump an entire platter of fried potatoes down Maynor's back, raising blisters, the spuds were so hot.

Late into the evening and through the night, the celebrations continued, filling the hills with music and merrymaking until the first hint of dawn. Nina remarked the early absence of the newlyweds. They'd lingered only long enough to receive the congratulations of the well-wishers who had been at the very front of the throng. Throughout the ceremony, Wolfram was hard put to keep his hands off his dancing bride. With law and custom satisfied, he wasted no time whisking Jacca away, but not to the splendid suite of rooms that Galen had retained for the couple in the finest travelers' inn on the high street. Wolfram and Jacca preferred instead the deep shadows of the pine groves on the highest moonlit ridge of the Ore Hills.

Deep in the night, after Nina had retired alone to her borrowed cottage, a gentle wind ruffled the curtains in her attic bedroom. Carried upon the breeze was the exultant howl of a satisfied wolf.

Nina smiled. She rolled over on her side, wincing as she landed on her bum hip. She'd been on her feet all day and had reaggravated her injury from slipping on the ice of "Fire Lake," as the locals had already dubbed the flooded lava-pit in the mountains. But as soon as her eyes closed, Nina was asleep.

Chapter Twenty-Two

In the early dawn four days later, Nina made her way up to the spring-fed pool on the hillside above the lodge that Galen had once shared with his mortal wife Sheyla. That woman had left the hills. The local gossips claimed Sheyla had run off with the itinerant bricklayer she'd hired to raise the height of the already imposing stone wall around her back garden. If that were so, Nina suspected the haughty, embittered woman would be left destitute. The bricklayer would no doubt end up with all the gold that Galen had showered upon Sheyla during the many years of what had been a happy marriage, until the woman learned of Galen's affair with Taji.

As Nina passed the property's securely locked back gate, she noted that the grounds were well kept and the house appeared to be in good order, from what was visible of it through close-set iron bars. Galen was keeping the lodge maintained, she surmised. If Sheyla grew disenchanted with her bricklayer, the woman would have a home to return to. Galen would never abandon his old sweetheart entirely, however much he might prefer to win back the affections of his one-time lover Taji.

Nina wished him well in his current attempt to do so. As he had promised, Galen was riding with Jacca and Wolfram on the first leg of their journey to Ruain. They were heading north up the valley to call on Taji and her mother at the old lady's home on the flanks of the mountains. Nina had noted the sparkle in Galen's eye at the prospect of being with Taji. Though he might be sleeping in the stable while the newlyweds got the only spare bed in the old woman's cottage, still he would be near the woman who had given him the gift of an extraordinary daughter. With romance filling the air around the passionate young couple, Nina had urged Galen to open his heart to Taji and profess the love he had felt for the hillwoman, for the better part of two decades.

Galen and the young people had been gone a day now. Nina had seen them off yesterday morning, declining their invitation to accompany them. She needed to stay in the hills and supervise Legary and Dalton, or so she had said, making her younger brothers her reason for staying behind. Legary had nearly finished rebuilding the Sky Trail, and the devout pilgrims among the local folk were planning a grand celebration to mark the cross-mountain walkway's reopening.

Many of them had already made the steep climb up the more southerly trail, the bridleway that led directly to Fire Lake. As Nina had predicted, every visitor marveled at the beautifully laid stepping-stones which curved along the top of the formerly precarious, knife-edged rim. But Galen knew his people: he'd been correct that their deeper admiration would be for the expanse of water so crystal clear that the lake bottom of begemmed black rock appeared near enough to touch, its every ripple and fold distinct and discernible from the rim-top. In a desert landscape, such a great quantity of pure, fresh water could only be deemed a miracle. The lake was proclaimed sacred. From now on, the pilgrimage path would not end where it met the South Trail. Ever afterward, those who crossed the face of the mountain would also climb to the lake, and there they would raise their voices in gratitude for the mountain snows and occasional rainstorms that fed the river in the valley and made life possible in these hills on the edge of sun-blasted badlands.

Nina waved Galen off on his journey, therefore, with the claim that she must keep an eye on Legary to be sure he didn't fall off the mountain while he finished the final miles of the skyway's restoration. She hinted, also, that she might sail east with the stonemason and Captain

Dalton as soon as the work was complete and Legary had taken his bow as guest of honor at the forthcoming reopening.

In truth, however, Nina had no idea what to do next, or where to go. Returning to the granny flat was a deeply unattractive prospect. And the more she contemplated that path, the more ill-advised it seemed. What damage would repeated trips through the void do to her memory? She knew from her mother's experience that traveling the void could disorder the traveler's mind. Lady Carin had needed decades to surmount the feeling that she'd become unstuck in time. Carin had lost some memories entirely, and others had drifted piecemeal, requiring years of effort to stitch together into a coherent mental picture of the lady's life.

Nina suspected her own memories had been similarly disturbed. The longer she remained in her native world, the hazier her recollections of Earth, and the more tenuous her connection to that place. Her life in the islands felt increasingly distant, as if her time there was only a half-remembered dream.

And might the fading of memory work both ways? The people of the archipelago had once regarded Nina as an almost mythical figure, a goddess of water and the sea straight out of traditional island belief. But now the people seemed hardly to see her when she moved among them. She'd become insignificant in that world, and all but invisible.

So be it, then. Earth was off the list.

But the thought of going home to Ruain held little appeal either. What would she do there? Dalton had his work as chief steward of the province, and Vivienne was occupied with the day-to-day affairs of the realm that would one day be hers to rule. Their father Lord Verek had increasingly withdrawn from active oversight of his lands and sovereignties. He had taught Vivienne well, and now he was free to enjoy a life of leisure, wrapped in the love of his devoted and revered wife, Carin.

Nina supposed she could keep to her original plan, and offer herself as governess to Jacca's children-to-come. But such a role would have her living in her childhood home as little more than a dependent on her baby sister.

Similar difficulties would arise if she sailed with Dalton and Legary. She could return east with the stonemason to his huge house in Granger. Drisha knew, he and Willow had plenty of room to take in a wandering widow who was, at present, homeless and penniless. Nina had made her own way in the world far too long, however, to be comfortable living on the charity of any of her siblings.

She mused on all of this as she reached the hot spring in the hillside, and sat on a rock to pull off her boots and stockings. Idly, not paying attention to what she was doing, she brought her long raven braid over one shoulder and undid the scrap of fabric that tied it. As she rested at the edge of the spring, staring into the water and mulling her options, Nina absentmindedly swished the ribbon through the water. The ripples this produced helped to focus her thinking, but she had not yet reached a decision about her future when a rustling off to the side made her turn her head and look.

She expected a rabbit nosing through the undergrowth. Or perhaps a bird that had winged down from a pine tree to search out a tasty morsel in the carpet of shed needles.

But no: What appeared at Nina's side was a boulder—a huge boulder that had not been there when she sat down. It was smooth, bald and unweathered, and almost perfectly round. Large blue eyes looked out with a liquid sheen from an otherwise featureless face.

"Grog!" she cried.

Nina's first impulse was to jump up and hug the giant. But he presented no waist or neck that she could get her arms around, only an enormous head that had materialized out of solid rock with no more noise or upset than a rabbit foraging for fresh green twigs. Nina contented herself, therefore, with flattening her hands below Grog's clear blue eyes and leaning her weight against what would have been his cheekbones, if he'd had the usual complement of facial structures.

"How you have changed, my friend," Nina murmured as she drew back and settled on the ground facing the boulder. "Can you no longer speak?" She touched her lips, then stroked her fingers across the boulder where Grog lacked a mouth. "I suppose it doesn't matter. When we traveled the plains together, you didn't say much anyway, beyond an occasional grunt." Nina leaned close to finger a stony ridge on the side of Grog's head, a ridge that resembled the curved outer rim of a human ear. "But you heard and understood every word I said," she added as she traced the hard, glossy rim.

"That's fine, then." Nina lifted her fingers and leaned back. "I'll talk enough for two, since I have a great deal on my mind. If you get tired of listening, just rattle pebbles at me."

Grog's response was a lazy half-wink, a slow lowering of one stony eyelid. Nina smiled, and commenced.

First, she expressed thanks to the giant and his people for saving her and hers from the *savitar*. Nina described how she and Galen had been coaxed up the mountainside, how they'd been given a trail of hot sparks to follow until they reached the *savitar*'s lair in the cauldron of boiling lava. She repeated Labéht's speculations about the creature's motives.

"It seemed to be probing our defenses." Nina thought back over the looping, zigzag journey she had made from valley floor to mountain height. "In myself and my brothers, alas, the *savitar* uncovered a great many weaknesses," she admitted ruefully. "I could not drown the creature. Dalton couldn't freeze a firedrake. And Galen had to abstain from firebolts, for the power of his element was like hot fuel poured upon the flames of hell." Nina paused as she felt again the shock that had washed over her with the realization that, even working together in a way they never had before, she and her wizardly blood-kin could not overcome a primordial power of destruction.

"I'm glad," she went on, "that Legary was kept busy with you, Grog, shoring up the lower mountain. If he had been on the rim with the rest of us, he would have attempted to seal the *savitar* in a rocky tomb of his own magical devising. But Legary would have burned in the creature's fires before he had set the first stone of such a burial vault."

As she talked, Nina pictured each of her brothers in their desperate struggle against an invincible foe. It came to her then, that Galen would certainly continue on north with his daughter and Wolfram, all the way to Ruain. He would want to consult Lord Verek, whose knowledge of wizardly lore and craft surpassed his. From that elder master of fire, Galen might learn how to fight hellfire with magian flame, if the goldsmith's home in the hills was ever again menaced by an ancient terror. And of course, the legend that had come to life in the southwestern mountains must be recorded at first hand in the *Book of Archamon*, the magical tome in the library at Weyrrock in which every significant event in the long history of Ladrehdinian wizardry had been written.

"It may be," Nina mused as her thoughts turned to the three riders who were even then wending their way northward, "… it may be that my niece Jacca will someday have the skills to prevail against a winged terror from the underworld. She is a gifted young adept, and she goes now to feed the flames of her knowledge. But Jacca is not yet ready for such a test." Nina met the clear blue gaze of Grog's great eyes. "I will ask you, therefore, to set a watch upon the realms that you rule, my king of the down-below." She pressed her hands together and nodded respect to him. "Remember your friends who walk in sunlight and place us under your protection, for all the people of this world must be counted your subjects, my lord."

As she looked into Grog's eyes, Nina saw a deep awareness—such an intellect of mind as had been wholly absent from the red gaze of the *savitar*. She'd detected nothing in that creature's glare except rage and bloodlust. And yet, both she and Galen had sensed an intelligence which had taunted them on the mountain slopes, like a wily adversary goading them just enough to keep them in the hunt for an "arsonist."

She wondered: Were the sparks, the firebirds—even the *savitar* itself—only the visible, aboveground manifestations of something too dark, deep, and secret to ever be seen in the light of the upper world? Nina recalled an old conversation with Nimrod the merchant, when she had scoffed at the notion that Grog might battle demons in the down-below. Now, she suspected that was exactly what he did.

On impulse, Nina got to her feet and bowed to Grog. He accepted her obeisance with a majestically slow blink of both huge eyes, leaving her momentarily silenced by a feeling of awe when she realized she could not see over the top of Grog's bald head. Were he to rise out of the hillside to his full height, Nina would not stand taller than his shinbone—assuming that he still bothered to adopt the semblance of a bony internal skeleton when he was, in fact, made of stone.

She guessed that the giant and his people might be easy and instinctive shapeshifters when young, but they hardened into granitic figures as they got older. During her time with Grog on the grasslands, Nina had heard him described as a great bull and a towering tree. To her, he had been like a whale, a leviathan of the deep. At Granger, Legary had seen him as a gigantic salamander, and Nina had also glimpsed the mudpuppy when she swam with Grog in a magical desert lake. But now her friend seemed literally set in stone, his head permanently a boulder atop shoulders that were as wide as the world itself.

"Ah, my dear colossus, I talk your ear off," Nina murmured as she settled back on the ground to resume their one-sided conversation. "But if I may impose upon your patience a little longer, there is the matter of my future."

She listed off her options, adding a new idea to her earlier thoughts of going as a governess to Ruain or becoming Legary's permanent houseguest. She might instead stay in the Ore Hills and live in Galen's cottage while he betook himself north to deliver his account of the *savitar*'s hatching, and arrange for his daughter's further education in spellcraft.

"But I am a creature of water," she decided as she spoke. "I think it best that I return to the ocean, although not to my island world across the void. Rather, I will sail with Dalton to the Eastern Sea, and there seek a coastal town or fishing village that needs a skilled healer. A good wisewoman can always earn her keep, and I am disinclined to live upon the wealth of my very wealthy family."

Nina reached as she had before, to stroke the stony curve of the ear-like projection on Grog's head. Again he closed one eye in a dreamy half wink. Nina had the impression that he enjoyed her touch. All this time, she had held her hair ribbon laced through her fingers, and it had dried in the warmth of the summer morning. She held the ribbon up to Grog's view.

"I am never parted from this token of our friendship." Nina swept her hair over one shoulder and braided the strands that had come loose, retying the ends with the frayed scrap of fabric. Tattered as it was, the material still gleamed, changing color with every change of light. "This token will remind me always, my lord," Nina whispered, "that I owe you my life and the lives of my loved ones."

She stood and gave another low bow, taking her leave of the king from the stony deeps. Nina did not look up until a soft rustling in the undergrowth signaled the sinking of the huge boulder back into the buried bedrock. But as she straightened, she saw that Grog had not slipped entirely from view. A five-fingered hand, enormous and rock hard, thrust upward out of the ground ... and tied like a ring around the smallest finger was a strip of the same lustrous fabric that Nina wore in her hair, a scrap of the giant-sized tunic that she had once gifted to the infant Grog.

She wrapped the stony finger in a hug. Absent a waist or a neck that she could get her arms around, this pinnacle of rock would suffice. Nina laid her cheek against the cool, smooth stone, and then stepped back as the hand gently withdrew. It sank soundlessly into the hillside, the ring of fabric disappearing with it, down into the underworld.

Chapter Twenty-Three

Nina sat with Mother Labéht on the Elder's front porch. She'd come to say her good-byes, but she found herself speaking, instead, of Corlis. Labéht wanted every detail of the maggoty infestation that had afflicted the nomad in the desert seven years ago, when Nina preserved the man's life by cutting sandfly worms out of his swollen backside.

"I trust he has fully recovered?" Nina asked when she'd concluded her account of the remedies she had applied to draw out the poison. "Has he consulted you on the matter? I left him in good health, but I'd had no previous experience with pestilential desert sandflies, so perhaps he suffered aftereffects that I could not foresee."

Labéht shook her head. "The man is tough as the hills. He does occasionally call upon me when he rides in from the badlands or the wilds of the south. But he seeks mostly to buy produce from my garden, for he develops a craving for fresh greens after months of living on little more than beans and beef."

Nina smiled and rubbed her throat. "I remember those meals. I grew so desperate for something green that I fought my horse for a melon that Corlis conjured from the bare sands of those canyons." She stared into the middle distance, her gaze dreamy and drifting as she recalled the refreshing sweetness of the fruit that Corlis had lobbed her way even while he continued to pretend she wasn't there.

"Did you notice the three blue feathers that Jacca wore in her hair on her wedding day?" Nina asked, refocusing on the Elder. Labéht had attended the ceremony, but the Old One had mounted her mule and ridden away before Nina could offer her refreshment from the groaning tables of food and drink. "Corlis gave Jacca those feathers when the girl was just a child living an unhappy lie in the home of Taji and Maynor." A wistful sigh escaped Nina. "I'm sorry he wasn't here for the wedding. I would like Corlis to know that his gift to a lonely child has been cherished through the years. Jacca has not forgotten him ... nor have I," Nina couldn't help adding, her voice barely above a whisper.

"It's unfortunate that your brothers have made their plans to leave at dawn on their eastern sailing," Labéht commented in an offhand way, but with her gaze locked on Nina's face. "If you travel with them tomorrow as you intend, you will miss the return of Master Corlis by only a matter of hours."

"What?" Nina sat forward in her chair of woven willow. "He's on his way here? And so close already?" She stared at the Elder and perceived a glint of knowing amusement in the woman's eyes. "Begging your pardon, my lady," Nina ventured breathlessly as she fought to keep herself in her chair and not racing up the nearest hillside. She longed to climb the highest hill above Labéht's cottage in hopes of catching a glimpse of Corlis riding in. "I do not mean to misdoubt you, but how can you possibly know the hour of the nomad's return?"

Labéht waved her hand, a gesture of airy dismissal. The Old One was enjoying Nina's sudden fluster.

"Oh," she said in a careless tone, "we of the Power have our little ways of delivering tidings, one to another. Corlis generally lets me know when he's about a day out from the hills." With one raised finger, Labéht tapped her chin as she directed at Nina a look that was meaningful, almost conspiratorial. "Corlis is not a man much given to observing such civilities as are common in society at large. But he extends to me the courtesy of sending word from time to time ... as I would expect and indeed require from a grandson of mine."

Nina gaped. Silence filled the tree-shaded yard at the side of Labéht's cottage, the afternoon stillness broken only by the clucking of the Old One's busily contented hens. Nina tried to shape a question, but nothing in her swirling thoughts lent itself to words.

Labéht laughed, pleased with the effect she had produced. "Are you doing calculations in your head, lady of far waters? Does the elapse of time not tally as you would think it must?" She leaned from her chair and refilled the glass of purple-black sunberry juice that her guest held in a now nerveless hand. "Do not overtax your faculties," the Elder cautioned with a sympathetic smile, "in trying to number the years that not even I may trace with any certainty. When I say that Corlis is my grandson, I mean rather that he is my fourth or fifth or sixth great-grand ... something like that." The woman shrugged. "I cannot tell you exactly how many generations separate him from me, but I can assure you that he is my direct descendant." Labéht fixed Nina with a significant look as she added, "Though you be a daughter of an ancient house of wizardry, Corlis comes from a magian lineage that traces back nearly as far as your own."

Nina raised her forgotten glass and gulped the cool, mildly tart juice. When she'd got it down, she managed to splutter, "Water in the desert. That's how he finds it." She remembered the impression Corlis had made on her, their first night on the trail, when he guided her off the barren high desert and down into a ravine that, at the bottom of a steep descent, held a narrow pool. For a time that evening, she had been half inclined to ascribe supernatural powers to the nomad for locating water when there had been no visible sign to suggest its presence, clear to the sun-blasted horizon.

"I should have trusted my instincts," Nina murmured when she'd regained the power of coherent thought and speech. "No mortal could thread a way through that maze of canyons without getting hopelessly lost and dying of thirst, long before he reached the other side." She shook her head. "Why did I not realize what was so obvious, now that I look with opened eyes upon that journey?"

"Perhaps you saw what Corlis wished you to see," Labéht replied. "It pleases him to pretend that he has no trace of the Gift. His ego is flattered when all who know of his reputation believe that no one and nothing gets the credit beyond his own grit and wit, his unbending resolve to prevail against the dry bones of the desert." Labéht lifted her hands in a ritual gesture that Nina recognized as wordless praise and tribute to the Elementals who gifted the *wysards* of Ladrehdin with magical potency. Nina copied the gesture, and for a moment the two women sat in reverential silence as each privately acknowledged the debt they owed to the ever-bountiful Powers of Eternity.

"Corlis will change his tune, in time," the Old One continued when the moment passed and her hands came down, to reach again for the flagon of juice that waited on the porch in cool shade. "As the years go by, he'll be hard-pressed to explain why he does not age. Mind you," Labéht added as she leaned to refill Nina's glass a second time, "I do not say that Corlis will enjoy the near-immortality of a *wysard* like yourself ... you who are born of two prodigiously gifted parents. But he will live—and he will retain his manly vigor—for all the decades that it may take, I suspect, for you to tire of him ... if it be your wish, Lady Karenina, to join yourself to that nomad."

"More than anything," Nina breathed, and she knew the truth of her words before ever they passed her lips.

Labéht nodded. "Then remain here tonight. I have a spare bed for you. In the morning, let your brothers leave without you."

"They won't. They'll want to see me ... to say good-bye."

If, indeed, I have a reason to stay behind when they go, Nina brooded in silent apprehension. For she was well aware that seven years had passed for Corlis. Perhaps he had grown cold toward her. Perhaps she meant nothing to him now.

* * *

Nina slept poorly. She was up at first light, helping Labéht tend the woman's large gardens of vegetables and herbs. By noontime the summer heat had driven them back to the cottage to prepare a light meal of cold chicken and mixed greens. They ate on the shady porch, and after the few dishes were washed and put away, Labéht declared her intention to have a nap. The Old One retired indoors, leaving Nina to sit on the steps and maintain a restless vigil for the foretold coming of Corlis.

As the afternoon wore on, Nina succumbed to nervous fatigue. She stretched out on the porch and fell asleep. It seemed a dream, therefore, when a voice spoke three clear words in her head:

"He is here."

Nina sprang up, awake in a moment. Wildly she looked around, but saw neither Corlis nor Labéht. It had not been the Old One who had whispered those words into her ear. Who, then?

"Thorn," Nina breathed as she realized she had heard that voice before, sounding inside her head when the desert mare challenged the gelding, Traveller, in the streamside glade halfway up the South Trail. Yesterday evening, Nina had pastured the mare with Labéht's mule after accepting the Elder's invitation to stay the night in the tucked-away canyon.

Nina flew off the porch and around the corner. She raced for the tree-shaded paddock where she had left Thorn unsaddled and un-bridled, grazing peacefully.

She saw the white of the mare's coat, bright in the shadows under the trees ... and then through the leaves, Nina saw Corlis. He was standing with Thorn, his head bowed as if deep in thought.

Nina shouted the man's name.

Up came his head, and Corlis stepped away from the mare, out into the sun. He had taken time to wash before calling upon his great-grandame. At the end of Nina's journey with him through the badlands, Corlis had been shaggy-haired, mustachioed and bearded. Now he was clean-shaven, his sandy hair cropped short just as it had been when Nina first laid eyes on him in Granger. The man looked exactly the same as at their initial meeting, from the boots on his feet to the slouchy, buff-leather hat that hid his eyes.

Nina took all of this in as she sprinted toward him. At her foot-pounding approach, Corlis whipped off his hat and held it over his heart. He barely had time to clap the hat back on his head before Nina was up and over the paddock's top railing, launching herself into his arms.

This was not the "hello" she had planned. She'd meant to greet him courteously but with as much detached reserve as she could muster. In the kiss she gave him, however, there was no detachment, no restraint. She took his mouth as if starving for him. He tasted like fresh parsley, as though he'd chewed a few leaves on his way here.

Time lost all meaning as they clung together under the westering sun. Nothing existed except heat and the man's sinewy arms around her, and under Nina's hands the hard muscles of his back. She was tugging his shirt out of his waistband, threatening to rip the fabric in her eagerness, when Corlis eased out of a tongue-deep kiss and set Nina down on her feet.

Panic stabbed her. Did he not want her?

Panting, her breath coming short, Nina looked up into his face, searching his gaze. His gray-green eyes had often filled her dreams, especially the way they darkened at the peak of arousal. Nina's anguish fled as she looked into the man's eyes. They were such a charcoal gray, they showed black.

Corlis fingered a loose strand of Nina's hair. "Mount up, lady." His voice was husky, little more than a whisper. "Let's ride."

Nina did not bother saddling the mare, or even putting a bridle on Thorn. Corlis opened the paddock gate for the pair of them as she rode through, bareback. He sprang into the saddle of his own mount, a white horse of the same breed as the mare, and led the way into the shadowy canyon behind Labéht's cottage.

The land was not a dead-end pocket in the hillside, as it had appeared from the Old One's dwelling place. The narrow canyon continued for a distance southward, then opened into a wooded dell, well watered and green with more grass than Nina had seen anywhere in the Ore Hills except along the river.

"It's beautiful!" she exclaimed as she slid from Thorn's back.

She'd barely caught a glimpse of a rustic door set into the hillside before Corlis was lifting her in his arms and carrying her through that door. He laid her on a bed of scented rushes and soft furs.

Moans of the most exquisite pleasure escaped her as Nina opened herself to him, body and soul. Their coupling was even sweeter than she had remembered, rising to a rapture that no mortal could begin to know. They did not rest that evening or through the night, nor for much of the following morning. But in the forenoon, spent at last, they fell asleep, their bodies still joined.

* * *

After a sumptuous, early evening meal of grilled goat and baked sweetroot, Corlis gave Nina a tour of his homestead. He had enough pasturage for all of the horses and pack animals that he required in his work of guiding merchants through the desert and on as far east as Seawood at the coast. His abode was little more than a cave set into the hillside, but it was a pleasant cave with a wall of windows that looked out onto woods and glades. His kitchen was a separate structure, a stone-built room with an iron spit in a huge hearth. A surprising number of pots and pans hung on the walls. When he was at home, Corlis seemed able and willing to indulge in cookery that approached the lavish. A nearby store-shed, however, bulged with dried beans and jerked meat, his standard diet on the trail.

"Lady, you're the only person alive, other than Labéht, who knows where I live," Corlis said as they ended the tour back with the horses. He patted Thorn's neck, then pointed at a cleft in the far wall of the dell. The slim gap was barely visible amid shrubs and overhanging trees. "There are only two ways in or out. You've ridden the path from Labéht's, and it's how you must go if you choose to leave me. That yonder"—Corlis nodded at the dark cleft—"is set with traps and snares and deadfalls. No one makes it through. As for the other path, Labéht guards it, and she keeps my secret."

"As shall I," Nina murmured, looking up at him and hardly able to speak for the emotions that filled her. "I thank you for the warning," she added when she could better trust her voice. "But I'll not stumble into your pitfalls or deadly contrivances, for I do not intend to leave you ever again. If you want to be rid of me, you'll have to throw me out."

"Never that, lady," Corlis murmured.

He ran his calloused hands through the silky curtain of Nina's hair. Her braid had come undone in the first moments of their lovemaking, and all these hours later she had not bothered to put it back.

She was gazing into his eyes, losing herself again in their darkening depths, when Thorn stepped close and gave Nina a nudge, firmly demanding attention.

"Jealous!" she exclaimed with a laugh. Nina scratched the mare's ears, mollifying her. "You have only yourself to blame, Mistress Thorn, for it was you who told me he had come."

"The mare speaks to you?" Corlis asked, watching quietly.

"She does. Not often, but I can hear her when she chooses to share a thought inside my head. I don't quite know what to make of Thorn. Where did you get her?"

"Bought her from a shaman. A priest, or something like, in a wild tribe down south." Corlis clicked his tongue. "The fellow let her go cheap. She terrified him."

"Such an uncanny ability ... it *is* a little unsettling. You've heard her?"

He nodded. "Thorn and I had a talk before I left her with Galen. I figured if you ever came back to the Ore Hills, you'd see the goldsmith for sure. So I set the mare to watch for you, and I told her not to let you leave before I got back. I told her to break your leg, if she had to, to keep you here."

"Break my leg!" Nina exclaimed. "Quite unnecessary. All you needed was to leave a message at Galen's shop. One word from you that you had not forgotten me, and I'd have ridden into the desert searching for you." Nina left off scratching the mare's ears and reached for her lover's hand, to rub her thumb across his hard calluses.

"I never forgot you, lady," Corlis murmured. "A man does not forget a goddess." He paused, gripping the hand that held his. "I am glad I did not leave a message," he continued softly, "for if you'd gone out looking for me in the sand, you would have died." He nodded at the mare. "A broken leg was safer. It would have kept you off a horse and under your brother's care, or Labéht's. You'd have healed quick enough," he added with a shrug and the ghost of a grin. "A broken bone must be hardly worse than a hangnail to a witch like you."

"Witch!" Nina scoffed. "Like you aren't a warlock? Labéht told me of your magian blood."

"An old wives' tale," Corlis retorted. "I deny every word."

Nina tilted her head, eyeing him thoughtfully. "Say as you will, sir. But in my womb, the blood of my ancient house will join with your own wizardly lineage, going back to Labéht and generations older. I intend to have your baby. I'm telling you now so you can get used to the idea, for in less than a year's time, you will be a father."

"A baby!" Corlis exclaimed, his feigned objection not hiding his delight. "Lady, I'll be back in the badlands as soon as the weather cools off. I've already been paid for my next job. What in Drisha's twisted beard am I going to do with a baby in the desert?"

"*We* will raise it as a native child of that place," Nina replied, with emphasis on the *we*. "It will know how to find water as you do, and it will learn the secret of those mysterious melons you summon from bare sand." She slipped her hand under the open front of the man's shirt and caressed an old scar across his ribs. "Perhaps it will even learn to play that pocket instrument with which you made music when you were otherwise so stubbornly silent, ignoring my existence."

"Lady," Corlis said, leaning close to stroke Nina's cheek, "I was aware of your existence every second of our journey ... painfully so at night, when I ached to the marrow of my bones. I've been aching for you ever since, all these past years."

"And I, for you," Nina whispered.

She did not try to explain that, for her, their separation had lasted only months. She only pulled him to her. In a grassy glade under the trees, they twined together, and at the height of her pleasure, Nina knew the moment she conceived. She threw her head back in a spasm of ecstasy, and dug her fingers into the nomad's shoulders so hard, he cried out.

And then Corlis was kissing her, and together they rose toward a shared release that flooded Nina with the heat of a thousand desert suns. Her sweat ran. Corlis, his chest heaving, gasped her name with every panted breath until Nina put her lips to his, kissed him from the depths of insatiable desire, and left him wordless once again.

Chapter Twenty-Four

The nomad had gold burning a hole in his pocket. His recent trip into the barbarian south had been profitable. He wished for Nina to accompany him into the village so that he might present her with a token of his esteem, as he put it. Although Nina protested that such was unnecessary, Corlis soon had her on her horse and riding the path to Labéht's cottage.

The Old One was at work in her garden. She greeted Nina with a nod, and received from her "great-grand" not only his salutations but also silver and gold in payment for the fresh foodstuffs that she supplied for his table when he was off the trail and holed up at home. Their visit was brief, and in the early afternoon Nina found herself dismounting in front of Galen's shop. Corlis meant to buy her the best, which meant buying from the Hills' master goldsmith.

As Nina entered the shop's glittering showroom, she yelped in surprise, for on display were most of the bangles, bracelets, and other treasures that Jacca had worn on the girl's wedding day.

"What's this?" Nina exclaimed, turning to the woman who was Galen's capable shopkeeper, minder of the money box in his absence. "Did Mistress Jacca not take these with her?"

The woman raised an eyebrow. "The young missus took what was hers, but these are not. Master Galen only ever lent them to her." The woman's slightly defensive manner relaxed when Corlis entered on Nina's heels. At sight of him, she came close to cracking a smile. The nomad had been in Galen's shop many times before, and he had spent lavishly. The shopkeeper was anticipating a substantial sale.

"Galen lent them to Jacca," Nina echoed, redirecting the woman's attention, "only to make a good show for his daughter's wedding? In hopes that customers would clamor then, to buy the pieces?" She shook her head. "The ways of the mercantile south remain foreign to me. But I suppose I will learn, for it's here I mean to stay."

With a sigh, Nina leaned over the display counter, studying the pieces she had not had time to fully appreciate in the bustle and rush of getting Jacca to the altar on the girl's wedding day. All were exquisite, but most carried a fire motif in tribute to Jacca's gift, and Galen's own. Red gemstones sparked flames from yellow gold and copper settings.

Nestled in amongst the blaze of fire, however, Nina spotted blue sapphires encircling a bangle of white silver. The effect was oceanic, like sea spray and azure waves.

"That one," she said, and pointed.

The shopkeeper withdrew the piece from the case. As she handed it over, the woman looked expectantly at Corlis.

He said not a word. He had not spoken since taking his leave of Labéht that morning. Corlis made no attempt to haggle down the price. From the purse at his belt, he produced a stack of coins and clinked them on the counter. Then he took the bangle from Nina's hand and slipped it over her wrist, his gaze never leaving hers.

It was not a ring on her finger, but it had the significance of one. Nina left the shop at the side of the man who would be her mate for life.

* * *

"Sister, you are a water-sylph!" Dalton exclaimed. "How can you live in a desert?"

Nina shrugged. "What better place for a summoner of water? No land is more in need. I can quench many a thirst in these sands and dry hills."

Her brothers grumbled, but they stopped arguing, for it was plain that Nina had made up her mind. Corlis said no word to either of the men, but he rode with the party across the narrow neck of desert that separated the Ore Hills from the southwestern seacoast where Dalton's ship lay at anchor.

Nina bade her brothers good-bye with a hug for each, and a promise to see them regularly. In the cooler months of the year, she would cross the desert with Corlis as he guided traders through the badlands and onward. Such crossings would have Nina calling upon Legary at frequent intervals, to visit him and his wife at their home in Granger.

She would also have opportunities to catch up with Dalton at coastal ports nearer than Seawood. On his scudding voyage of the Southern Seas to join her in the Hills, the captain had sighted several promising harbors along a coast that he had never before explored. One particularly lively hamlet lined a waterfront due south of Granger. During his return voyage, Dalton proposed to drop anchor there, for Legary to disembark nearer his home, and for both men to scout potentially lucrative openings for expanded business dealings. Unlike Nina, the brothers were full participants in the money-making ways of the mercantile south.

She did not demur, therefore, when both men pressed gold into her hands as they took their leave.

"You'll need something for the upkeep of Galen's house," Legary said, evidently not understanding that Nina no longer resided there. "His roof might leak ... if it ever rains here again," he added, squinting at the sand that rippled between the foothills and the beach where they stood.

"You must also buy yourself some clothes," Dalton put in, looking with faint disapproval at Nina's attire, the last surviving garments of the few she'd brought with her from the island world. "Those are little more than rags."

"I thank you, my dear brothers, for your care of me," Nina said, smiling as she hefted the bags of gold they'd bestowed upon her. "But at this moment you can better serve me by handing over the water bottles from your saddles." She gestured at their canteens. "You'll have food and drink aboard ship. Pray, spare me a bag of bread and cheese, or whatever's in the ship's stores. Master Corlis and I are not going straight back to the hills."

Her brothers looked askance at this, but in the end all was done as Nina asked. A dinghy took the two men across to Dalton's sailing vessel, with their horses swimming the short distance to then be hoisted securely aboard. The small craft rowed one more quick trip to deliver to Nina the supplies she'd requested.

"Is our lake still out there?" she asked Corlis when she had waved the men off on their return voyage and she stood with her lover in the sand, alone with only his two white horses. Nina wasn't entirely sure of her bearings. This stretch of coastline lay south of where she had emerged from the badlands on her previous travels with Corlis. But she thought their magical lake in the desert must be relatively close by, if it still existed.

Corlis nodded. "It's there. Four days' ride. That lake has never gone dry since you filled it. But it was a little low, last time I saw it. It would profit from your revisit, my lady."

Nina sorted through the foodstuffs from the ship's galley. There was plenty for a journey of that length. She retied the bags and slung one on her saddle, leaving two others for Corlis to pack on his horse. They mounted, and headed north.

"What would you say," she asked as they rode stirrup to stirrup, "if I told you that we owe our reunion to a dragon?"

Corlis twisted in his saddle to study her, his gaze narrowed against the sun. "I'd ask to know the story, to know how I might thank the dragon."

Nina fingered the sapphire-studded bangle on her wrist. "If the Powers so will it—and by the grace of the stone-people—you'll never get a chance to address a firedrake of this world. But you shall certainly hear the story. It will pass the time." Nina paused, gathering her thoughts, then added, "It's a tale that I would have our child learn by heart—to be ready, in case there *is* a return of the *savitar* or its kind, some day in the future. But I would have our offspring know the story also for the lessons that I learned while clinging to a mountain, facing death from a winged terror. I learned that everyone needs someone who will come when they're called and not ask why. And it's neither a sign of weakness nor an admission of failure to seek help when you're in over your head."

She fell silent, riding beside Corlis and wondering what her words might mean to him, a man who had long been a taciturn loner. "Enough philosophizing," Nina said, waving away her pensive mood. "Prepare to listen, man of the silent desert, for it's a long story and I aim to tell you all of it. But the first patch of shade we find, these rags I wear are coming off. And for storytelling, I will then have no breath to spare. For I'm minded once again, sir, to join my body to yours and leave the marks of my fingers upon your flesh."

Corlis made no reply except to doff his hat and bow so low to her that he nearly left his saddle. With the hat's slouchy brim no longer hiding his gaze, Nina could see the color of the man's eyes. They were a deep gray-green, shading charcoal.

But the sun was hot, and no shade offered. Corlis swept his hat back on. In the daylit hours, at least, the desert would have its due. Nina accepted the necessary postponement of their pleasures. She touched a finger to the brim of her own hat, and wished she still had the dark glasses that had shielded her eyes from the tropical sun of her Earthly islands. When next she saw Galen, she would have the metalsmith make her a pair: lenses of smoky quartz, thinly flaked and set in rims of silver or steel. Nina tapped her thumbnail on her teeth, sensing a money-making opportunity. Galen could craft sunglasses for sale to the perpetually squinting, desert-neighboring hillfolk, and Nina could share in the profits. What a charming idea for an income of her own.

But that business could wait. She settled her hat lower over her eyes, and launched into the story of the fire-breathing dragon at the gates of hell.

Through the afternoon, she talked, until her tongue grew tired of forming words. Nina broke off, and flung a little misty water into the air. The sun shining through the conjured droplets showed every color of the rainbow. She caught wet beads on her fingertips and moistened her lips.

Corlis looked at the rainbow, and then at Nina. When she gave him a nod but remained silent, he rode through the floating mist, with his face turned up to catch its dampness on his tongue. Then from his pocket he took the small mouth-instrument upon which he made music. The tune he played seemed to shimmer in the air, so luminous that Nina could see the intertwining of the notes.

As she journeyed beside him into the desert, her heart beat in time with the melody that Corlis played, and she knew:

The goddess of distant oceans was home.

END of BOOK 6 of WATERSPELL

About the Author

CASTLES IN THE CORNFIELD provided the setting for Deborah J. Lightfoot's earliest flights of fancy. On her father's farm in Texas, she grew up reading tales of adventure and reenacting them behind ramparts of sun-drenched grain. She left the farm to earn a degree in journalism and write award-winning books of history and biography. High on her bucket list was the desire to try her hand at the genre she most admired. The result is Waterspell, a complex, intricately detailed fantasy comprising the original four-book series (*Warlock, Wysard, Wisewoman, Witch*). In the "Nina sequels" to that earlier quartet—*The Karenina Chronicles* and *The Fires of Farsinchia*—new generations of powerful *wysards* carry the saga into the magical future of an ancient world.

Having discovered the Waterspell universe, the author finds it difficult to leave.

Deborah is a professional member of The Authors Guild. She still lives in rural Texas. Find her on Instagram @booksofwaterspell and explore her overflowing, catch-all website at waterspell.net.

Thank you for reading. If you've enjoyed this book, or any of the books of Waterspell, please leave a review at a bookseller's site, or on Goodreads. Reviews are so important, and deeply appreciated. ⌐